SEDUCING THE SUN FAE

A FADA NOVEL

REBECCA RIVARD

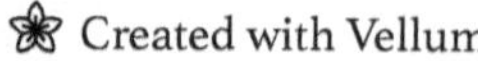 Created with Vellum

PRAISE FOR REBECCA RIVARD

"**Bewitching!** Great paranormal romance filled with sorcery and magic and erotic scenes that kept me reading!" ~Amazon Vine Voice

"Primally exciting, sexy and downright fun...**an absolute winner!**" ~*InD'Tale Magazine*

"A **powerfully written paranormal romance** with an alpha male who takes no prisoners..." ~Goodreads review

"This is the first of her books for me and **I am hooked.**" ~Amazon review

"There is sex and suspense and everything you could hope for in a shifter book. **I can't wait for more.**" ~Paranormal Romance Guild

THE FADA SHAPESHIFTER SERIES

BEST SHIFTER SERIES OF 2018 ~ PARANORMAL ROMANCE
GUILD REVIEWER'S CHOICE AWARDS

The fada.

Shapeshifters created during Dionysus's infamous bacchanals from a mix of fae, human and animal genes.

They're ruthless, untamed—and when they love, it's forever.

Stealing Ula: A Fada Shapeshifter Prequel (Nisio & Ula, set in Ireland)

The Rock Run River Fada
Seducing the Sun Fae (Dion & Cleia)
Claiming Valeria (Rui & Valeria)
Tempting the Dryad (Tiago & Alesia)
Sea Dragon's Hunger (Cassidy & Nic)

The Baltimore Earth Fada (The Darktime Trilogy)
Saving Jace (Jace & Evie)
Charming Marjani (Marjani & Fane)
Adric's Heart (Adric & Rosana)

Fada Shapeshifter Short Reads
Lir's Lady (#3.5—Lir & Isleen)
Shifter's Valentine (#3.6—Jenny & Chico)

Find out more and read exclusive excerpts: https://rebeccarivard.com/shapeshifters/

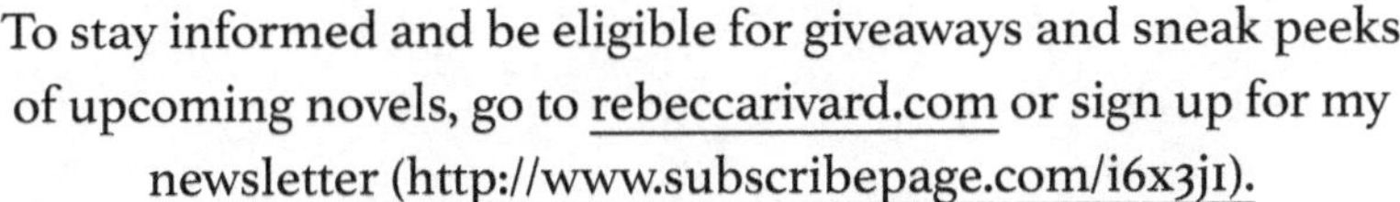

To stay informed and be eligible for giveaways and sneak peeks of upcoming novels, go to rebeccarivard.com or sign up for my newsletter (http://www.subscribepage.com/i6x3j1).

DEDICATION

This book is dedicated to my family, from my parents to my husband to my children to my siblings, who have supported and encouraged my writing in ways too numerous to count.

I love you all.

1

———————

*D*ion's breath hitched.

Damn, the sun fae queen was hot. And not just because she, like all her people, carried a touch of the sun's radiance within her.

No, she was tall and lithe with hair a gleaming river of sunshine, nicely curved hips, and breasts that would fill his hands perfectly—and he was a large man.

Her dress was a barely-there scrap of gauze the color of ripe apricots. He forced his gaze back to her face, but even that drew him in: exotically tilted eyes and lush red lips that begged a man to taste...suck...even bite.

She came closer, flanked by a regal copper-haired lady and two hard-faced blond guards. The short skirt fluttered around her legs, revealing smooth golden thighs.

His whole body heated despite his hiding place in the cool stream.

He scowled. It wasn't the first time he'd seen the queen, but he'd been careful not to get too close, knowing she used her looks as a weapon.

He hadn't bargained on his immediate, gut-level response. The woman was pure, undiluted sex.

She strolled past, so close he could've reached up and dragged her into the stream with him. It was a hot afternoon in late May, and she paused to cool herself by lifting her hair. The movement raised her breasts, pressing her nipples against the apricot gauze.

Dion drew a slow breath, his eyes riveted on those tempting points, and she glanced in his direction. He ducked beneath the surface so all she'd see was a ripple in the flowing water. He was a river fada, with a Gift for blending into water and wetlands, but Cleia was a powerful fae. She probably could've penetrated the illusion if she'd tried. Luckily, she believed herself safe on the lush grounds of her clan's compound.

With a shrug, the queen turned back to her copper-haired companion.

Dion slipped between the cattails edging the stream and lifted his head to watch her pass. Her scent filled his head, sweet but tart, like a fresh-plucked orange.

She was close...so close. His gaze fixed on the vulnerable curve where her hair fell forward over one shoulder, exposing her nape and the delicate pointed ear of a pureblood fae.

His fingers flexed on the stream bed.

It would be so easy to take her. He was a master of the quick, silent death. But it was too risky with her big blond guards just steps away. If he was caught, his clan would be embroiled in a war, and weakened as they were, they just might lose.

Besides, killing a woman didn't sit right—even a heartless siren like Queen Cleia. No, he had a better idea.

The two women continued past and he angled his body upstream after them. As he flowed into the dappled shade beneath a massive willow, Cleia threw back her head and laughed at something the other woman said. Her throaty chuckle stroked down his body like a promise.

His cock hardened—but damn if his lips didn't lift, too.

He blinked and hardened his jaw. She would *not* hook him like a foolish young fish.

This was the bitch queen who'd lured and used some of his best warriors before casting them aside. The men returned home pale and worn out. And with each man she drained, the clan's fishing grounds grew less fertile, the children weaker and sickly. Even Rock Run's vineyards produced half of what they once had.

And it had been going on for twenty fucking years.

Enough. No more would Queen Cleia take his men to feed her royal ego. She'd revealed a weakness to his youngest brother, Tiago, and Dion intended to take advantage of it.

He'd seen all he needed. But he hesitated, reluctant to leave.

When he realized he was waiting for another burst of laughter, he growled and turned abruptly downstream. Water slapped against the bank and the guards rushed toward him.

Power rippled over his skin, cool and refreshing as a summer storm. His limbs changed to fins and a tail, his gills grew more prominent, and scales formed a shimmering armor.

By the time the guards reached the stream all they saw was an enormous silver fish.

They snarled. "Thrice-damned river fada."

A fae ball seared through the air in a fiery arc, just missing Dion's head. He flexed his tail and dove deep, heading back to his river.

Soon, whispered the water as it slid past his scales. *Soon.*

THE WAY back took Dion across the Flats, a shallow area at the top of the Chesapeake Bay. As he swam, he plotted his strategy. The sun fae were at their weakest during the dark nights of the new moon. The moon had been full just last night, so for his plan to succeed he'd have to wait two weeks until early June.

He turned up the Susquehanna River. From there it was a short swim to Rock Run Creek and home. As Dion entered the creek, a sentry in river-dolphin form whistled hello. Dion flicked a fin in greeting and continued on his way to the Rock Run base.

The entrance was six fathoms beneath the surface. He arrowed down through a narrow underwater passage to surface in a small grotto that appeared to be a dead end. Even if human divers—or fae—made it this far, they'd never realize this was Rock Run's main entrance.

He shifted back to man and slipped through a hidden door into the system of caverns that made up the base. Shaking himself dry, he pulled on the shorts he'd left on a shelf.

As he headed for his quarters, Luis, his second-in-command, stepped out of the operations room and wished him a formal good evening. "*Boa noite, meu senhor.*"

Dion nodded. "*Boa noite.* Something wrong?"

Luis had been the fourth Rock Run warrior ensnared by Cleia. She'd kept him as her lover for a little more than a year. He'd returned more or less intact, but his subsequent mating had produced only one child in five years and he'd never regained his full strength.

Luis had always been wiry, but now he was gaunt, his cheeks bruised hollows in his face. The clan's healers had done what they could, but the man was growing weaker by the month.

Somehow the queen was still draining his energy even years after his return. She had to be stopped.

"Perhaps," his second replied. "You know the new earth fada alpha?"

"Lord Adric?"

The Baltimore earth fada were longtime rivals of Rock Run who'd been rocked for years by a bitter internal struggle for clan leadership. Apparently some young whelp—this Adric—had at last come out on top.

He wouldn't last long—not if he was as young as people said.

Unlike the river fada, who shifted to water-based animals, the earth fada changed to land-based animals like cougars, wolves or even deer, but in every fada clan, the predatory animals far outnumbered the non-predatory.

Adric didn't stand a snowball's chance in Hades. He'd be dead within months, murdered in a back alley or exhausted from fighting off challenges.

"Rodolfo saw Adric and a couple of his men on our land near the western border," Luis said. "In animal form, but Rodolfo recognized their scent. The three of them spent about an hour scouting around—checking out the vineyards, looking over the local humans."

"He's sure it was Adric?"

"*Sim*. He saw him just last week in Baltimore."

"Damn." Dion's heart sank. The last thing he needed right now was a clash with the Baltimore shifters. They'd been sniffing around Rock Run for years, waiting for a chance to grab a piece of it. "They must have heard we're in trouble."

Luis nodded. "I'm afraid so."

"Someone must have talked, damn it. I thought I made it clear—"

"Someone always talks. They don't mean to, but—." Luis shrugged. "And hell, if I was Adric, I'd pounce. As the new alpha, he needs something big to hold onto his followers. If he could grab a piece of our territory—or better yet, kick us out of Rock Run altogether—they'd crown him fucking king."

"Not going to happen. I'll slit his throat myself if I have to."

"So what do you want to do?" Luis leaned against the wall, awaiting instructions. His shoulders slumped, exhaustion pinching his face, but at Dion's sharp look, he pushed himself upright again.

Dion hesitated, tempted to tell Luis to get some rest, but the other man would take it as an insult. He sighed inwardly and let it go. "What have you done so far?"

"I ordered the sentries to double their patrols in that sector."

"Good. Keep the double patrols for the next few days and inform the *tenentes* we're on alert. Warn the locals as well."

The local humans were farmers and employees of the vineyards and winery, descendants of the people who'd emigrated with his parents from Portugal, and the clan took their protection seriously.

"And notify me immediately if anything else happens," Dion added. "I don't care what time it is, I want to know."

"Will do." Luis headed back into the operations room.

Dion turned toward his quarters. The past few years, he and his men had been forced to hire themselves out as mercenaries and assassins just to keep the women and children fed. It was a role all too easy for them to fill. Every fada male had a cold, ruthless animal inside of him—literally.

Sometimes Dion felt uneasy at what hard bastards he and his warriors had turned into, but right now he was glad of that ruthless streak.

Because if young Lord Adric proved to be a problem, Dion would have no qualms whatsoever with taking the S.O.B. out.

2

———

Two Weeks Later

Cleia revved her sport bike and shot across the Susquehanna River bridge, pushing the solar-powered motor to its limit.

Her bodyguards raced to keep up. She was being irresponsible, but she just didn't give a damn. She'd woken up that morning edgy, wanting...something, she wasn't sure what.

She turned down a dirt road and went another mile or so before turning up a narrow path—straight into Rock Run River Fada territory. Behind her, she felt Artan and Grady's disapproval, but to hell with it. They were her bodyguards, not her brothers.

The shapeshifter was planted in the center of the path, big and broad and arrogant in jeans and a sleeveless T-shirt, a scarf wrapped around one bulging bicep. She had to swerve to miss him.

For a heart-stopping moment she fought for control of the bike before screeching to a halt just beyond him. She whipped around.

"You ass—" She swallowed. Hard.

Holy mother, he was gorgeous. A mane of black hair, bold

Mediterranean features, a heavily muscled chest that strained the fabric of his T-shirt. Bare feet, a dead giveaway that he was a river fada. They hated shoes.

Not that she wouldn't have known he was a river fada anyway. Not with that big body and screw-you attitude. She'd bet her favorite jewels that if she'd ridden past, he'd have laughed and turned away—leaving her the one wondering.

Excitement sparked low in her belly. She was a two-hundred-year-old fae, and with her powerful glamour, could have just about any man she wanted. But she was tired of men who came too easy.

Something whispered that this man was dangerous...and she was jaded enough to want him even more.

She activated her glamour and swung off the bike, removing her gloves and helmet and shaking out her hair.

"*Olá, Senhor,*" she said in Portuguese, his clan's preferred tongue.

He stared back with eyes the same silver-blue as the river in spring, startling against his olive skin. "*Bom dia,* Cleia."

No "Queen Cleia." She raised a brow. "You know who I am?"

"Of course." His gaze swept insolently down her body, clad in brown biker's leathers and a yellow top.

Heat jolted through her. She stared back, caught by those odd light eyes as if he'd thrown a net over her. All her senses came alive. Her lips parted and her breath skidded in and out.

Then Artan and Grady pulled up on either side of her and the river man shuttered his gaze.

Her fingers clenched on her gloves. He seemed somehow... less. But why should that bother her? She'd already decided she wanted him.

With a shrug, she amped up her glamour and beckoned him closer. "Come, ride with me." It was an order and they both knew it.

He glanced at the guards and remained where he was.

Waiting for them to back off. She hesitated. But what could he do in the split second it would take Artan and Grady to get back to her?

"Move back," she ordered. The two men grumbled but did as she asked, wheeling their bikes to a spot several yards away.

She turned back to the river fada. "Ride with me."

He stepped forward to take her hand. Electricity shot up her arm and she jerked, but he firmed his grip. Not hurting her. Just letting her know he'd release her when *he* decided.

Their eyes met, clashed. His nostrils flared.

"Cleia?" Artan started forward, Grady on his heels.

"Stand down," she snapped without taking her gaze from the man before her. Stars, they acted as if she were a defenseless little girl, not the most powerful sun fae in the world.

The guards halted but remained where they were, midway between their bikes and her.

The river man stared at her lips. It felt as if he'd tasted them; they tingled and ached for more. She moistened her bottom lip with the tip of her tongue. He followed the motion with his gaze and then gave her a slow, knowing smile.

A tremor fluttered up her spine. It was as if he saw through her glamour to the woman beneath. The real woman, the one she never allowed outsiders to see.

"Who are you?" she whispered. She swallowed and repeated the question more forcefully. "Who *are* you?"

He turned her hand in his. After that first jolt, his fingers were cool; his touch, like all the river people, as soothing as rain.

"Dion." A low voice that slid over her skin like rich, raw silk. "Dion do Rio."

Dion of the River.

She tugged at her hand and this time he let it go.

Shoving her hands into her pockets, she regarded the big, barefooted man, wondering if she were about to make a huge mistake. Certainly, Artan and Grady were glowering at him suspiciously, but their family had guarded hers for centuries and trusted almost no one.

Most fae looked down on the fada, said they were little better than animals. Descendants of Dionysus and his wild followers, the fada were shapeshifters created during the god's infamous bacchanals, a mix of fae, human, animal and the god himself. Insular and clannish, they lived closed to nature in underground caverns and dens.

The other fae were right. Fada were dark, untamed...ruthless. But what the other fae didn't know was that fada made the best lovers.

And it had been a long time since a man's touch had affected her so strongly. A very, very long time.

She drew in a breath. "Well, Dion of the River, will you come with me? Of your own free will, you agree?"

"*Sim.*"

"Say it. Say you will come with me freely."

"Yes." She watched as those firm lips spoke the words. "I come with you of my own free will."

3

———

*D*ion settled onto the bike's pillion and placed his hands on Cleia's waist.

She was clever, he'd give her that.

She lured a man with that seductive glamour—he'd sensed her turn up the power and had had to draw on his own strength to resist falling under her spell—and then she drew promises from the unlucky bastard's own lips, binding him as certainly as if her surly blond guards had wrapped him in iron chains.

But Dion, a powerful lord and alpha in his own right, wasn't so easily bespelled. And wise to the tricks of the purebloods, he'd been careful to promise nothing but the truth. He *was* going with her of his own free will. What he planned to do with her once they were alone was his own business.

She set her helmet on her head. This close, he could see her bright hair was made up of individual strands of gold, platinum and copper, braided into a single gleaming plait. He nudged the braid out of the way and set his lips to the downy skin beneath.

She stilled and then with a low laugh, put the bike in gear and roared off.

They rocketed up a hill and he tightened his clasp on her,

intensely aware of her lithe, warm body. A sun fae's metabolism burned hot and fast. He could feel her heat through his jeans. His muscles tightened and his cock, already half-hard, lengthened even more.

He gritted his teeth and leaned into a curve as she accelerated into it with a dizzying nonchalance. He'd been surprised to see a fae on a motorcycle, but the metal frame was encased in plastic and she wore leather pants and gloves to further protect her skin from iron's poisonous effects.

She took another sharp curve and for a heart-stopping second, they hung on the edge of a ravine with nothing before them but blue sky and a steep drop to the boulders below.

She tossed him a taunting glance. "Having fun?"

He grinned back, enjoying himself more than he cared to admit. Like her, he preferred motorcycles to cars, and he could tell she was in complete control of the speeding machine.

"Faster," he growled against her velvety nape.

With a delighted gurgle, she opened the throttle. "You asked for it."

His mouth took a feral curve. "I did, didn't I?"

They crossed the Susquehanna River and entered the Rising Sun Fae Clan's territory. The very atmosphere changed, growing brighter, airier.

They zoomed through a patchwork of rolling hills, green forests and newly planted fields, and then turned up a smooth dirt road flanked on either side by fruit trees. To the left was a cornfield with the plants already knee high and to his right marched rows of plump red strawberries.

Everything reeked of fertility, promising a bountiful harvest.

The contrast to Rock Run's struggling lands left an acrid taste in his mouth. He wanted to wrap his hands around his hostess's pretty neck and demand she cease whatever she was doing to his people. But her big blond guards were right behind them and even though he was pretty sure he could take them, they'd be enough of a distraction that she'd escape and then he'd never again get within a mile of her.

"Here we are." Cleia drove up the hill to the compound he'd seen the other day and halted before a large mansion built of cream-colored granite.

Dion dismounted the bike and looked up—and up. Set on a circular foundation, the mansion rose four stories, each layer a circle smaller than the one below and set with rows of windows crowned by gilded arches. From a pole at the top, a flag fluttered —a gold sun spreading its rays across a midnight-blue field.

It figured. He set his hands on his hips and took in each of the four cream-colored layers. The woman didn't live in a sensible, easily defended cave or bunker, she lived in a damned wedding cake.

She parked the sport bike herself in the garage. A surprise, that. He'd have figured she'd leave it for a servant. When she returned, they walked together up the mansion's wide marble steps and into a huge circular foyer. Large windows let in bright sunshine and a door marked each of the four cardinal directions.

Presiding over the foyer was an enormous gold-and-crystal chandelier. The thing had to weigh several hundred pounds. Sunlight sifted through the dancing crystals, casting rainbow shards across the walls and the floors.

He followed the show with his eyes, entranced, even his lip curled at yet another example of sun fae excess.

Two women crossed the foyer toward them, Cleia's housekeeper and the copper-haired fae she'd been with two weeks ago.

"This is my cousin, Lady Olivia," she told Dion.

The fae lady favored him with a curt nod before pulling Cleia to one side. "What are you doing?" she demanded, low-voiced. "He's not what he seems. The man reeks of power. You can't mean to take him to your apartment. Especially tonight. Have you forgotten what time of month it is?"

Dion tensed, but Cleia just retorted, "Of course not."

The two engaged in a whispered argument. With his shifter hearing, he could hear every word. They had to know that, but apparently didn't care. *Idiotas.*

"This one's even more dangerous than that one a couple of years ago—that do Mar man. Damn it, Cleia, you're playing with fire."

Dion came alert. Rui do Mar had been his second-in-command before he'd fallen prey to the fae queen's glamour. The man had been Rock Run's best hunter and tracker. Now he was fit for little but wine and women.

"But you're forgetting one thing," Cleia retorted. "I'm a sun fae. I *like* the heat."

"You're going to regret this…"

"Enough." Cleia's power flared, turning her face blindingly beautiful—and as cold as a marble statue. And then as quickly it subsided and she patted her cousin's arm. "I know what I'm doing. Do you really think he's stronger than me—even at this time of month?"

Olivia shook her head. "If you say so."

"We'll have dinner in my apartment," Cleia told the housekeeper while Dion scrutinized her surreptitiously, unsure if that flare had been as powerful—and dangerous—as it appeared. "Don't disturb us unless absolutely necessary."

"Very good," the housekeeper replied.

Lady Olivia's mouth firmed but she remained silent.

Cleia reached for Dion's hand. Once again, there was that small shock as their skin touched. Her expression didn't change but he scented her jolt of arousal. It acted on him like an aphrodisiac. His grip tightened on her fingers, but he kept his face blank.

"This way." She guided him toward a spiral staircase that ascended through the mansion's center. Together, they mounted to the top, her guards on their heels.

Her apartment took up the entire fourth floor. Built on an

open plan with only a few low partitions between sections, it was large and airy with pale yellow walls, billowing white curtains and floor-to-ceiling windows that made the cave-dwelling fada in him uneasy.

The furniture was a warm oak with curving legs and carvings of flowers and trees. At one end of the apartment was a large bed, its headboard carved with a rising sun picked out in gold leaf.

He was aware of the queen's gaze on him, but he released her hand to walk onto the balcony. This high up, the view was dizzying. He instinctively looked southwest. He could see all the way to the Susquehanna, eight miles distant, and the place where Rock Run territory began.

He gazed at the shining ribbon of water for a long moment. It steadied him, bringing home what was at stake here—and it was *not* this constant, inconvenient hum of attraction between him and the sun fae queen.

When he came back inside, she was sending her guards to dinner.

"We'll station someone outside the door." The big blonds scowled in Dion's direction.

"As you wish," she said with a shrug.

They bowed and left, closing the door behind them. A wave of her hand locked it.

She turned to him. "Welcome to my home, Dion do Rio."

He inclined his head, having decided the best way to induce Cleia to let down her guard was to appear harmless. He wanted her to think of him as just another adoring slave.

"Thank you, my queen."

To his surprise and puzzlement, disappointment flitted across her face. She dragged a hand down her braid.

"Erika will bring dinner in a few minutes. Would you like to clean up in the meantime?"

"I would, thanks." He was dusty from the ride and besides, a river fada rarely turned down a chance to get into the water. He stepped closer to trace a finger down her cheek. "Will you join me?"

Her eyes drifted shut. Her lashes were a dark brown tipped with gold, as if dipped in fairy dust. His heart thumped. Unable to help himself, he cupped her nape and pressed a kiss to each soft, delicate eyelid.

"*Por favor,* my beauty?"

Her pulse thrummed under his thumb, but she shook her head. "You go ahead. I'll wash up and see to your dinner."

"Very good." He stepped back.

Careful. Remember what she is.

The bathing room could have been designed by a water fada. The windows were a tinted glass that cast a calm blue-green light. The bathtub was the size of a small pool, and the walk-in shower was composed of earth-toned tiles set with multiple shower heads that rained water over him from five directions.

Dion took his time showering. There was no hurry. It was best to wait until full dark when the queen would be at her weakest.

By the time he rejoined her, twilight had fallen and the apartment was lit by golden balls of fae light floating near the ceiling. To his left, a table had been set with a heaping platter of fresh fish and a basket of crusty bread, as well as salad, fruit, a cheese board, and several bottles of Rock Run's own vinho verde.

His stomach contracted—he was always hungry these days. Whatever food there was went first to the women and children. He glanced at Cleia but she was on the balcony, gazing out over the fields, so he helped himself to a large helping of bread, cheese and fish.

His hunger assuaged, he poured a glass of wine for them both and moved to the balcony. Cleia had freed her hair from the braid and changed into a dress the intense blue of a summer sky.

A storm was coming. Far-off thunder rumbled.

Cleia gripped the rail and raised her face to the wind, hair streaming behind her in a glossy flag. Her round bottom faced him, the flimsy blue skirt whipping about her thighs to expose tantalizing glimpses of smooth golden skin.

Holy mother of *Deus*. She was naked under the dress.

Dark talons of lust sliced at him. His eyes went night-glow, his animal rising to the surface. He fought the desire to bend her over the rail and take her, hard and furious as the coming storm.

And if her people saw, well, it would only demonstrate that her unchecked reign was at an end.

He drew in a breath, took that single step forward. Then he halted, hands tightening around the wine glasses. The press of the glass under his fingers reminded him to rein himself in, that it was not yet night.

Cleia glanced over her shoulder at him, a tiny line between her brows.

He shuttered his eyes and offered her the wine. She accepted it with a smile, but he sensed her wariness.

He moved back into the apartment and took a seat on the floor, pretending to be calm while inside, his mind worked over-time. If she called her guards, he could grab her and escape down the wall. But it would be a hell of climb, four stories down and with a struggling woman over one shoulder—not to mention the fact that she had her own powers to call on.

She had that faint frown on her face again. He gave her a weak smile that was only partly feigned. She returned it with a half-hearted curve of the lips.

Outside, the wind blew harder and the sweet scent of rain filled the air. Inside, his heart slapped in hard beats against his rib cage as he waited to see what she would do.

She glanced around one last time and then came back inside. "It's going to storm soon."

He released a breath he hadn't known he was holding. "*Sim*."

She relaxed onto a nearby chair, one leg slung over the chair arm in a pose so casual it bordered on insulting. "Did you eat?"

"A little. But food can wait—unless you're hungry?"

"I had something while you were in the shower."

Taking a sip of wine, she propped her head on one hand, regarding him as if he were a tasty fillet about to be served to her on a platter.

He deliberately tamped down his power even further, sending it instead into the gathering storm, which would also increase the cover for the two Rock Run warriors stationed just outside the compound. The sun fae hated getting wet. Everyone but the guards would've taken shelter by now.

Cleia sighed and suddenly he understood what was wrong. She didn't want harmless. She wanted danger.

The lady was bored with men who danced to her tune.

Ah. He'd be happy to provide the queen with a little...excitement.

He crouched before her and put out a hand. "Give me your foot."

She hesitated and he waited, unmoving. In this dance, she would learn that he was the leader, she the follower.

She slanted him a look from under her lashes and then, setting her wine on the floor, placed a slender foot in his palm. It was clad in a jewel-encrusted sandal: rubies, emeralds, diamonds. The fae loved bright, glittering things.

Gods. A good-sized family could live on the proceeds of just one of those pretty stones for a year. It was yet another weakness, something he could use against the shallow, party-girl queen.

Right now she wasn't thinking about jewels, though. Her gaze was all for him. Her hands clenched on her lap, but she held herself still, waiting to see what he'd do next.

Keeping his eyes on hers, he undid the sandal strap and slid his finger under her arch, tracing a slow path down the sensitive skin. Her breath hitched.

He removed the sandal and pressed a kiss to her instep, then placed her foot on the chair seat so that her knee was bent, opening her to him.

"Keep it there."

Her throat worked but she obeyed.

He removed the other sandal and kissed that instep as well. Her breath released in an audible whoosh.

His lips curved against her soft skin. "You like that."

Their eyes met and he inhaled sharply. *Deus*, her irises were beautiful: a tawny, sun-touched brown.

"Mm," she murmured. "More." Their gazes locked, but when he simply stared at her unmoving, she added, "Please."

Triumph streaked through him. He'd won. She just didn't know it yet.

"As you wish, *querida*," he said, and sucked her big toe into his mouth.

4

───────

$\mathcal{C}$leia moaned and gripped the armrests.

By the sun and all the stars, could anything be more erotic than the sight of the big man crouched at her feet, suckling her toes?

He hadn't bothered to put his shirt back on after bathing, leaving him naked from the waist up. Dark hair curled over his broad, hard-muscled chest and arrowed down the warm olive of his abdomen. His erection strained against his pants.

One hand held her foot while the other caressed her calf. With each pull of his mouth, electricity arrowed straight to her womb.

His gaze collided with hers...intent, crystalline blue with a hint of silver.

A predator's eyes. Wild. Dangerous. Untamed.

His eyes went night-glow. The silver deepened, blotting out the blue as his animal rose to the surface.

Even as a sensual shiver skated down her spine, she knit her brows. What was going on? One minute he seemed so unassuming, almost weak; the next hard and powerful.

And there was something familiar about those eyes...

He nipped her toe and she gasped and forgot everything but the sensations he was inducing. Her hips rocked restlessly, her skirt bunched up around her thighs. She burned for more, was desperate for his touch—there, between her legs.

She opened her mouth to tell him so, and then closed it again.

He'd made it clear he liked to be in charge. She'd never admit it, but it was exciting to have him direct her, to allow him to decide when and where to pleasure her.

The dark, hard-faced fada seemed to read her mind. He draped both of her legs over the armrests so she was wide open to him, then pushed her skirt up and studied her, his gaze hot.

"You're wet. I can see your heartbeat...here."

He touched a finger to her throbbing clitoris and she sucked in a breath as another bolt of electricity shot through her. He smiled but kept his gaze on her flushed, glistening labia, sliding the finger through their center, stroking teasingly in and out of her sex, before bringing it to his mouth.

His lids lowered and he sucked the finger clean.

She moistened her lips. "Please," she rasped, forgetting to power her glamour, forgetting Olivia's warning to be careful, that this man was more than he seemed. Forgetting everything but the desire searing her in slow, sweet waves.

"Please—?" he prompted huskily.

He touched a thumb to her clit, pressing lightly. She waited for him to move—to slide, circle, *anything*—but he held still.

He was playing games with her, she knew that. He wanted her to beg; she'd played such games herself countless times, although usually with herself as the tormentor.

She should resist. Who was he to toy with her?

But she couldn't stop herself from giving him the words. "Please...touch me."

"Here?" His thumb circled once, teasingly.

Her stomach muscles jumped. "Yes. Right there."

But maddeningly, he stilled again. She flexed her hips,

silently asking for more.

He leaned forward to give her a light lick. She felt his breath, cool against her burning cleft, and nearly shot out of the seat.

"Yes," she managed to say. "Do that, please."

"Good girl," he purred against her skin, his accent thickening. "I like to hear you beg. Tell me. Tell me what you want."

A small voice cautioned that this was risky, that she shouldn't allow him to seize too much power. But she was safe on her home grounds, a guard stationed outside the door. What could happen?

She arched into him and begged.

DARKNESS REARED UP IN DION, churned in his veins. His cock, already impossibly hard, throbbed against the confining pants.

He longed to rip the damn things off and thrust himself deep into that hot, lush mouth.

He drew a harsh breath and forced himself under control. There would be time enough for that when he had Cleia safely back at Rock Run. For now, it was enough to drive the proud, jaded queen wild.

Taking hold of her hips, he held her still for his mouth. She moaned but allowed it. He rewarded her by taking her needy bud into his mouth and suckling it, swirling his tongue over the sensitive nerves.

She gripped his head and tried to force him closer, but he lifted his head and took hold of her wrists. He set her hands on the armrests.

"Keep them there or I'll stop."

Her eyes narrowed but he stared back, refusing to relent. Her throat worked. "All right." She waited until he brought his mouth back to her sex before adding, "Bastard."

He smiled. "You have no idea," he murmured against her tender flesh.

She gasped and gripped the armrests.

He settled in to bring her to climax. She was so hot and wet, it wouldn't take long. He could almost believe she hadn't had a man since Tiago had returned two months ago, wrung out from a mere week with her.

She'd been merciful in that, at least, rather than keeping him for years as she had his other warriors. Tiago believed he'd escaped, but Dion found that hard to credit. More likely Cleia had tired of the youth and planted the idea of escape in his mind. Lord knew he was irritating, constantly questioning and arguing.

And he was Dion's youngest brother, which was the final straw as far as Dion was concerned. The fae queen had overstepped her bounds once too often.

Cleia was staring down at him, a pucker creasing her brow. He put his brother from his thoughts and settled in to blow her fae mind.

The first thing was to get rid of the dress. He wanted her naked—in every way.

He came to his knees and pulled the skirt up to her waist. "Raise your arms." When she obeyed, he removed it and tossed it aside.

She put her hands back on the armrests without being directed to and his lips quirked. She was a quick learner; he'd give her that.

But she'd had time to come back to herself. A glamour shimmered over her body, giving her a damn-near irresistible radiance.

He frowned. "Drop the magic crap already. You're fine as you are."

"Am I?" She lifted a brow, her expression world-weary and a little sad.

His scowl increased. What game was she playing? Surely she knew how sexy she was?

"Have you never had a man without your glamour?" He

raised his hands to her hair, sifting the silky strands through his fingers and running his thumbs over the delicate points of her ears.

She tilted her head into his hands, catlike, reveling in his touch. "A few times. When I was very young."

"And didn't anyone tell you your hair holds all the colors of the sun's rays? That your breasts are full and firm as ripe fruit?" He weighed the lush orbs in his hands, lightly pinched the tight copper nipples.

"No..."

Her eyes were bright with pleasure, her cheeks flushed. Her body gave off the salt-touched musk of desire.

He glided his palms over her torso. She was narrower than he'd realized, more fragile. He had the discomfiting notion that a large man like himself could easily break her—and wasn't that his intention?

He shook off the thought and moved his hands to her hips, smoothing over her succulent bottom. Indulging himself in the shape and feel of her.

"And didn't they tell you that your ass is round and *linda...*" His voice was gritty as the shifting seabed now. "*Muito, muito linda.*"

"No," she whispered. "No, they didn't tell me that."

"*Idiotas.*"

He captured her face in his palms and thrust his tongue into her mouth, taking her in a hard, dominating kiss. She moaned and sucked on his tongue, drawing him deeper inside.

Heat balled low in his belly.

He fisted his hand in her hair and drew her head back. A pulse beat in her throat. He brushed his lips over the fluttering skin and nipped her. She jolted and he soothed the bite with his tongue before moving on, giving her another love bite, then another.

Marking her as his, if only for tonight.

He brought his mouth back to hers, unable to get enough of her. Her taste was hot, enticing, more addictive than Rock Run's finest wine.

When he lifted his head, they were both breathing raggedly, and he was through with teasing. He released her hair to stroke a thumb over her kiss-swollen lips.

"Bend over the chair."

She hesitated, her gaze searching his face. He waited impassively, hands at his side. He wouldn't force her, however hard lust rode him. Despite what he had planned, whether or not he fucked her was her choice.

Her gaze dropped to his erection. Her lips curved in a slow smile and she turned around.

He exhaled audibly. *Thank all the gods.* Despite his good intentions, he wasn't sure what he'd have done if she'd refused him.

He guided her into position over the chair, her long legs spread, that lovely round bottom lifted to him. He pressed a palm on her lower back, silently directing her to remain where she was, and shucked his pants.

"Dion?" She glanced over her shoulder at him, her expression a mix of excitement and apprehension.

He raised a brow, his flushed, very ready cock in his hand. "*Sim?*" He glided his fingers up and down the stiff stalk.

Her eyes darkened. She touched her tongue to her full lower lip and he stifled a groan. His hand tightened on himself.

Her lips curved in a sultry smile. "I'd like to touch you...taste you. I'm good—you'll like it."

His mind swam with enticing pictures of her on her knees, those coral-colored lips enclosing him, but he shook them off. If he wasn't careful the woman was going to regain control.

"Next time. Right now I have something else in mind."

She tossed her head, the queen never far from the surface. "But—"

He'd counted on her objecting. "I see I have to convince you."

He crossed the room for the scarf he'd left draped over a chair. When he turned back, she was on her knees watching him, her body half turned so that he had a profile of firm, pointed breasts. He smiled darkly. He was going to enjoy this.

Crossing back to her, he lifted her by the waist and bent her over the chair again. He looped the silky length of material under her hips and caught hold of the ends. "Now I can ride you," he informed her.

"Oh." A quiver went down her spine, her eagerness for what came next palpable.

His slow smile would've frozen all but his clan's most dominant members in their tracks. "*Sim, minha bonita*. Yes, my pretty one."

He took the ends of the scarf in one hand, holding her where he wanted her, and with the other grasped his cock so he could rub the tip over her sex.

She let out a broken moan.

Good. He wanted her feverish with desire, unable to think... unable to resist.

He positioned himself at her entrance and pressed inside.

His lips parted on an involuntary groan. *Lord, she felt good.* Tight, slippery and incredibly hot.

He pumped slowly in and out, reveling in the feel of her fisted around him, all thoughts of revenge temporarily forgotten. She gripped the edge of the seat and pushed back, undulating on him in leisurely circles.

Heat slammed up his spine. His thighs clenched and his balls tightened painfully.

"*Deus*," he gritted. "That's—"

He inhaled deeply and focused on giving her pleasure, bending forward to run his free hand over her, playing with her nipples, rubbing her swollen clit. "Having fun?" he taunted, echoing her question as they'd swooped around the ravine's edge.

She moaned. "Stars, yes."

"Let me see...should I go fast"—he thrust quickly in and out of her several times—"or slow?" He stroked in at an excruciatingly slow pace and paused.

"Dion." She flung back her head and he dropped the scarf to bury his hands in her hair, tugging just enough to give her the added spice of pleasure/pain. Her inner muscles clenched on him. She arched her back. "Oh, Goddess. Take me. Now. Hard, Dion."

Still giving orders, he thought with the small corner of his brain still able to form words. But she'd recalled him to his purpose.

His lips peeled back in a grin that betrayed his animal roots as he reached for the scarf again.

She ground herself against him. "Please. I need—"

"*Sim, sim,*" he crooned. "I'll give you want you want, *minha linda.*" He reached a hand under her to swirl his fingers around her needy little nub until she keened out her pleasure and began to convulse around him.

He slowed his thrusts and as she sobbed out his name, he wrapped the scarf around her eyes. It had been prepared with a binding spell cast by another powerful fae, impossible for anyone but him to break.

"Dion?" She reared up under him. "What—?"

He knotted the ends tightly and then gripped her shoulders. His balls exploded and he came, pumping into her in powerful, euphoric bursts. He barely remembered to draw on the power of the storm.

Lightning flashed, and all over the mansion, fae lights shattered. He opened to it, using his Gift to harness the huge surge of power so as not to harm her more than necessary, then released it, sending the current sizzling through her.

The pleasure spiked impossibly high.

Cleia screamed in ecstasy and then slumped forward, unconscious.

5

____

leia returned to consciousness in slow stages.

From somewhere nearby came the sound of running water, but she was warm and dry, tucked into a large, comfortable bed. She smoothed a palm down the cover. A soft, woven cotton, it rested lightly on her naked body.

Her brow furrowed and she turned her head restlessly side to side. Something was wrong. Her bedroom was airy, light-filled. But everything was dark, the air moist and smelling of earth and stone.

She forced herself the last few degrees to consciousness. When she opened her eyes, the world was still an unrelenting gray. Horror skittered up her spine and her hands flew to her face. Then she gave a sob of relief.

She wasn't blind. Something was covering her eyes, preventing her from seeing.

She frowned, trying to recall what had happened. The river fada—Dion—had given her a climax that had all but fried her brain, and then...nothing.

She inhaled sharply. The bastard must've knocked her out, and then brought her here—wherever "here" was.

She tugged at the light silk, tentatively at first and then harder, then hooked her fingernails under it and tried to rip it off, but it stayed put as if made of the strongest iron. And if anything, it was getting tighter the more she tugged on it.

Even though she knew it was hopeless, she delved deep within for her magic.

Nothing.

Her breath sucked in and she scrabbled frantically at the binding. It tightened painfully around her head.

Footsteps sounded. She froze.

"Easy now." *His* voice, calm but firm. "It's bespelled. No one but me can remove it. The more you pull at it the tighter it gets. Let it be before you injure yourself."

She swallowed. He was almost certainly telling the truth. The fae, even the fada with their diluted blood, found it difficult, not to mention extremely painful, to lie. And now that he'd mentioned it, she detected the faint scent of binding herbs: apple, cedar, ivy.

She panicked in earnest then. Without her sight, she couldn't perform even the simplest spell. She was helpless, at the mercy of this man. This *fada*.

"*No.*" She clawed at the scarf. "Take it off, you, you—"

He remained silent but she sensed him standing there, watching and waiting. Her lungs seized. Everything bad she'd ever heard about the fada raced through her mind: their dark rituals, their animal nature. The way they treated their women.

She'd never fooled herself that her Rock Run lovers were tamed; they'd only been under her spell. Without her magic to protect her, who knew what this man would do to her?

She gave a last, despairing tug at the scarf but it only tightened more until she whimpered and let go to curl into a ball. Her chest heaved. Panic was a vise clamped around her rib cage, compressing it so that she couldn't get enough air.

She gasped, her mouth opening and closing soundlessly as she desperately sought oxygen.

A light touch on the binding. She flinched, but the pressure eased.

"*Acalme-te*," Dion murmured. "No one's going to hurt you." He placed his palm on her bare upper back where she lay curled onto her side. "Breathe." He rubbed the skin. "There you go. Now another. That's it..."

Her breath whooshed in. For several endless moments she lay there panting, humiliated at her loss of control.

"Are you all right now?" he asked.

She jerked her chin. *Yes.*

"All right then." He removed his hand.

She struggled to sit upright while keeping the blanket around her. Now that she was calmer, she realized the scarf wasn't opaque. She could discern light and dark, and while she couldn't see Dion's face, she could make out his general shape.

She turned in his direction. "Where am I? What have you done, *fada*?"

"Still the haughty bitch, I see." His tone was amused, but there was an edge to it. "We're nothing but beasts to you, are we? Good for nothing but to get your gold-plated *buceta* off."

"I—you—bastard. That's not true—"

"No?" he scoffed. "But to answer your question, you're in my own apartment deep underground where your people will never be able to track you. In my territory—which means you, *minha senhora*, are in my power."

Her hands fisted on the blanket. "Who are you? And I want the truth this time."

"I didn't lie—my name is Dion do Rio. But you can call me Lord Dion—or Dionísio, to give you my full name."

"*Dionísio.* Stars, I'm an idiot."

Not the original god of wine and ecstasy, but a direct descendant on his father's side, who'd been a Portuguese river fada with a lineage stretching back to the dark, wild god himself. Which meant this man was indeed a lord—and the Rock Run alpha.

Goddess, what had she done?

"Don't be too hard on yourself," Dion remarked in condescending tones. "I was using a sort of glamour as well, only I tamped down my power to make myself appear less than I was."

She absorbed that in silence. She should've sensed his power. She was a sun fae, and more to the point, her people's Conduit. Power, energy, was her stock in trade.

Perhaps she *had* grown arrogant over the years. Certainly, she'd been willfully blind, drawn to the man's dark sensuality. She was angry and afraid, but even now a small part of her couldn't help noting that if that was how he appeared with his power tamped down, he must be as beautiful as a god when it wasn't.

He touched her shoulder. She tensed, painfully aware she was naked and defenseless beneath the thin blanket.

He growled. "Calm yourself. I don't force myself on helpless women."

Her hands clenched. *Helpless?* She itched to unleash her full power, a radiance that could literally blind him.

But she couldn't. Her magic was dependent upon her ability to see. With her eyes bound she was as helpless as any mortal.

It was her Achilles' heel—and no one but Olivia knew that. And Olivia would die before she told anyone.

So how in Hades had he found out?

"Here." He slid a big arm around her shoulders and brought a cup to her lips. "Drink this."

She shook her head and pressed her lips together. The blanket slipped, exposing the tops of her breasts. He stilled and she concealed her triumph.

The man wanted her even without her glamour; she could practically smell his lust. Maybe she could use that. She let the cover remain where it was.

The cup nudged her mouth. She turned her face away. She was so thirsty her tongue felt thick and too big for her mouth, but she was even more afraid of being drugged.

"It's only water," he told her.

When she still hesitated, he blew out a breath. "For God's sake, drink. You have to be dehydrated—you've been out since last night. I don't need to drug or poison you. The binding keeps you prisoner."

He was right. With her eyes bound, not only was it impossible for her to access her magic, she couldn't see to escape an underground cavern anyway. She took the cup from him. The water was cool and sweet. She drank thirstily, draining the cup before handing it back.

"More?"

"Yes, please."

He refilled the cup. When she was finished, he took it from her, saying, "That's enough for now. You don't want to make yourself sick."

He set the cup somewhere nearby and then came back to stand next to the bed. She felt him considering her.

A chill slid over her skin. All of a sudden, trying to seduce her way out of this seemed like a bad idea.

Unbidden, she thought of the only bacchanal she'd ever attended. She'd been barely out of her teens and too curious for her own good. Fortunately, Artan and Grady had tracked her down and brought her home. Her parents had confined her to her room for a week with no visitors save a servant who brought her food and water. When she'd begged to be let out, her dad had said she was lucky he hadn't turned her over his knee.

But she'd been punished worse than he knew. The nightmarish scenes had lived in her mind for years: wine and magic and dancing that turned primitive...carnal...frenzied. Women—and men—taken against their will. Harsh whippings for the slightest resistance.

The baccha brought out all that was wild and dark in the fada, allowing their feral side full rein so that a fada in the grip of the *Delírio* was more beast than human.

She'd watched from a dark corner, using her glamour to take on the appearance of an old, sick crone until Artan and Grady found her. By then she was curled up with her hands over her face, praying no one would see through her disguise.

The silence thickened. Cleia drew the blanket up to her chin and firmed her jaw, hoping the fada wouldn't notice her trembling fingers.

"Why?" she asked.

"You know why, *minha senhora*."

My lady, not *Queen Cleia*.

The nuance made it clear she was a prisoner.

"But I don't. You say you're not going to force me—and that's the only way you'd have me now." He chuckled darkly but she ignored him. "So if you haven't brought me here for sex, then why? Without my magic, I'm not much good to you. Unless you intend to hold me for ransom—"

He made scornful noise. "I wouldn't risk war for a handful of pretty stones."

"Then why?"

"You've developed a taste for river fada. Of your last ten lovers, eight of them were my men."

"So? They were adults. They came to me of their own free will and were treated like honored guests while they lived with me, and then were returned to you unharmed."

"Like hell," he snapped. "Rodolfo was the first. You kept him three years, and then took Miguel soon after. They both returned home with half their strength, and are as yet unmated. Emanuel and Luis you kept for a shorter period of time, and they've managed to mate, but only Luis has had a child from these matings—and just one in five years. I don't know yet with Jorge and Benny because they shifted to their dolphin form as soon as they returned and are lost to the currents.

"And Rui"—his voice tightened and she guessed Rui do Mar was special to him—"was about to mate with a fada woman. You kept him for a year. By the time he came home, he'd lost interest in his woman and is as yet unmated. He was my second-in-command—a strong, capable warrior—and now he's a drunk, fit only for fishing."

"I'm sorry. I had no idea—" Something struck her: those oddly familiar silver-blue eyes. She felt a sinking sensation in the pit of her stomach. "And Tiago?"

"My youngest brother."

"Your...brother?"

"*Sim*," was the grim reply. "You only kept him a week, and he appears healthy enough. But the *idiota* thinks he's in love with you. He mopes around the base like his life is over."

"But—" She shook her head.

She'd been shocked to find out that Tiago was only twenty-one—an adult as the fae counted these things, but just barely. She wasn't the evil succubus the Rock Run alpha seemed to think her, draining men dry and then tossing them back, so she'd sent him home. "He's very young," she said lamely.

"*Exatamente*," Dion gritted out. "But you couldn't resist him, could you?"

"He approached me. It was a few days before I realized he'd done something to make himself appear older—bought a spell, cast a glamour...I'm not sure what. He said he'd fallen in love with me. I—there was something about him..."

She trailed off. Tiago had radiated the same untamed power as his older brother, except that in the youth it was weaker, still developing. But oh, what a man Tiago would be. She'd promised he could return in seven years if he wished, then cast a spell that made him think he'd escaped and set him free on the banks of the Susquehanna.

His feelings must have been stronger than she'd realized if he was still pining for her. She frowned. She'd genuinely liked the boy—had never intended to hurt him.

Something occurred to her: Tiago had seemed so young and naïve that she hadn't taken him very seriously. Had she been careless enough to let him discover her deepest secret—that her power depended on her ability to see?

Silence fell. She felt the alpha's gaze on her, his dark, brooding presence filling the cavern. The skin on her nape tightened. She rubbed her upper arms, wishing she could see his expression.

"Are you all right?" he asked abruptly.

"Yes." A little shaky, but she'd crawl across a bed of nails rather than admit it.

"Good. I kept the voltage low so as not to harm you."

"How kind," she muttered.

Something about the joining of a sun fae and a river fada could cause a power surge—probably the mix of water and energy. She'd occasionally experienced a low voltage sizzle with her river fada lovers. It made the sex that much more exciting, which was why she kept seeking them out. But the current that Dion had sent through her had been a hundred times more powerful.

How had he done it?

She remembered the sex, wild and earthy...him thrusting into her, deep and hard, filling her until she was sobbing with pleasure...binding her eyes...and then lightning. Her very veins had burned with it. Even now she hummed with remembered ecstasy.

But the power...that had exceeded anything she'd ever experienced. She suspected he could've easily killed her—but he hadn't, which meant he wanted something.

"I understand you're upset," she said carefully, "but what's done is done. My people have a saying: *The sun cannot reverse its path across the sky.* I—"

"I want it back," he ground out. "What you stole from my men, you will return. You owe us. For twenty years you've stolen from us. *Twenty years.* And not just the men. We're all weaker—the women and children, too. Even our vineyards are affected."

"What are you talking about?" She scraped her fingers through her hair. The man was as crazy as his wine-swilling, fornicating namesake. "I stole nothing. How can I return the time we spent? How can I return the lovemaking? And even if I could, what does that have to do with the rest of you? I haven't touched your women and children and I've never even been in one of your vineyards. You're out of your mind."

He slapped his palms on the mattress and leaned in close so that she felt his breath on her cheek, hot and dangerous.

"Don't lie to me," he said in a low, hard voice, "or put me off with your fae half-truths. Or I'll make you sorry you were ever born."

She stilled, excruciatingly aware of how vulnerable she was. The only sounds in the room were the running water and his jagged breathing.

Instinctively, she tried to call on her magic...but of course, nothing happened. It was like shouting into a dark, echoing void.

She tightened her grip on the blanket, her heart rapping like a wild thing. Her magic had always been there. Without it she was merely a woman in the sights of a large, furious man.

He blew out a breath and drew back. When he spoke again his tone was calmer.

"You stole life-energy from my men, and what is stolen can be returned. Think on it, my lady. Maybe a few days as my guest will prod your memory. For now, I'll send someone to attend you. You'll want for nothing, I assure you."

She heard his footsteps receding even as she opened her mouth to protest that she could consider it until the sun fell from the sky, but that didn't mean she could accomplish the impossible.

Thrice-damned, irrational fada. She growled and, snatching up a pillow, threw it across the room.

She heard another dark chuckle. Then a door closed and she was alone.

She tossed the cover off and sat on the edge of the bed. With one hand she grasped the headboard. It was made of stone. In fact—she traced the headboard with her fingers—it had apparently been carved from the cavern wall itself. She put her feet on the floor. It was stone as well, cool under her bare feet.

For some reason that brought it home to her: she was being held prisoner in a cavern. Deep underground, far from the sun.

Panic threatened again. Her hands went to her blindfold, tugging at it even though she knew it was hopeless.

She couldn't stay here. *She couldn't.*

The door opened and she heard footsteps again. Not Dion's. These were slower and somehow comfortable sounding. She took a deep breath and straightened her shoulders. She might be a prisoner, but she was still a queen.

A kind, motherly voice spoke in Portuguese, as had Dion, although Cleia had been too upset to notice it. Thank the Goddess, her Gift for tongues was intact.

"Good afternoon, Senhora Cleia. My name is Isa."

Cleia peered at her through the blindfold. She could see enough to tell that the newcomer was short and wide. "Peace to you and yours, Senhora Isa."

"Peace to you and yours," she returned. "And how are you, *minha senhora*?"

"Fine," Cleia found herself replying, although that was ludicrous, considering she'd been kidnapped, stripped of her power and left naked in a strange bed by a pissed-off fada.

"Good, good. Now, what can I do for you?" The pillow she'd thrown was replaced on the mattress and Isa continued talking without waiting for a reply. "Why don't we get you dressed first? Raise your arms now."

Isa dropped a dress over Cleia's head as the woman continued to mutter soothingly. Unlike the fada, sun fae preferred to go about fully clothed, but their metabolism ran fast and hot, so they wore light, airy attire year-round.

Cleia fingered the skirt. It was a soft cotton gauze, and a perfect fit.

"Lord Dion brought some of your dresses back with him," Isa said, reading her mind.

"I see."

"That's better now, *sim*? Aren't you *linda*?" Isa patted Cleia's arm as if she were a child. "I nursed Lord Dion, his three brothers, and his sister, too. The alpha is a good man. I'm sure the two of you will work this out."

Cleia snorted disbelievingly but Isa just took her hand. "I'll get you a snack—how does bread and cheese sound, *minha senhora*? And then you can take a nice, long soak in the alpha's pool. It's right over there—do you hear the waterfall? And in a few hours we'll be having dinner—fresh trout tonight. Won't that be a treat?"

So she was in alpha's own quarters, in the heart of the Rock Run base. Even though it was what Dion had told her, her heart sank. The base was notoriously well protected by both concealing spells and the fada themselves. Even if Olivia somehow tracked her to the base, she might not be able to rescue her.

"You do like fish?" Isa was asking.

"Yes," Cleia murmured, allowing herself to be swept along.

Now that she thought about it, she *was* hungry—her fast metabolism burned through calories at a rapid rate—and still shaky. If she was going to escape, she needed to be at peak strength.

And she *would* escape.

Because if she didn't return home by the summer solstice, not just her life was at risk, but the life of every sun fae on the planet.

6

———

The woman was going to be difficult. Dion expelled a breath as he exited his quarters.

He'd expected her to crumble into a hundred pleading pieces as soon as she understood how hopeless her situation was. She was a sun fae, shallow and frivolous. She should've caved as soon as she realized she was alone, stripped of her magic and completely in his power.

But after that momentary panic, she'd sat there, that proud chin raised, and refused to let him intimidate her. A part of him couldn't help admiring her spirit.

But his darker side had wanted to keep pushing, to take what she'd so recklessly offered when she'd taunted him with those high, firm breasts, teach her how risky it was to provoke a man who was part animal. He'd wanted to pin her to the bed and tease her mercilessly with his mouth and hands until she was writhing with pleasure and begging to give him anything he wanted...

Then he'd scented her fear.

His insides had twisted in self-revulsion. Queen Cleia owed him and his clan, big time—but when he realized she was truly afraid of him, he'd immediately backed off. And then, to his disgust, he found himself directing Isa to treat the woman as an honored guest, although he'd also ordered that she be kept confined to his quarters.

Tiago stepped out of a doorway, causing Dion to swerve so as not to bowl him over.

"She's here?" his brother asked. "Queen Cleia?"

"Yes," he replied shortly without breaking his stride. He was damned if he'd encourage the young whelp's infatuation.

At twenty-one Tiago was nominally an adult, but just barely, since the fada had a lifespan of four or five centuries. A younger version of Dion, he had the same mane of curly black hair and broad face with high, hard cheekbones, although on a youth's wiry frame. But already his shoulders had begun to broaden, and his hands and feet were big boats of appendages, intimating that someday he'd match or even surpass his oldest brother.

Dion just prayed his hair didn't turn silver before that happened. At a hundred turns of the sun, he was in the prime of his life, but Tiago seemed determined to make him old before his time.

When he'd disappeared, Dion had been frantic. He'd had every man he could spare out searching, and damn it, they should've been able to find him. The fada were the best trackers in the world.

But Tiago had deliberately covered his scent—as he'd been taught by Rock Run's own trackers—and they hadn't found a trace of him until he'd been discovered swimming as his otter in the Susquehanna Flats, tired but unhurt...and sick in love with Cleia.

"She's okay?" Tiago demanded. "You didn't—"

"Of course she's okay. She's in my own quarters and Isa is looking after her."

"And you?" His brother's eyes narrowed. "Where will you sleep?"

"On the couch in my *sala*. Not that it's any of your fucking business."

Tiago ignored that to turn back toward Dion's quarters. "I'll just say hello."

"The hell you will." Dion snagged his arm. "Stay away from her, *entendes*? She eats pups like you for breakfast."

Tiago's smile was sly. "She liked me well enough until she found out how old I was."

Dion blinked. It seemed the boy was turning into a man. But of all the women he could've chosen, did it have to be the sun fae witch?

"For God's sake, you saw what happened to the other men. Do you want to end up like Jorge? Or Benny?"

His brother hunched a shoulder. He was too young to recall what some of the older men had been like before Cleia, but Jorge had been his mentor, giving him his first training in the fighting arts. Then one day Jorge had left on a mission and never returned, surfacing a few weeks later along with Benny as Cleia's latest lovers. Tiago had seemed to take it in stride, but Dion had seen the naked hurt on his face when he'd first found out.

"Of course not. But she didn't hurt me. She'd never hurt me."

"You think you're a match for a two-hundred-year-old fae? You're a child compared to her. Whatever she does, it takes time —months, even years. You were damn lucky to get out of there when you did."

"Maybe. But maybe I'm the one she wants too much to hurt."

"That's just her glamour. She makes every man think he's the only one for her."

"You can say what you want," his brother said with a defiant lift of his chin, "but I know what I know. And I'll tell you one thing, I wouldn't be here if she hadn't sent me home. I didn't want to leave, but she said the whole clan was looking for me. And then she did something"—Tiago's dark brows drew together —"and suddenly, she wasn't so beautiful anymore, and I knew it was time to go home. But she said I could return in seven years—and I will."

Like hell, Dion thought, but he had the brains not to say it aloud.

Instead he said, "What are you doing here anyway? Shouldn't you be training with your cohort? If you want to make warrior, being my brother won't be enough."

"You think I don't know that?" Tiago shot him a hostile look. "I've been your kid brother my whole fucking life. I have to put in twice the work to get any respect."

Dion returned his stare. Maybe someday his brother would be his equal in dominance, but that day was still far in the future. "Then why are you here, sniffing after a woman who's already turned you down?"

Tiago flushed and dropped his gaze, suddenly appearing very young. Dion felt a twinge of remorse, but he didn't know how else to get through to the lovesick idiot.

"I'm sorry," Tiago mumbled. "I just—" He broke off, said, "*Adeus, meu senhor*," and hurried away.

Dion passed a hand over his face. *Deus.*

It was times like these that he realized just how much he still missed his parents. They'd disappeared ten years ago en route to visiting relatives in Europe. He and his men had searched for weeks, but they'd vanished somewhere in the ocean near Iceland. Eventually he'd been forced to call off the search and declare himself the new alpha.

His two middle brothers had been adults and had left soon after—the two of them were too dominant to live in the same clan with him as alpha. Nic and Joaquim made their living as mercenaries, visiting only rarely.

So it had fallen on Dion to raise his two youngest siblings. Tiago had been just eleven and Rosana even younger at five. He did his best, but it wasn't easy being both their brother and their alpha.

He blew out another frustrated breath and continued on his way.

TRUE TO HER WORD, after showing Cleia to the bathroom, Isa called for a meal of bread, cheese and fresh fruit. When it arrived a few minutes later, she settled Cleia at a table in what she called the *sala de estar*, or living room, and poured her a glass of grape cider.

Cleia applied herself to the food with the intense concentration of someone who hasn't eaten for almost twenty-four hours. But with her appetite satisfied, she sipped the tangy cider and questioned Isa as unobtrusively as possible.

Unfortunately, other than confirming what Cleia already knew—that Dion had brought her to the river fada base because he believed she was stealing energy from his men—Isa had little to add.

"You'll have to ask the alpha," she kept saying until Cleia gave up. If Isa knew anything more, she wasn't going to divulge it.

From what Isa had said, Cleia gathered that Dion's quarters consisted of the two rooms—the *sala* and the bedroom—that she'd thus far been in. Apparently the clan did most of their dining and playing together in a large hall, which went with what Cleia knew about them: fada lived communally, as much a pack as wolves or dolphins.

Dion was not only alpha but the oldest of a family of five, of which Tiago was the fourth and youngest brother. The sister, named Rosana, was the youngest. It had been left to Dion to raise his young brother and sister when his father, the previous alpha, had disappeared along with his mother.

"And Lord Dion just became alpha?" Cleia asked. "No one challenged him?"

Fada were known for their bloody successions. It was a rare

alpha who didn't undergo a series of challenges to prove his worth.

"No," was his former nurse's proud reply. "Everyone was content to let him rule. We always knew he'd be the next alpha—and not just because his *pai* wanted it. The young lord has always been tough but fair. But listen to me running on. I promised you a bath, didn't I?"

Isa set Cleia's hand on her arm and led her back into the bedroom to the far wall. The sound of running water grew closer, and Isa explained that a small waterfall ran down the wall on one side, feeding the pool in which she was going to bathe.

The water was apparently comfortable for a river fada but to Cleia it was only a shade above freezing.

She gritted her teeth and immersed herself anyway, needing to wash away the scent of sex and sweat still clinging to her. If she could smell herself, Dion certainly could, and she was damned if she'd wear his scent any longer.

Isa helped her wash her hair, then Cleia used a washrag and soap to scrub every last trace of him away before immersing herself a second time.

When she emerged from the pool, Isa enveloped her in a large and blessedly warm towel and helped her get dressed again before guiding her to a couch in the *sala*. "I'm afraid I have to leave now," she told Cleia, "but I'll be back in a few hours with dinner. You're sure you'll be all right here? Alone?"

She shrugged. "What choice do I have?" Then she felt ashamed when Isa apologized—several times—for leaving her. At last the older woman took herself off.

As soon as she was alone, Cleia rose to investigate her prison. She started with the *sala*, working from the outside walls in and utilizing both touch and what sight she had through the gray silk. The walls were stone, cool and slightly damp under her fingers. She'd heard the entire base had been excavated from a system of natural caverns.

Now, as she moved around the room, she formed the impression of a plain, utilitarian space, large enough to hold a table and a few chairs and a couple of couches. There was nothing in the way of frills: no table cloth, no pictures on the walls, not even a rug to cover the hard stone floor.

She moved into a beam of sunlight. Startled, she lifted her face to its warmth. She was sure she was underground, so there must be a shaft in the cavern ceiling to let in light and air.

Smart. She tipped her head back and drank in its energy. It was weak, too weak, but better than nothing. She would've remained beneath it except she wanted to finish exploring before Isa—or Dion—returned.

She continued around the room until she arrived at the door to the hallway. It was locked, of course, but she was surprised at how disappointed she was. After all, what would she'd do even if the door were open? She had no idea where the exits were, and besides, a blindfolded woman would stick out like a sore thumb. They'd catch her before she'd gone ten yards.

But there was something about knowing she was locked in that had the panic clawing at her again, fighting for purchase...

She drew a deep breath and released the doorknob.

About a quarter of the way around the room, she found another locked door. She guessed that was the door to Isa's apartment; Isa had explained that in Dion's father's time, the alpha's apartment had been one large space made up of both her apartment and his, but Dion lived alone now, with Isa and his younger sister next door.

Cleia continued until she came to a small kitchen with a sink, a stove and a built-in stone cooler that held wine, juice and cheese. A few yards from the kitchen, she turned another corner and felt her way along the wall until she once more reached the bedroom.

As with the *sala*, she methodically worked her way around the outside walls, noting the placement of the bathroom, the bed and the pool, as well as the room's size—about twenty by twenty feet.

Two rustic bentwood chairs flanked the pool. She ran her hands over them, marveling at the clever way they'd been formed from willow and thick vines. They were the only furniture, save for the alpha's sturdy stone bed.

With that done, she then moved through the center of each room, locating each of the skylights in turn. There were five in the bedroom, four in the slightly smaller *sala*.

Suddenly, she was exhausted. She made her way back to the bed. At its foot was a sheepskin rug, the only floor covering in either room. She leaned against the bed and curled her toes into it, instinctively seeking its warmth after the cool stone floor. She would've liked to take a nap while she waited for dinner, but she was damned if she let Dion catch her in bed again. Instead, she returned to the *sala*, found a sunbeam, dragged a couch beneath it and dozed curled up in its warmth.

But she didn't see the alpha again that evening.

Isa brought her dinner, which Cleia ate in solitary splendor in the *sala*. She forced herself to eat a decent amount, knowing her body needed nourishment. When Isa had opened the door, she'd heard the clink of dishes and the murmur of what sounded like a crowd dining elsewhere in the caverns.

A wave of homesickness washed over her. If she were home, she'd be eating with her family: Olivia and several other cousins, including little Gracie, who lived with her parents on the mansion's second floor and never failed to have a hug and a kiss for her "Aunt" Cleia.

She set her fork down and paced restlessly around the *sala*, counting the steps from the table to the wall, from the wall to the couches, from the couches to the door to the hallway. Anything to keep her mind off how alone and helpless she felt. Without her sight, she couldn't even read.

If this was Dion's idea of torture, he was doing a good job of it.

She might've been tempted to give in to him—if she only knew what the blasted man wanted.

To hear him talk, she was some kind of night fae, the pale-skinned, black-haired energy-suckers of the fae world. She would've been insulted if it weren't so serious.

She thought of that crowd of people eating while she was left by herself in a strange apartment and to her horror, hot tears pricked her eyes. Dropping onto the couch, she pressed the heels of her hands to her eyes through the scarf and took a deep breath.

Calm down. Feeling sorry for yourself isn't going to get you out of here.

Footsteps sounded in the hall. She sat up and scrubbed her hands over her cheeks and put a serene expression on her face. The key turned in the lock.

"*Ah, bom,*" Isa said in her kindly voice. "I see you ate your dinner. It was good?"

"Very good, thank you."

"Lord Dion didn't think to bring you a nightgown, but I borrowed a shift from one of the women. She's about your size." Isa chuckled. "You'd swim in one of mine."

"*Obrigada,*" Cleia said politely.

With Isa gone, Cleia could barely keep her eyes open. The food had helped, but what she really needed was to spend a few hours in full sunlight, recharging her energy. But that was impossible as long as she was held underground; the little she could pick up from the skylights wouldn't be enough.

The longer Lord Dion kept her prisoner, the weaker she'd become.

She braided her hair, climbed into bed and pulled the covers up to her chin. For the hundredth time, she tested the scarf's strength, but it was still as firmly attached as the other ninety-nine times she'd tried it.

She curled up and wrapped her arms around her abdomen to

comfort herself. But even as tired as she was, it was a long time before she fell asleep.

7

After leaving Cleia, Dion spent a couple of hours drilling some of the younger warriors and cadets. The entire clan was on alert in case the sun fae attacked, although Dion considered that unlikely. First, they had to make sure Cleia was with him—and he'd been damn careful to muddy the trail—and second, they had to locate the base, concealed by some of the best spells money could buy.

No, if he were the sun fae, he'd move cautiously. An attack could result in Cleia's being spirited away to another location, or even in her death.

Meanwhile, just spending time with the alpha served to calm the younger ones, who were understandably agitated by the news that he'd kidnapped a powerful fae.

To add to that concern, he'd never discovered what the Baltimore shifters had been doing on Rock Run's lands. As far as he knew, they hadn't returned since that single incursion a couple of weeks ago, but they might have simply been clever enough not to be caught.

Something would have to be done about them, but right now Dion couldn't let himself be distracted.

He washed up and entered the large cavern that served as Rock Run's dining hall. It was filled to the brim with people talking in low, worried voices. When they saw him, the sound stopped for a moment before resuming. He stifled a sigh and moved through the tables, reassuring the clan by word and touch.

Even dinner didn't provide a respite. He spent the meal explaining himself to Luis, his five *tenentes*, and a few other brave souls, including Isa. Not everyone had agreed with his decision to kidnap Cleia, and now that he had, there was even less support for keeping her indefinitely. After ten years as alpha, he wasn't accustomed to being questioned. He sought advice, yes—and often took it—but once he decided on a course, he expected it to be accepted.

The objections to him holding Cleia prisoner ranged from Rodolfo's, "We don't make war on women," to Luis's opinion that Dion was inviting the wrath of the sun fae down on their heads. Tiago regarded him as if he'd kicked a kitten, while Isa seemed inclined to bring Cleia under her maternal wing, which was a bit like a seal trying to mother a killer whale.

Rui simply lifted a glass to him from across the cavern. Dion wasn't sure whether he was congratulating or mocking him. When Dion arched a brow, Rui dropped his gaze and went back to his dinner, although as usual he was doing more drinking than eating.

Dion's mouth tightened. Once, he and Rui had been as close as brothers, raised together after Rui's mother died birthing him. When Dion became alpha, the only man he wanted as his second was Rui, a tough, seasoned warrior who could've challenged him for alpha if he chose—and even Dion wasn't sure who'd have won.

Now, the man's belly was bigger than his chest and he was fit for little but chasing women and netting fish—and frankly, he was the worst damn fisherman in the clan.

Seeing Rui only fueled Dion's resolve to hold Cleia until she agreed to fix whatever she was doing to his people.

This was her doing. It was up to her to make it right.

He set down his fork. As usual, he hadn't gotten enough to eat, but for once he didn't notice.

"Enough," he barked when Davi, his youngest *tenente* and eager as a puppy to prove his worth, asked leave to scout the sun fae defenses. "We're not going to attack the sun fae—that would be suicide. And by the time they figure out where Cleia is, she'll have given in. Does anyone doubt I can break her?"

He rose to his feet and looked around him.

"No, my lord," Davi replied quickly. Luis and the other *tenentes* murmured their agreement and, around the hall, others nodded as well.

"But will it be worth it?" Isa's dark eyes were shrewd.

He slapped his hands on the table. The entire room went silent.

"All I know is we can't go on like this. Twenty years that bitch has been stealing our life-energy. Look around you—how many children have been born in recent years? Not to mention the warriors she's drained—" He inadvertently glanced at Luis.

The other man looked stricken, and Dion swiftly looked away.

His second-in-command drew himself up. "If you're asking for my resignation—"

Dion sighed. "Of course not. You're a good man, Luis, and I'm fortunate to have you at my side."

Luis gave a taut nod, but he glanced at Davi, who was listening avidly. Unless Luis recovered soon, the younger man would be within his rights to challenge for second and everyone present knew it.

Dion dragged a hand through his hair. It felt as if he'd spent the entire day fighting in some way or the other—first Cleia, then Tiago, and now this.

"I'm going for a swim," he muttered and strode from the cavern. He desperately needed to get in the water. It was either that or explode—or return to Cleia and take his frustrations out on her hide.

Changing to his river dolphin, he swam down Rock Run Creek to the Susquehanna and from there into the Chesapeake. A couple of warriors joined him, no doubt sent by Luis to guard him.

But he was glad for the company, taking comfort from the pack—as long as it wasn't arguing with him. Together, they cruised the bay, snacking on fish and spying on the humans who were in sailboats enjoying the early summer weather. When he returned a couple of hours later, he felt much better.

Most of the clan had retired to their quarters. Other than the sentries, the only people he passed were a courting couple who had eyes only for each other.

His apartment was dark save for a few dim fae lights floating in the gloom. His eyes went night-glow, adjusting to the reduced light. He trod softly through the *sala* to find his captive fast asleep —in his bed.

He stared down at her hungrily. She'd kicked off the blanket and was curled onto her side, one arm hugging the pillow, her shift rucked halfway up her thighs.

She was soft-skinned, vulnerable, desirable.

He wanted to protect her.

He wanted to rip the shift the rest of the way off and take her until she was sobbing with pleasure.

He clasped his hands behind his back to keep himself from touching her. But he couldn't stop his gaze from roaming over her, taking in the soft curve of her thighs, the thick braid that fell over one shoulder, and her full, perfect breasts, outlined beneath the thin white cotton. He knew he should return to the *sala* but he couldn't make himself take the first step.

Had it been just yesterday that he'd had her? It felt like another lifetime.

He hated that he wanted her even now, when she was doing nothing to entice him. *Deus*, the woman merely had to take a deep breath and he got hard.

She whimpered in her sleep.

Something in him tightened at the unhappy little sound. He disliked making war on a woman as much as the rest of the clan. Why didn't they understand that he had no choice?

She whimpered again. "No...no..."

He couldn't hold back any longer. He told himself it had nothing do with sex. She was having a nightmare. She needed comforting.

He smoothed a palm over her hair. "Easy there, *menina*. You're all right. It's just a bad dream."

Cleia gave a sleepy murmur and pressed her head into his hand. Then she went taut.

He removed his hand and melted back into the shadows, but she jerked upright, the blanket clutched to her chest.

"Who's there?" she croaked, tearing at the scarf with her free hand.

"Lord Dion. I was just checking on you."

Her tight shoulders eased. She took her hand from the scarf.

"As you can see," she returned flatly, "I'm still here."

He moved nearer, grateful that she didn't seem to realize he'd been stroking her. "Do you need anything?"

"No. No, I'm fine."

"You ate? Isa brought you dinner?"

"Yes. She's been very kind."

"*Bom*." He hesitated, curiously reluctant to leave her. "You're warm enough? I can get you another blanket."

"No. I'm all right."

Still he hesitated. The silence stretched until he said, "Well, good night then."

"Actually," she said, halting him, "there is something."

"*Sim?*"

"I—I wondered if I could join you for dinner tomorrow."

"You want to eat with the clan?"

She nodded, and he narrowed his eyes, trying to make out her expression. "Why?"

She moved a slim shoulder. "I could hear you all talking tonight. I...never mind."

He considered her, wondering what was behind her request. Did she simply want company? Or did she think she could somehow engineer an escape, perhaps prevail on one of the young, hormone-addled males to help—like his brother?

"I don't trust you," he said. "But I have you confined here for your own good. They know what you are, what you've done. The women especially have no reason to like you. You took eight of our best men."

"I see. Forget I asked."

Lying back down, she curled up on her side again, her back to him. This time, she was careful to cover herself.

Damn it, he would *not* feel sorry for her. For all he knew, this was another one of her tricks. But he found himself saying he'd think about it.

"*Obrigada.*" A whisper in the dark.

And the fact that she'd thanked him made him feel like the world's biggest S.O.B.

Jaw tight, he strode back to the *sala* and flung himself onto a couch. But it was too short and narrow. He tried first one position, then another, until finally, he rolled onto his stomach, his left arm and foot dangling over the side, and resigned himself to a sleepless night.

8

———————

"Senhora?" A rap on the door.

Cleia blinked and pushed herself upright from where she'd been napping on the couch. "Come in."

The door opened and Cleia realized it wasn't the outer door but the one to the apartment adjoining Dion's. Quick, light footsteps approached. Not Dion or Isa then, her only visitors since being taken captive two days ago.

"Senhora Cleia?" A young girl's voice.

Cleia could see enough to tell that she was slender and of average height, most likely Dion's young sister. Not that she cared—at this point, she'd have welcomed pretty much anyone.

Isa checked in from time to time, but Cleia had spent most of the day alone. Thus far she had eaten a solitary breakfast, taken another plunge in the cold pool, spent several hours sunbathing under one of the skylights (although the energy she'd received wouldn't have powered a light bulb), eaten a solitary lunch, moved through a combination of yoga and Pilates, and then ended on the couch, where she'd dozed off more out of boredom than because she was tired.

She aimed a grateful smile in her visitor's direction. "Yes, I'm Queen Cleia. Peace to you and yours."

"Peace to you and yours." The girl plopped herself on the other end of the couch. "I figured you'd like some company—you must be bored, stuck in here all day. I'm not supposed to be here, but I wanted to meet you. If you don't tell my brother, I won't."

She paused for breath long enough for Cleia to respond. "I'd love some company, but are you sure—"

"Oh, Dion will growl," was the airy reply, "but he won't do anything. He doesn't know how to handle me now that I'm almost grown up."

Cleia's lips twitched. "I see."

"I'm Rosana, by the way. Rosana do Rio. The youngest of the family," she added unnecessarily. "Which means I've got four older brothers who won't let me do *anything*. Well, Nic and Joaquim don't live here anymore, but that still leaves Dion and Tiago. They can't seem to remember that I'm almost sixteen—especially Dion. He's the worst."

"Ah..." Cleia felt a reluctant twinge of pity for the absent alpha; he clearly had his hands full with this one. She gently turned the conversation. "I remember when I turned sixteen. My parents threw me a ball and fae came from all over the world to celebrate. It was the first time I was allowed to attend a dance with the adults."

"A ball? What did you wear?"

"Oh, it was beautiful..." Cleia settled in to describe the three-day party to her rapt audience.

When Isa returned an hour later, they were sitting beside the pool, dangling their feet in the water and still talking. For an almost-sixteen-year-old, Rosana was surprisingly clear-eyed about her family and clan and she had a droll wit to match. Cleia couldn't remember the last time she'd laughed as much.

Isa clucked her tongue. "You know the alpha doesn't want you in here."

"For heaven's sake," Rosana retorted, "does she look dangerous to you?"

"No, but—" Cleia sensed both of them glancing at her. *She's a fae*, Isa had been about to say.

Cleia swallowed her hurt. Goddess, even the nice ones didn't trust her.

"Besides," Isa demanded, "aren't you supposed to be in the kitchen helping the cooks?"

Rosana leapt to her feet. "Is it four o'clock already?"

"Fifteen minutes ago," was the dry reply.

"Uh-oh. I'd better get going or Dion will kick my butt."

"*Rosana*," Isa scolded. "He would not—"

"No? Maybe not literally, but figuratively—"

"Go," the older woman commanded. "Now."

"I'm going, I'm going."

Cleia heard her kiss the other woman and then with a cheerful goodbye to them both, she was gone.

Isa shut the connecting door behind her. "The alpha spoils her," she said with a sigh as she returned to where Cleia was still sitting by the pool. "We all do. But without her parents to take her in hand..."

Cleia found it hard to picture the hard-eyed alpha spoiling anyone. But then, Rosana was a loveable young thing.

"You don't have to apologize. She reminds me of one of my cousins—she's a ball of energy just like Rosana."

"She'll be the death of me." Isa heaved another sigh. "But that's not what I came for. I brought you something to do."

Helping Cleia to her feet, Isa guided her back to one of the couches in the *sala* where she set a large bundle of what felt like thick, coated string on her lap.

"There. We thought you could help repair the nets."

Cleia caught the faint scent of the river. She ran her hands over the bundle. It was some type of webbing.

"A fishing net?"

"The alpha ordered me to find you something to do," Isa said a little defensively. "One of the women reminded me the nets always need mending. Valeria." She said the name as if Cleia would recognize it. "She's one of our best fishers," Isa added.

"I see," Cleia replied, none the wiser. But she guessed Valeria was one of the women who had cause to resent her.

She fingered the net. She was the sun fae ruler and Conduit, as well as one of her clan's best healers. She could breathe life and energy into a sick child—or stop a man's heart. Even amongst the fae, her powers were legendary. Some of the most powerful people in the world fell over themselves to please her. But she'd been raised to honor all the clan's workers, even the most humble.

And she just *knew* the Rock Run women—especially this Valeria—were hoping she'd refuse to do something as menial as mending a fishing net.

She nodded at Isa. "Show me what to do."

9

———

Cleia was gone.

Dion swore under his breath and glanced around his quarters again as if he'd somehow missed her the first time. Where in Hades was she?

It had been a long day. He'd started at Rock Run's largest vineyard, examining the young grapes along with its manager, Gaspar, the descendant of a Portuguese viticulturist who'd immigrated to America along with Dion's father.

He'd left Gaspar feeling cautiously optimistic—it looked to be the best harvest in two decades. A harvest they desperately needed, having lost much of last year's grapes to black rot. But much could go wrong between now and autumn.

Next, he'd gone to the huge cavern where his warriors trained and worked them until even the strongest were groaning for mercy. He'd finished with a swim in the bay, but instead of relaxing, he'd found himself thinking about Cleia and her long, golden body. Upon his return, he'd been drawn to her like a fish to a beautiful yet deadly lure.

Now he halted, irritated and a bit worried. Cleia *had* to be somewhere nearby—there was no way she could've escaped.

Still, he'd expected to find her where he'd left her, as she'd been the previous three evenings.

He glanced around his quarters one last time, but from where he stood he could see into both rooms, and he'd already checked the bathroom.

He frowned. The sparseness had never bothered him before. But now, with Cleia gone, the apartment seemed as devoid of personality as a hotel room, save for the five colorful dresses hanging from sturdy wood pegs.

He crossed the floor and fingered one—a soft rose pink shot with gold thread. The material slipped silkily through his fingers, giving off the faint scent of oranges...and the woman herself.

He rubbed the skirt against his cheek, taking her distinctive aroma onto his skin and marking the cloth with his own scent in turn until he realized what he was doing. His cheeks heated. He dropped the dress and strode out of the apartment in search of his missing captive.

"*Boa noite,* Dion." Isa stepped from the apartment next to his. She'd moved into this section several years ago to share quarters with Rosana after she'd grown too old to live with Dion. Normally they kept the door between their apartments open, but with Cleia there, he'd ordered it kept locked at all times.

"*Boa noite,* Senhora Isa," he replied a little impatiently but with the respect due an elder. "I'm looking for Senhora Cleia."

"That's what I was coming to tell you. She's with Rosana."

"Rosana?" he repeated, unable to believe his ears.

He didn't ask who'd let Cleia out of his apartment. Only his sister would dare. But Isa should know better.

"What are you thinking," he asked in a low, dangerous voice, "to leave her alone with that woman?" He brushed past her into her apartment.

"Dion." His former nurse's voice was sharp. Even after all these years, she could still halt him in his tracks.

"What?" He turned to face her.

"*Acalme-te*. It's not what you think. Senhora Cleia needed the company—and your sister likes her."

"*Deus*. Have you forgotten what that woman is?"

Isa's round, kind face firmed into stern lines. "Of course not. But you've bound her powers. Without them, she can't hurt anyone. It's cruel to leave her alone all day, blindfolded and with no one to talk to. I do my best, but I can only spare a little time here and there."

Unbidden, he recalled Cleia's forlorn whimper the other night as she lay sleeping. He passed a hand over his face. "I suppose it can't hurt anything. But I still want to check on them."

Rosana's door was open. Through it he heard a sound he hadn't heard much lately—his sister giggling. Rosana was his greatest joy—and his biggest headache. At least Tiago he could understand, having been an adolescent male himself.

But his young sister confounded him. One minute she was wildly happy, the next she was sobbing as if her heart would break—or furious at his attempts to rein her in. Isa said it was only hormones and would pass, but that didn't make Rosana any easier to live with.

He knew he spoiled her, but he couldn't help himself. To him she'd always be the skinny little girl with a mop of black curls and eyes too big for her face who, after their parents had disappeared, had clung to him like a limpet, afraid she'd lose him as well.

But now she was at the age when she could've used a mother. Isa did her best, but she had other responsibilities and *Deus* knew he was clueless where fifteen-year-old females were concerned. So he gave in to her, more than he should.

He found Rosana and Cleia on his sister's bed, heads together and chuckling at whatever was amusing them. Then Rosana saw him and the grin slid from her face.

"Dion's here," she said.

He swallowed his hurt. "*Boa noite*, Rosana. *Minha senhora*."

Cleia turned her bound face toward him. As usual, she'd set herself under one of the light shafts. The sun lit her hair, hanging in a thick braid over one shoulder, and gilded her fine features with gold. Even with the gray silk obscuring her eyes, she dazzled.

"I know," she murmured to Rosana. "I recognized his footsteps." To him, she said, "Good evening, my lord. I've been getting to know your sister. What an interesting young lady—you must be proud of her."

She tilted her head and smiled straight at him.

His heart lurched. It was the first true smile she'd given him— he didn't count that first day when she'd been trying to lure him with her glamour—and he found himself smiling back even though he knew she couldn't see him.

He blinked and swallowed hard. *It's all part of the seduction*, he reminded himself. But he couldn't help responding to it.

He glanced at Rosana. He should scold her—she knew damn well she should've asked permission to release Cleia from his apartment. But his sister's glower said she was expecting just that, so instead he murmured, "I *am* proud of her."

Rosana sent him a startled glance. He ignored it to take a seat on a chair next to the bed.

"I see Isa put you to work," he remarked to Cleia. He'd told Isa to find her something to do—nobody sat idle in the fada base. But it had also been a kindness after he'd caught her restlessly pacing his *sala* and realized she was all but screaming from boredom.

Her beautiful mouth twisted self-deprecatingly. "Mending fishing nets—and not very well, I'm sure. But it's something to do. Rosana volunteered to help me."

"*Ah, bom.*"

He watched as Cleia knotted a string and then held the end for Rosana to cut. Mending nets was usually done by the old people or those who couldn't contribute any other way. It seemed somehow wrong for Cleia's long, delicate fingers to be working with the tarred black string.

He brushed the thought away. Let the woman do some real work for a change.

"You're not doing so bad," he admitted. Actually, she was doing a surprisingly neat job for someone working by feel alone. "But it seems you're doing all the work." He raised a brow at Rosana, whose only contribution seemed to be wielding the scissors.

"*She* doesn't mind," his sister retorted. "*She* says she'd rather stay busy than sit around and worry."

"If *she* would only cooperate," he returned, "*she* could go home and she'd have nothing to worry about."

The queen's lips moved. No sound came out, but he was pretty sure they formed the words, "pigheaded fada."

His lips twitched in spite of himself.

Aloud, she said, "I don't mind mending them. As for Rosana, she doesn't have to do anything—I'm happy just to have her company."

His sister sent him a triumphant look. He sat back, fingers interlaced behind his head, and replied with the air of someone making a discovery, "She's not bad for someone who's only seen fifteen turns of the sun."

"*Di-on*." Rosana scowled at him.

He gave her a wink and a grin.

She tossed her head, but he could tell her heart wasn't in it. For the first time in what seemed like forever, she returned his smile. "And fifteen isn't so young. It's about time you noticed I'm almost grown up."

"Oh, I noticed."

And so had a good number of the unmated men. She was going to be a beauty, with their Celtic mother's elfin features and unusual sapphire eyes. So far, she didn't seem to be interested in anything other than a little flirtation, but he dreaded the day she started dating in earnest.

"Yeah?" She hopped off the bed and, in one of her quicksilver mood changes, knelt on the floor to fling her arms around him. "Lady Cleia has been telling me about the sun fae. Did you know her parents threw a ball for her sixteenth birthday? Fae came from all around the world. And every year, she throws a ball to kick off the midsummer festival. They wear dresses that shimmer when you move and jewels in their hair, their ears...even in their navels." She giggled. "The men too—although not so many. Everyone glitters—it's like the stars come down to earth, she says. Right, Lady Cleia?"

"Yes, but I'm sure your brother isn't interest—"

"Why not? I'll be sixteen in August. It doesn't have to be a ball, but why couldn't we have a dance?" She placed her hands on his knees and used those big blue eyes to their full effect. "Please, Dion? I promise I won't ask for anything ever again."

"A dance?" He caressed her shoulders. "I don't know, *minha pequena*. That's not our way—"

"I knew it," his sister said in tragic tones. She jerked away and threw herself on the bed next to Cleia. "He never lets me do *anything*. He says the old ways are past, that the bacchanalia were an excuse for drinking too much and giving in to our animals. But I don't want to go to a baccha. I just want to have some fun like other girls my age. I wish...I wish that Mama and Papa would come home."

She burst into tears.

"Rosana," he said helplessly. "Don't, *querida*." He made a move toward her, but Cleia lifted her hand to halt him. He obeyed only because he didn't know what else to do.

But to his surprise, Cleia took his side. "Hush, now." Setting the net on the mattress, she stroked Rosana's wavy black hair away from her face. "Your brother's right about the bacchanalia— they're too wild for all but the most feral fae or fada. And trust me, little one, you don't want to fall under the power of such a one."

"A dance is not a bacchanal," his sister insisted, her voice muffled by the mattress.

"No, it's not," Cleia agreed. "I'll tell you what—when I go home, if your brother says it's all right, you can come for a visit and we'll have a ball just for you. My dressmaker will make you a dress in any color you want and you can wear some of my jewels. Would you like that?"

"Promise?" Rosana lifted her head.

"Promise."

She turned to him. "Can I? Please, Dion?"

Over my dead body, he thought, any gratitude he'd felt toward Cleia evaporating.

"When the lady leaves—*if* she leaves—the last thing she'll want is a visit from my sister. Unless"—he crooked a brow at the queen—"she intends to use you to pay me back."

Cleia's spine went stick straight. "How dare you?" she hissed. "Truth"—she touched her heart—"Rosana can visit Rising Sun and she will be returned unharmed whenever she wishes."

"Like my men were?" he shot back.

"Damn it, *that wasn't me.* And if I promise your sister will be safe, then she'll be safe. Unlike you, I don't sneak around and tell half-truths to get what I want."

He was on his feet now. "By *Deus,* if you were a man—"

"What?" she taunted. "What would you do, *fada?*"

Anger bloomed in his chest, hot and red. He stared down at her. If she were a man, he'd knock her across the room for such an insult.

But she was a woman, and he ached to push her down on the mattress and show her just who was master here...and who the captive. He might have renounced the bacchas, but that didn't mean his ancestors' dark blood didn't course in his veins.

Rosana shifted uneasily. "It's okay," she muttered. "I didn't really think he'd let me go."

But neither of them paid attention. Cleia pressed her lips together and lifted her chin. He knew damn well she sensed the danger she was in, but the woman was too proud—and stubborn —to back down. Then he noticed her fingers clamped on the mattress's edge, knuckles white.

Shame twisted his belly.

He exhaled harshly. "Not one word I told you was a lie. And the only sneaking around I did was to protect my people. I acted in self-defense. Twenty years you've drained us. *Twenty fucking years*. I had to stop you. We have nothing left to give."

Cleia's chin went up another notch. "Then release me. I swear I won't take another of your warriors as a lover. You don't under-stand. You can't keep me here. I have to go home."

"Ah, but I do understand. I met with your cousin Olivia yesterday. She told me you have to return by the midsummer festival for your people's sake."

"That's what she said? That my people need me back by the midsummer festival?"

"Yes." Dion scrutinized her face, wishing he could see her eyes. "Why? Isn't that true?"

Lady Olivia had implied they required Cleia for some cere-monial purpose. All seven sun fae clans, along with much of the fae world, gathered at Rising Sun to celebrate midsummer with a huge, three-day festival, kicked off by a ritual attended only by the sun fae to mark the summer solstice. As queen, Cleia led the ritual, but surely someone else could take her place.

Now he wondered if there was more to the ceremony than an excuse for yet another extravagant fae revel.

"It's true." Cleia kept her face blank, but he was learning to read her. She was worried beneath the expressionless façade. "My cousin—Lady Olivia—she's well? Did she have a message for me?"

"She seemed well, *sim*. But there was no message. Surely you don't think I'm so *estúpido* as to admit you're here."

"But she knows you're the last person to see me."

"She can't prove anything. After you passed out, I sprinkled concealing dust on you."

Rare, precious stuff for a fada. Only the fae could create that kind of magic, so he'd had to barter five of his best warriors as mercenaries for a month to obtain it—but it had been worth it.

"I waited until everyone was asleep," he continued, "and then carried you out of the mansion. A couple of my men brought you back to the base while I returned to your apartment. The next morning, I was as 'surprised' as everyone that you'd disappeared during the night."

And he'd made damn sure he got the hell out of there before Lady Olivia had a chance to question him more deeply. Even so, the small lies he'd told had cost him; he'd spent the first few hours after his return curled up in a ball in his *sala*, wracked by pain.

"Olivia will find me," Cleia stated confidently. "She would've sensed the moment I left the compound."

"The storm was at its peak—and your energy was at its weakest. She didn't come looking for you until the next morning. And one of my men laid a false trail to make it look like the Virginia night fae were involved."

"No one outsmarts my cousin," Cleia returned, but she sounded less certain now. "She's an old fae and one tough mother when someone she loves is threatened. You have no idea who you're dealing with."

"*Não*? We'll see." He nodded curtly before he recalled she couldn't see him, and left the apartment.

HE SPENT that night in the river.

He was tired of tossing and turning on the couch, knowing Cleia was in the next room, so close he could hear when she murmured in her sleep...so close that her sweet-tart scent penetrated his dreams. But he didn't sleep any better than he had the previous three nights.

He shifted to river dolphin, his favorite form, and dozed. To breathe, a dolphin had to keep one side of its brain awake at all times. If he'd let himself fall completely asleep, he would've drowned. Instead, he had to swim slowly and surface every so often for a breath.

His drowsing mind meandered here and there. He found himself wondering if Cleia actually attended a bacchanal. There had been a note in her voice that made him think she was speaking from experience.

The thought shouldn't make him go hard—he fully agreed with his *pai*'s decision to ban the dark, alcohol-soaked orgies— but he couldn't help flashing on an image of her clad in nothing but that bright mane of hair, kneeling before him and taking his cock between soft, wine-stained lips...

He groaned and then sputtered as he took in water; he'd unconsciously changed back to man as he'd envisioned sex with her. He shifted to dolphin again and spent what remained of the night with his animal riding him.

She wants it.

The words beat in his brain, primitive, sly. After all, it had been Cleia who'd invited him to her bed, not the other way around.

She's yours to take, the animal murmured.

Mine...mine...mine...

With the coming of the day, he surfaced and took his human form again, trying to still that insistent chant. He hoisted himself onto a rock in the river's center. It had rained somewhere upriver. The water rushed by, a dark shimmer in the pre-dawn light.

He propped himself on his forearms to watch the sunrise, but even the hazy pink and gold rays reminded him of Cleia and her gauzy dresses, seated on a chair before him as he inched the material up her long, tanned thighs...

He swallowed. Having her in his own apartment—in his bed, yet—was an unholy temptation.

But he couldn't take her. Not like this. Not while she was his prisoner.

He might be a ruthless S.O.B. but there were some lines he refused to cross.

His animal would have to accept that. It moved beneath his skin, disgruntled but resigned.

A breeze rippled across the fast-flowing water, caressing his damp skin. To anyone but a water fada, it might seem chilly, but to him it felt...suggestive. His already partially-erect cock twitched as if a silk scarf had been drawn over it—or a woman's long, glossy hair.

He wrapped his fingers around the rapidly stiffening stalk and stroked up and down.

Recalling Cleia as she'd been last night, arguing with him, her face flushed with anger.

Then picturing her on her knees, sweetly begging his pardon, her mouth full and red, the blindfold gone so he could see her tip-tilted eyes go hazy with arousal and those long fingers reaching for him...

He stroked faster, visualizing her in all sorts of darkly erotic positions with him controlling her, taking her, until she was screaming with ecstasy. His heels dug into the rock and he groaned as his seed shot hotly onto his abdomen. He dropped an arm over his eyes and slumped back onto the rock, the breath jerking in and out of his chest.

She wants it. Why don't you take her?

Deus. What was he going to do?

He lay there for several minutes but was no closer to a solution when he gave up and rolled off the rock into the water.

Back at the base, Isa was lying in wait for him outside the dining hall. She always gave him the respect due her alpha, but also managed to make sure he never forgot he'd had a part in the gray which streaked her rich brown hair.

Now she greeted him politely, and then informed him just as courteously that he needed to allow Cleia to take her meals with everyone else.

"I do?" he replied in dangerous tones.

But the problem with a woman who's known you since you were a pup is that she isn't easily cowed.

"*Sim, meu senhor*. She's lonely and homesick. Last night she barely touched her dinner. I don't care what she's done, I'm not going to stand by and watch her starve."

He scraped his fingers through his wet hair.

Damn Cleia anyway. He hadn't expected her to hold out for more than a day or two. She was a sun fae. They lived for fun, parties, excitement. Take her away from her people and her pampered lifestyle, force her to do menial work, threaten her subtly as only a man could a woman—and yes, he knew he was a bastard but he was desperate—and she should be begging to give him anything he wanted.

But it hadn't worked.

She'd proved tougher than he'd expected, stubbornly maintaining she'd done nothing wrong. Although in hindsight, he didn't know why he was surprised. She might be a self-indulgent, party-loving fae but she was also a queen, a ruler in her own right.

"Did she put you up to this?" he demanded.

Isa's look told him not to be a fool. "It's plain to see she's unhappy."

"You say she's not eating?"

"She ate less than half of what she usually does. You know how the sun fae are—they're not that different from us; they need their clan. What could it hurt? She can't do anything with her powers bound."

He blew out a breath, concerned in spite of himself.

Yes, he knew how the sun fae were. The most gregarious of the fae, their compound was a constant stream of activity, with fae from all around the world coming and going. If they weren't having a party, they were hosting a festival—or throwing one of their fucking balls.

As Isa said, they needed their clan—although they'd probably turn up their aristocratic noses at any comparison to a fada.

He'd known keeping Cleia isolated was cruel, but damn it, what choice did he have?

Still, Isa was right; they couldn't stand by and let the blasted woman starve. It was bad enough that he was keeping her underground when she was a creature of sunlight.

"Fine," he said. "She can eat with the clan from now on. However, inform her that if she goes anywhere other than my quarters and the dining hall without my or Luis's permission, she'll be immediately confined again—and this time, I'll tie her to the damn bed."

Isa pursed her lips. He had the feeling she was struggling not to laugh, but all she said was, "Yes, my lord," before heading down the hall toward his quarters.

The dining hall was filled with people eating breakfast. Coffee scented the air and the serving tables held large platters of fried fish; the fishers had had a good catch yesterday. There were baskets of dark peasant bread and big bowls of strawberries, as well as cereal and milk for the children. When times were better, the menu might include more variety, but at least for today, he was pleased to see that no one would leave hungry.

He gulped a double shot of espresso and then made himself a hefty fish sandwich before taking a seat at a table with some of the other unmated warriors.

He knew the instant Cleia entered the hall.

A shock went through the crowded room. Whispers fluttered from person to person and the kids stared at her with open-mouthed curiosity. Several of the women flashed her looks of pure hatred, and even the friendlier ones frowned.

Cleia couldn't see them, of course, but she must have sensed the stares. She faltered and then lifted her chin with that proud little movement he was coming to recognize.

He felt an unwilling admiration: even in a casual summer dress and borrowed rope sandals, she looked every inch a queen.

Mine.

Isa touched her arm, guiding her to a table near the door. Rosana immediately jumped up and sat down next to her. A moment later, Tiago picked up his plate as well and made his way across the room to take seat across from the two of them.

A few people resumed talking in soft voices, but there was a tense silence as everyone else waited to see what Dion would do. He took his time, finishing his sandwich before strolling across the room to greet the new arrival. It was a move designed to show that while Cleia's presence in the dining hall had his approval, he was also the alpha, and her dominant as long as she was in his territory.

He heard a flurry of whispers, but it worked: the clan lowered its collective hackles and resumed eating.

While Isa went to fix a plate for herself and Cleia, he greeted his brother and sister and then took a seat next to his captive.

"*Bom dia.* You slept well?"

She was sitting rigidly upright, fingers intertwined in her lap. So she'd sensed the animosity in the hall. Well, he'd never believed her a stupid woman.

"Good morning," she replied. "I slept well enough. And you? I wondered where you were."

Did you miss me? a foolish part of him wanted to ask.

But all he said was, "I spent the night in the river. I thought it for the best."

She didn't pretend to misunderstand. "I see."

Across the table, Tiago's gaze moved from Cleia to him, a frown creasing his brow.

She spoke again. "I want to thank you for inviting me to share your meal. I can see that it's not a...popular decision."

"They'll do as I say."

She inclined her head.

"Besides, it's Isa you should thank, not me. She's worried you're not eating enough."

"Of course," she murmured wryly. "You'd look bad if you let your prisoner starve."

He absorbed the jab in silence. It was true, after all. It just wasn't the whole truth.

"From now on you'll eat with us. Isa will arrange it. And you can move between the dining hall and my quarters—that's safe enough."

"*Obrigada*. It will be nice to have some exercise."

"I can bring her to meals," Rosana volunteered.

"And me," added Tiago.

"Take it up with Senhora Isa," he told them. To Cleia he said, "No thanks are necessary. As you say, you're worth more to me alive than dead."

Rosana gave an outraged gasp and Tiago's frown darkened.

He ignored them to rise to his feet, giving Isa, who had returned with two plates, back her seat.

As he walked away, he happened to glance at Davi. He was staring at Cleia with unconcealed lust. In fact, half the unmated men in the room were casting surreptitious looks in her direction.

Mine.

His animal growled, a low but unmistakable warning.

Startled looks swung his way. He ignored them to raise a hand for attention.

"You"—he jabbed a finger at Luis, his five *tenentes* and the men and women in his top warrior squad—"meet me in the training cave in ten minutes. You other warriors, find the people in your squad and engage in training exercises in the river. The rest of you, have a good day."

The training cave was a large, open space with exercise equipment and several rings in which men could engage in one-on-one combat, or fight with several at a time. A stream bubbled up at one end, providing fresh drinking water.

He greeted his men—and two women—as they assembled, and proceeded to work them for four straight hours, starting with calisthenics and intense stretching based on a boot-camp style of yoga, then moving on to a form of marital arts, fighting both barehanded and with knives, until his hard-assed warriors were bent over and gasping for breath, muttering among themselves about crazy S.O.B. alphas.

Dion swiped at the sweat stinging his eyes and eyed the groaning, winded group. His lip curled.

"You call yourselves warriors? Don't make me laugh. Maybe you should go home to your mamas and leave the fighting to the grownups."

Davi growled under his breath but when Dion swung his way, he ducked his head.

It was Rodolfo who came to his feet, brow lowered. A big bull of man, he rumbled, "Bite me. You've just got a wasp up your ass because of Cleia."

The cavern went still. Everyone knew Rodolfo had been the first Rock Run man to have the queen.

Luis rose slowly from where he'd been drinking from the stream. Dion had been careful not to push him as hard as the others, but his face was taut with exhaustion. His gaze went from Rodolfo to Dion but he remained silent.

"Maybe I do," Dion allowed. "But I'm not the one whining for mercy."

"I don't whine—and I don't ask *anyone* for mercy." Rodolfo's lips peeled back and he met Dion's gaze full on. "Not even you, *my lord.*"

Dion's claws sliced out. "Then show me why I should allow your fat carcass to take up space as a *tenente*," he snapped.

"*Com prazer,*" Rodolfo snarled.

"No weapons. Bare hands only." Dion retracted his claws. He didn't want to kill the man, just teach him a lesson.

The two of them handed their knives to Luis and squared off in one of the rings with the others forming a circle to watch. It wasn't a ritual challenge, but if Dion lost, anyone unhappy with his place in the hierarchy would want a chance at him and he'd be fighting off challengers for the next six months.

Dion circled Rodolfo, his muscles loose and ready. He was the alpha; let Rodolfo make the first move.

The big man looked uneasy now. He had a quick temper that tended to burn itself out just as rapidly. Dion suspected he hadn't intended things to go this far.

But he welcomed the chance to fight. Everyone present knew this wasn't about the insults he'd tossed off—they were warriors, used to ribbing one another. No, this was about Cleia and who, ultimately, had a right to her, whether as a prisoner or a lover.

Maybe Dion *did* have a wasp up his ass with regard to the woman—but that didn't mean he was wrong. She was the key to the strange malady plaguing his clan and he was damned well going to keep her until the problem was resolved. The others would just have to accept it.

And if a part of him wanted to claim her in other ways, well, that was his own damn business.

Rodolfo lunged at him, surprisingly fast for such a bulky man, but Dion simply stepped aside and then grabbed him when he was off-balance. They grappled with each other until Dion kicked out one of Rodolfo's legs.

The big man landed on his back with a thud, his breath sawing in and out.

Dion quirked a brow. "Had enough?"

Rodolfo grunted and rose back to his feet. Dion stifled a sigh. The man was stubborn as an ox. He'd have to be knocked down another couple of times before he'd yield.

Dion settled into a fighter's crouch and went after Rodolfo with a flurry of punches and karate chops. The *tenente* retaliated with some good blows himself. It wasn't the no-holds-barred combat of a true challenge, but they'd both be sporting some colorful bruises.

Dion saw an opening and slammed the heel of his hand into Rodolfo's jaw. His big head snapped back. He blinked and wavered but remained standing.

Dion waited for him to regain his equilibrium. Everyone knew the fight was his. Nothing would be served by pounding one of his best men into unconsciousness.

But Rodolfo dropped to one knee. "Enough," he said, head down and gaze averted. "My apologies, *meu senhor*."

"Of course." Dion stuck out his hand. When the *tenente* grasped it, he pulled him to his feet and into a bear hug. "Good fight, *irmão*."

They nuzzled each other's cheeks, exchanging scents and emphasizing there were no hard feelings. He rubbed Rodolfo's buzzed-cut head and released him to look around the circle of warriors.

"Anyone else have something he needs to get off his chest?"

Nobody said a word.

"Good," he said. "Now, all of you, in the frigging creek. The stench in here's enough to turn a man's stomach. Your mates won't let you in your dens." A ripple of laughter swept the group. "The rest of the afternoon is yours unless you're on sentry duty," he continued, "but I want to see everyone back here tomorrow, same time."

They nodded and headed toward an exit that led to Rock Run Creek, talking animatedly about the fight.

Dion followed, a hand to his jaw, gingerly working it back and forth. But the crisis was averted for now. That was worth a few bruises.

Luis dropped back to walk with him. He still looked tired, but he'd recovered his color. "You're pushing them too hard," he remarked. "If Rodolfo hadn't gotten pissed off, someone else would've."

"Perhaps. But they needed to blow off steam. Everybody's on edge, waiting to see what the sun fae will do. I'm counting on you to keep things calm."

Luis shook his head. "I just hope you know what you're doing."

"I do," Dion returned with more certainty than he felt.

Never show fear. Never show uncertainty. His pai had drummed that in to him.

But that didn't mean he was never afraid, or that he was always certain he'd made the right decision. Twenty years the clan had been in decline, and Dion alpha for ten of those. In his darkest moments, he castigated himself for not seeing sooner that Cleia was at the root of it.

They reached the creek. His hard-faced warriors were frolicking like pups, splashing and dunking one another.

Dion's grim mood lightened. Leaving Luis on the bank, he waded into the noisy knot, where he was immediately jumped by three men—all in fun, of course.

He grinned savagely and lashed out with his fists, giving as good as he got.

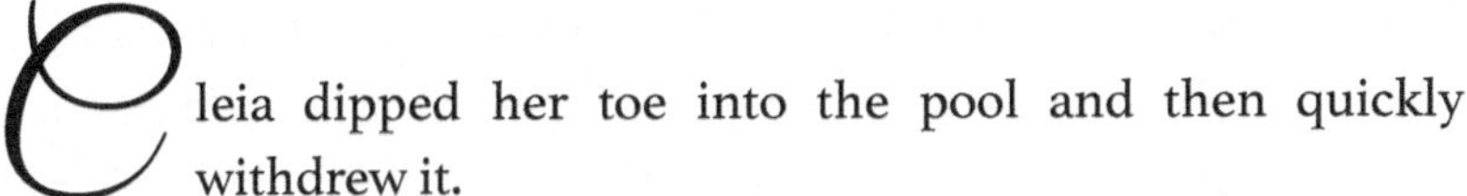

10

———

*C*leia dipped her toe into the pool and then quickly withdrew it.

"Haven't you people heard of hot baths?" she grumbled. "You know, the kind that melt your muscles, help you relax after a long day? Or even a hot tub—now there's a brilliant invention."

There was no reply. But then, she hadn't expected one. Rosana was out swimming with her friends and Isa was off doing whatever she did during the day.

Cleia paced her way toward the *sala*, automatically steering around the bed. It was day seven of her captivity and she was so bored she'd have even welcomed another net to mend. But she'd apparently repaired every damn net in the base.

Distracted, she went off course and bumped into the open door to the *sala*. She growled and smacked her palm against the hard wood.

"And where are you, Lord Dion? I could use some company here. Even yours."

But since their confrontation in Rosana's bedroom, the alpha had avoided being alone with her. Most days the only time she saw him was at dinner.

She knew why, of course: it was that damnable current between them. They might be captor and captive, but neither could forget that first night—and how good it had been.

At least he was allowing her more freedom these days. She could go to the dining hall on her own and she was allowed to take walks—within the caverns, of course—with Isa, Rosana or Tiago. She'd used the opportunity to familiarize herself with the base, in case by some miracle she managed to escape.

Of course, if she could break the binding spell, she could simply teleport herself out—she had the Gift of wayfaring—but barring that, she had to rely on more traditional means of transportation.

But her excursions out into the base had just shown her how hopeless her situation was. Rock Run was a maze of crisscrossing tunnels that would've been hard to navigate even if she'd had her sight.

Rosana said it was to discourage intruders. "Even if someone invaded," she'd explained, "they wouldn't get very far."

"Clever," Cleia had murmured. And it was.

She was coming to see that the fae—even friendly fae like herself—underestimated the fada. She'd unconsciously absorbed fae prejudices, believing that shapeshifters were a lower level of being, somewhere between the fae and animals. But Dion had easily outwitted her guards and was keeping her prisoner with apparently no one the wiser.

If he was an animal, he was smart like a fox.

She smacked the *sala* door again. "But if you're so clever, my lord, why are you afraid of me?"

The silence echoed, so loud she felt like she'd drown in it if she stayed alone in these two rooms another minute.

The hell with it.

She marched across the *sala*. She was busting out, even if it was just to go the dining hall. At least she'd have company there

—even if it were with women who treated her like a cross between a demon and a siren.

She tried the door and to her relief, it opened. She kept expecting to find Dion had changed his mind and locked her in again, something she wasn't sure she could bear.

The hall was quiet. Empty. Everybody had somewhere to be, something to do...except her.

She placed a hand on the stone wall and made her way to the dining hall: fifty-six steps, turn to the right, take another seventy-two steps and then make another right turn into the hall.

She was greeted by the low murmur of voices: the cooks, working in the large, open kitchen. Footsteps approached and then a woman spoke in polite but cool tones.

"*Bom dia, minha senhora.* May I help you? Some wine, perhaps?"

"That would be nice, thank you." Cleia felt her way to the nearest table.

The woman returned with the wine, placing it in her hand. Cleia thanked her again, and she said, "If that's all..."

"No, wait."

"*Sim?*" the woman returned impatiently.

It was a little lowering—Cleia wasn't used to being considered a nuisance. She swallowed her pride and said, "I wondered if you could use any help?"

The woman came nearer, close enough for Cleia to see she was almost as large and broad-shouldered as a man. "What do you want?" Her voice dripped with ice now.

"Just what I said—I'd like to help. There must be something I can do."

Work-roughened fingers closed on her wrist. Cleia stiffened but allowed it.

"With these hands?" the other woman asked scornfully. "I don't think so."

"I have something she can do, Gabriela," a voice called from the kitchen.

A couple of the women chuckled.

"I'll be right back," Gabriela told Cleia and walked away, leaving her to sip the wine and wonder if she'd regret this.

Gabriela returned with a large sack and a ceramic bowl, which she set on Cleia's lap. "Have you ever shelled peas?" she asked, clearly expecting her to refuse. "We need them for the *caldeirada*. The fish stew."

"No, but I can figure it out." Cleia fished a pod from the sack; anything was better than returning to those two empty rooms with nothing to do but worry about her people and that Olivia would attempt something reckless to free her.

Besides, these women were starting to annoy her. How did they think she normally spent her days—painting her nails and giggling with her friends? Not only was she the ruler of the seven sun fae clans, she was a well-respected healer.

"You just open it, right?" She dug her nails into the pod and ripped it inexpertly apart.

Gabriela clucked her tongue, unimpressed. "Here."

Taking Cleia's hands, she showed her how to break open the next pod by pressing on one end. When it opened at the seam, she guided Cleia's thumb down the opening to release the peas. They dropped into the bowl.

"There's more when you finish those," Gabriela said and walked off.

Cleia pressed her lips together and fought the urge to heave the bowl after her. She felt for the next pod and opened it with a snap.

From the kitchen she heard rapid-fire Portuguese, too soft for her to make out, followed by a burst of laughter.

She scowled and tore open another pod.

She was partway through the sack when she heard a child's light, rapid footsteps. They stopped next to her.

"Whatcha doin', lady?" a cheerful voice asked in Portuguese.

Cleia dropped a handful of peas into the bowl on her lap and smiled in her tiny interlocutor's direction. It was a boy, she guessed, about age three or four.

"Shelling peas for dinner," she replied in the same language. "Would you like some?"

"*Sim.*" The boy paused before tacking on a polite, "*Por favor.*"

Her smile increased. She had a feeling that was why he'd stopped. She held out the bowl. "Help yourself."

"*Obrigado.*" A small hand reached past hers into the bowl.

"*De nada.*"

"I likes beas," her new acquaintance informed her somewhat indistinctly as he chewed.

"Me too. You can have more if you like."

"Okay." He reached into the bowl again.

"What's your name?" she asked.

"Xavier."

"Sha-vee-err," Cleia repeated. "That's a nice name. I'm Senhora Cleia."

"Clay-uh," he repeated. "I know. Mama told me."

"Who's your mama?"

"She's over there." He pointed toward the kitchen. "We're having *cal'da* tonight."

His mother must be one of the cooks.

"You mean *caldeirada*?" The spicy mélange of fish, potatoes, peppers and other vegetables already scented the air.

"*Sim.*" Small fingers touched the scarf over her eyes. "Why d'you hafta wear that? Don't your eyes work?"

She smiled wryly. "They work fine. But Lord Dion wants me to wear it."

"Oh. How d'you see?"

"I can't. Not much, anyway. I can see light and shadows and that's about it. Enough to tell you're a big boy—about this tall." She raised her hand high above her head.

"*Não, senhora*. I'm down here." He chuckled and tugged on her arm.

"Oh, there you are." She tapped the top of his head.

He chuckled again. "I likes you," he announced. A small, sweaty hand touched hers.

"I like you, too." She ruffled his soft curls.

"If you want to go somewhere," he offered, "I can hold your hand so you don't bump things."

Stars, what a sweetie. He must have seen Isa or Rosana helping her to navigate the tables at dinnertime.

"*Obrigada*," she replied gravely. "If I need to go anywhere I'll be sure to ask you."

"Okay."

She sensed a change in the air, a rustle of energy, and then a cool, wet nose nudged her bare calf. She stifled a gasp. "Xavier?"

He chittered in reply. Two webbed paws settled on her thighs and a moment later a furry little animal scrabbled onto her lap. She caught him and then chuckled.

"You're an otter."

For answer, he butted her arm, demanding to be petted. She set aside the peas and combed her fingers through his warm, velvety pelt. "Is this what you want?"

He sighed with pleasure and flopped onto his back, his head a slight, warm weight against her arm. Her heart turned over. Gathering him closer, she pressed a kiss to the top of his downy head. He smelled puppy-sweet with a hint of river.

He rumbled low in his chest, which she guessed was the otter version of purring.

"Xavier!" A woman hurried out of the kitchen. "Don't bother the lady."

"He's no bother," Cleia returned, rubbing the soft little belly beneath her hand. "I'm happy to hold him."

The woman came closer, smaller and more slender than Gabriela. "I can take him now."

Cleia heard the wariness in her voice. She stifled a sigh and made to return him. "Of course."

But Xavier shook his head and burrowed deeper into her arms.

"Imp," the woman scolded, but there was a smile in her voice.

"I'm guessing you're Xavier's mother." Cleia gave his belly another rub and the low rumbling increased.

"That's right. My name is Marina. He keeps me on my toes, that one."

"I can believe it."

Xavier let out a sigh and his body went limp.

"Is he asleep?" Cleia whispered.

"Yes." The smile was still in Marina's voice. "He goes until he runs out of energy, then crashes wherever he is."

"He's adorable. I'd love to have one just like him."

Cleia tried to keep the envy out of her voice, but it crept in. Like the fada, the fae rarely had children outside the mate bond.

There was a short silence, then Marina said, "Do you know who I am?"

Cleia swallowed uneasily. "No. Should I?"

"Luis's mate."

"I see." She remembered Luis, of course: he'd been her lover for nearly two years. She recalled what Dion had told her—that in five years, Luis had only given his mate one child—and briefly closed her eyes. "So Xavier is his son."

"*Sim.* We pray for more, but so far—nothing."

Cleia nodded her head but remained silent. What was there to say, after all?

Marina touched her shoulder and she tensed, but all the other woman said was, "Maybe someday, you'll have one of your own."

Cleia stroked Xavier's fur. "If the Goddess is willing."

"Yes. Well, let me take him to the creche. I have to get back to work."

"If you're sure—" Cleia reluctantly handed the sleeping pup back to his mother.

He grumbled a bit, but she murmured something soothing and he quieted again. Marina left and Cleia went back to shelling peas.

But when Marina returned a few minutes later, she didn't go back to the kitchen. Instead, she stopped and addressed Cleia in a voice shaking with emotion, "You seem to be a nice person. Why can't you let Luis go?"

"But I did." Puzzled, Cleia strained to see her face, but all she could see was a damned shadow. "What are you talking about? He left me years ago."

"You really don't know, do you?"

Cleia's fingers tightened on the ceramic bowl. "Your alpha accused me of stealing life-energy, but I'm not."

"I wish you could see Luis, then," Marina said bitterly. "He's wasting away. The healers have done their best. He gets better for a while, but it always comes back. He has so little energy and he's gotten so thin that I'm afraid"—her voice caught—"I'm afraid I'm going to lose him."

She sat down heavily on the bench next to Cleia.

"Oh, Marina." Cleia thought of the Luis she'd known. Darkly handsome, with a hard, muscular frame and a sly wit that only emerged after you got to know him. It hurt to picture him sick, wasting away. "I'm sorry, more sorry than I can say. But I swear I'm not doing anything. Truth." She brought her hand to her heart.

She sensed Marina's scrutiny. "Maybe you're not doing it deliberately, but it all goes back to when he was your lover—"

"But he was perfectly healthy when he left me. It must have happened after he came home. I swear on everything I hold holy that it's *not me*. Don't you think I'd know if it was?"

"But it has to be you. There's no other explanation. What if you're doing it without being aware of it?"

"Do you think that hasn't occurred to me? I've spent the past week going over and over it in my mind. And I can think of nothing—I *feel* nothing—that makes me believe I am."

"Then Luis is never going to get better," Marina stated flatly.

Cleia instinctively reached out a hand to her. For a moment, she thought the other woman was going to refuse to take it, then her hand settled in Cleia's.

Cleia squeezed her fingers. "I'm a healer in my own clan. When I get back to Rising Sun, if there's anything I can do, I promise I will. And if it turns out I'm wrong—that I've caused his illness in any way—I'll do whatever I can to make him well."

Marina gripped her hand with both of hers. "You swear this?"

"I swear." Cleia touched her other hand to her heart in the sign of a sacred vow.

"*Muito obrigada, minha senhora.*" Her voice held an optimism that Cleia prayed wasn't misplaced.

"Marina?" Gabriela called from the kitchen. "I could use those peas."

"Coming." Marina took the bowl from Cleia and gathered up the almost-empty sack. To Cleia she said, "I have to go, but if you want, Xavier and I can come by tomorrow morning. If you want us to, that is," she added diffidently.

"I'd love it. And tell Gabriela I can shell more peas."

"That's all right. She's almost done with the rest."

Cleia's smile was rueful. "She didn't really need my help, did she?"

"No," Marina admitted. "But that doesn't mean it wasn't welcome."

She left and Cleia toyed with her wine.

Could she be draining life-energy from Rock Run's people? But how? Even the night fae didn't suck life-energy; instead, they fed on dark energy: fear, anger, hopelessness.

Marina was speaking to the other women. This time she was defending her, explaining that she'd agreed to help Luis.

A short while later Cleia once more heard footsteps approaching.

"Here." It was Gabriela, her voice gruff. "It's still a couple of hours until dinner," she said as she set a plate on the table next to Cleia. "I brought you some cheese and olives to snack on."

Surprised, Cleia started to thank her but Gabriela was already walking away.

Cleia felt for a chunk of cheese. She was always hungry these days, her body trying to make up for the nourishment it wasn't receiving from the sun by eating even more than usual. But it only worked up to a point. She was already weaker and she suspected she'd lost a couple of pounds.

She took a bite of the cheese. It was delicious, firm with a slightly nutty flavor, especially when paired with the olives.

Apparently she'd made a friend. She just hoped she hadn't made a promise she couldn't keep.

11

————

*D*ion strode into the dining hall, eager to see Cleia and despising himself for it.

The sun fae queen had been his prisoner for a week now and he was still no closer to a solution. In fact, he was meeting her cousin again tomorrow. He couldn't keep refusing Lady Olivia's requests to meet, but he had no idea what to say to her.

Meanwhile, he avoided Cleia as much as possible, except for meal times. He told himself that was because Rosana and Tiago usually ate with her, too, but the truth was he was as drawn to the woman as if she were still powering that glamour. Today he'd forced himself to stay away until dinner, when the clan gathered for a large, family-style meal.

He entered the hall as the sun set. The light shafts darkened and balls of fae light glowed on, floating over the crowd gathered for the evening meal. His gaze sought Cleia. In the roomful of dark-haired, bronze-skinned fada, her bright hair stood out like a beacon.

But he could've found her blindfolded. He always seemed to know where she was, as if he had an internal compass tuned only to her.

She was at a large table with Isa and his family. Cleia grinned at something Rosana said and his breath snagged in his chest.

Mine.

He set off in her direction.

As he threaded his way through the crowd, he was pulled into hugs by everyone from old women to giggling toddlers. Normally he enjoyed this time of the day, these physical touches as important to him as to the clan, cementing his position as alpha and providing reassurance to his people, but tonight he had to force himself to slow down and accept them.

He passed Rui draining a glass of wine, his latest woman cooing into his ear.

Worse, Valeria, Rui's almost-mate, sat a few tables away, watching him flirt with dark, wounded eyes. Catching Dion's look, she flushed and lifted her chin before turning to her neighbor, a sea fada visiting from Greece who'd been chasing her for the past couple of months.

Dion frowned. The old Rui would've kept Valeria close, making sure she was too satisfied to even think of taking another lover.

He dropped a heavy hand on his friend's shoulder. "*Idiota,*" he said in a sub-vocal voice. "Don't you see your woman with that Greek ass?"

Rui's mouth twisted in a derisive smile. "She's better off without me," he replied and held out his glass to his current woman to be refilled.

Dion saw Valeria's flinch even though her face was turned away. His fingers tightened on Rui. He itched to knock the glass out of his hand, but he knew the other man would simply shrug and get another drink.

"*Deus,* you sicken me."

"Yeah?" Rui took a gulp of wine. "Get in line."

His green eyes met Dion's. The self-loathing in them made

Dion's heart twist. Then his friend's gaze slid to the left. He was in no condition to challenge Dion and he knew it.

"Rui—"

The other man's claws sliced out, even though he kept his eyes down. "You may be my alpha," he said, this time in low tones that only Dion could hear, "but my mating is none of your damn business."

He was right. Dion blew out a breath and released him, continuing across the cavern until he reached Cleia's table.

Luis and his family had joined the others. Xavier stood on the bench next to Cleia, leaning against her shoulder and dipping a chunk of bread into her *caldeirada*. She had an arm around his waist, encouraging him.

Dion shot a glance at Marina—she was fiercely protective of her only child—but she was seated on Xavier's other side, chatting with Cleia as if they'd been friends for years.

As he wished everyone good evening, Xavier dipped his bread in Cleia's stew again. He shook his head at the pup, but he just flashed a toothy grin and popped it into his mouth.

"*Boa noite, meu senhor,*" he said around a mouthful of fish and bread.

Dion ruffled the boy's curly brown hair. "Leave some for the *senhora*, imp."

"She don' mind."

Dion glanced at Cleia, who had her lips pressed together, struggling not to laugh.

"Even so," he said sternly, then had to swallow his own laughter as Xavier stole a chunk of bread from his mama's plate and plopped it on Cleia's.

"There you go, lady."

She let out a husky laugh and pressed a kiss to his head. "Why thank you, sweetheart."

Dion gave up and sat down at the table's head, with Cleia to his right and Tiago on the left. The steward, an elder named

Monte, hurried to put food and drink before him. Dion thanked him and took a sip of wine before starting in on his stew.

Rosana was telling everyone that Cleia was teaching her the sun fae's favorite dances. "Lady Cleia says I'm a natural," Rosana added with a defiant look in Dion's direction. "We're practicing every day so I'll be ready when I visit the sun fae. She's going to throw a ball for me."

"Rosana," he said warningly, but Cleia gave a tiny shake of her head and nudged him under the table. He contented himself with saying, "We'll see."

Unfortunately, his sister took that as a yes. She brightened and began prattling about the dress she'd have—jade silk, whatever-the-hell color that was—and whether she should wear a silver or gold chain—or both.

He blew out a breath. His sister was going to drive him crazy with this talk of a ball. Didn't she know the fae weren't to be trusted?

But Cleia swore that Rosana would be unharmed. And whatever else she might be, she wasn't one of those fae who twisted the truth to suit themselves. For example, even though she'd used a glamour to lure his men, once she'd had them, she'd treated them fairly, allowing them the freedom of her lands and releasing them without penalty when she was through with them.

The hell with it. Let Rosana amuse herself preparing for a ball that would probably never take place. He had enough to worry about right now.

He concentrated on his meal, letting his sister chatter on, murmuring agreement where appropriate. But the whole time he was conscious of Cleia seated just a foot away. Her piquant scent...the warmth radiating off her skin...the grace of her fingers as she helped Xavier eat...

Somewhere deep inside, his animal let out a contented sigh, pleased just to be close to her.

Tiago had brought his otter friend Fausto and was feeding

him tidbits. He whispered something in Fausto's ear and the intelligent creature hopped on the table to offer Cleia an oyster on the half-shell, chattering in a language only he and Tiago understood.

"Lady Cleia," Tiago said, "Fausto has a gift for you—an oyster that he shucked himself."

The otter set it in her palm.

"Why, thank you." Cleia brought it to her lips, and with the help of a fork, tipped it deftly into her mouth. "Delicious," she proclaimed.

Fausto chittered, pleased, and scooted back across the table to shuck another oyster.

Meanwhile, Cleia continued to share her meal with Xavier, breaking bread for him when he needed help while still taking part in the general conversation like a seasoned parent, although he knew she didn't have any children.

She was going to make a good mother someday—and a fine mate for the man lucky enough to win her.

And why did that make his stomach squeeze?

Mine, that insistent voice stated.

He swallowed and shifted on his chair. Don't be an idiot, he told himself. Fae don't mate with fada. And even if she wasn't a fae, she's your enemy.

But she didn't *feel* like an enemy, and that was the problem.

Monte set a bowl of strawberries before Cleia. "Picked just this afternoon, my lady."

"Wonderful," she said with a delighted curve of her lips. "*Obrigada.*"

The steward smiled and bowed while Dion stared at him, jaw slack. Monte was a dour, ancient fada who ruled Rock Run's domestic affairs with an iron hand. Even Dion avoided going up against him unless absolutely necessary.

Cleia nudged the bowl toward Xavier, still on the bench beside her.

"Thanks, lady," he said and stuffed a whole berry into his mouth.

"That's enough, greedy one," Luis said. "If you're not careful, you're going to choke." He reached around his mate to snag Xavier and set him on his lap.

The small boy chewed manfully, determined to prove his papa wrong. Dion smothered a grin as Marina pushed the bowl back to Cleia.

"Here, my lady. You'd better eat some or Monte will have our heads."

"We can't have that." Cleia selected a strawberry and brought it to her lips. "Mm. It smells so good—like summer."

Dion's fork halted in mid-air as the berry touched her soft, full lips. "*Sim*," he murmured absently.

Her mouth closed around the lush red fruit and his whole body heated, his mind awash with salacious pictures. He glanced at Tiago and what he saw made him nudge his brother with his foot. Hard.

Tiago flushed and reached for his beer. Fausto, sensitive to atmosphere in the way of animals, chittered and dove across the table onto Cleia's lap. She chuckled and offered him a shrimp from her stew. He snapped it up and then rubbed his head against her arm, eyes slit with pleasure—and Dion found himself envying a damn otter.

He drew a serrated breath and focused on his meal. Hades take the woman, anyway. Bringing her here had been a terrible idea.

But releasing her was out of the question.

The fact remained that she was sucking his people dry. He had no choice but to see this through to the bitter end.

~

CLEIA WAS INTENSELY aware of Dion sitting beside her, eating. The man didn't speak much, but he didn't have to. He just had to be in the same room and her whole body started to hum as if her very molecules were attuned to him.

His hand touched hers and energy sparked up her arm. They both froze.

Then he inhaled harshly and murmured, "More stew, my lady? Or some bread, perhaps?"

"Some bread, please." She waited as he placed it on the plate, taking care not to touch her again.

She bit into the light, crusty baguette. If only she could see him. She knew from Rosana that he'd been swimming. He often did at the end of the day; apparently the long hours he spent training with his warriors weren't enough. No wonder the man was all muscle.

Somehow she knew he'd returned still damp and clad only in a pair of loose shorts, his typical attire. She flashed on an image of him sprawled on that big bed of his, his large, olive-skinned body slick with moisture, a smile playing on his hard mouth as he beckoned her closer—

She swallowed and squeezed her thighs together.

Damn the man anyway. She should despise him for how he'd tricked and captured her. But she didn't.

Other than keeping her imprisoned underground, he hadn't harmed her. In fact, she was treated more like a guest than a prisoner. She hadn't forgotten that night she'd had a nightmare and he'd tried to comfort her; hardly the act of the hard-ass alpha he was supposed to be.

With each day, she came to respect him more. He was an astute leader, guiding his clan with a light touch, encouraging his people to find their own solutions where possible. He spoke little, but when he did, people listened. And he had a huge soft spot where it came to children. How could you dislike a man who was as entertained by Xavier's tricks as she was?

Not that he didn't have a ruthless side—her capture proved that—but that was part of being a good ruler.

And what if he was right about her? The conversation with Marina had shaken her. Later, when Isa had walked her back to Dion's quarters to freshen up before dinner, she'd questioned the older woman closely.

Dion hadn't exaggerated—the men she'd taken as lovers weren't the only ones being harmed. The whole clan had been affected. Their vineyards and small farms produced less each year. The fishing wasn't as plentiful as it had once been.

Worse, the people weren't as strong, especially the children. A few had even died.

Goddess, that tore at her heart.

Oh, she'd heard rumors, but she'd dismissed them as the sort of lies people spread about the fae. After all, as she'd told Marina, wouldn't she know if she was draining energy from the Rock Run Clan? So she'd blithely continued to snap up their best men.

Because she could—and because she, like most fae, was a shallow, pleasure-loving creature.

Dion was right. She *had* been arrogant, thinking only of her own desires. She would've sworn she hadn't a bigoted bone in her body but she was as bad as the other pureblood fae, treating the fada as if they were created solely for her enjoyment. She'd never considered what the men were leaving behind, that Rock Run might need their skills as warriors or fishers, that the women might resent her for taking their best men.

And what had it gotten her? She'd grown increasingly bored, until after sending Tiago back home, she'd said the hell with it. She was going to try celibacy for a while.

Until she'd come across Dion standing on the road, that big hard body a sexual lodestone, his barely concealed insolence a potent spice...

If only she could give him what he wanted... But she'd told him the truth, she hadn't deliberately set out to drain his people's life-energy. However, she was an energy conduit, so there was a chance she was doing it without her conscious knowledge. She'd love to consult some of her own elders—another healer, perhaps, or Olivia, who might know if something like this had ever happened before—but Dion would never agree to that.

Her stomach tightened uneasily. Because even if it were true that she was stealing life-energy from Rock Run's people, she couldn't give it back. Any excess energy would've been absorbed by her own people.

The best she could do was to stop whatever she was doing—and she had no idea how to accomplish that when she wasn't even sure she *was* doing something.

Worse, if she didn't convince Dion to release her soon, she was going to miss the midsummer ritual, and no one else was strong enough to take her place as the Conduit. She was afraid Olivia would try anyway—and if she tried and failed, the energy surge would incinerate her.

But if no one took Cleia's place, the sun fae would miss their annual solar replenishment and start a slow, painful fade from existence. Already she grew weaker with each day spent below ground with nothing save the occasional feeble sunbeam to nourish her.

But that was nothing compared to what would happen if she missed the ritual, now just ten days away—and not just to her, but all the sun fae.

She set down her spoon, her appetite gone.

12

---

*D*ion perched on a rock in the middle of Rock Run Creek, mentally girding his loins for the coming skirmish with Lady Olivia. It was a tricky dance they did. Without actually lying, he had to continue to make her believe he knew nothing about Cleia's disappearance, while she in turn tried to trip him up and confirm that he had her queen.

He glanced out over the water. To the north and west was a mix of forests and vineyards, much of it owned by the fada and the humans who worked their lands. To the east the creek emptied into the Susquehanna River, which then flowed into the Chesapeake Bay, fresh water mixing with the sea to create an estuary rich in aquatic life: blue crabs, oysters, herring, rockfish.

He'd been a boy when his parents had led a small group of friends and family to America after their Portuguese home river had grown too crowded. They'd originally been headed for Rhode Island and its large population of Portuguese immigrants, both human and fada. But his father had happened upon this remote corner of the Chesapeake and the large river that fed it and decided it would do even better.

His father had been right. The clan he'd founded had had

room to grow and flourish. If they could just turn their twenty-year run of bad luck around...

He glanced toward the distant Rising Sun compound, moodily regarding its lush green forests and meadows. Sun fae had a gift for making things grow.

His father had been old-world Portuguese, proud and clannish, steeped in *tradição*. "Fada and fae don't mix," he'd said, his battle-worn face stern. "We're like oil and water. The fae are sly, tricky creatures who'll smile even as they're stealing the fish right out of your net—or the woman out of your bed."

Now Dion wondered if his *pai* had been wrong to keep the two clans apart. Maybe Rock Run should've made an effort to ally with the Rising Sun fae. Not only were they their nearest neighbors, they'd lived in this land for centuries and done well, better than the fada, for all that his people were hard, disciplined workers. Maybe the clan could learn something from the sun fae.

There was a splash nearby and two dolphins arced through the air—Rodolfo and Luis, right on time. Rodolfo kept his dolphin form, but Luis shifted to man so they could talk. He pulled himself onto the rock while Rodolfo traced lazy circles around them both.

"You ready?" Luis asked.

"As ready as I'll ever be. The meeting's at the stone house. Follow me upriver, but not too close."

Luis inclined his head. The stone house was a small dwelling used by the clan to receive visitors. For security reasons, it was upriver and on the opposite shore from the fada base. No one but their closest allies knew the base's location.

"I want Lady Olivia to think I'm alone," Dion added. "Stay out of sight. You two are just there as backup."

Olivia would be less guarded if she believed he was alone, and she might let something useful slip.

"Got it."

Luis dove back into the creek and Dion followed, the two of them not bothering to shift for the short swim.

The house was in a clearing fifty yards from the creek, set in the forest so that it wasn't visible from the water. A hundred yards in the other direction, a narrow dirt road ended at the garage that held the clan's vehicles. When they reached the shore, Dion went into the house to get dressed, while Luis and Rodolfo changed to otter and took posts on either side of the clearing, hidden in the trees.

Dion pulled on the black button-up shirt and slacks that he kept for times like this. Fae considered it an insult if you didn't arrive at a meeting shined up like a new penny. *Assholes.*

As he dragged his wet hair into a ponytail, he eyed a pair of wing-tips but decided against them. He was damned if he'd jam his feet into stiff leather shoes to impress Lady Olivia.

He'd deliberately arrived before the appointed time to emphasize he was the host and the sun fae lady the petitioner. Now he returned to the clearing to wait for Olivia.

She arrived soon after, early as well. The air several yards away shimmered and she teleported into the clearing.

So the lady had the Gift of wayfaring. Interesting. Her power must be nearly equal to Cleia's; only the strongest fae could teleport.

She hadn't come alone. She'd brought a man, an earth fada by the scent. He was young, not much older than Tiago, his slim, muscular body poured into a tight bronze shirt and black pants, his good-looking face arrogant under spiky black hair with the tips bleached blond. A chunk of quartz hung from a leather cord around his neck.

Definitely an earth shifter, then: they had some mystical connection with their quartz. Exactly how they used their quartz was a closely guarded secret. All Dion knew was that if he ripped it from the other man's neck, he'd be hurting.

The stranger eyed him with ill-concealed insolence. He

remained a step behind Olivia, deferring to her, but just barely. Dion's first thought was that the buff young shifter was Olivia's lover, but the man didn't have the scent of a male guarding his woman.

No, he was simply doing a job.

Dion's hackles rose. He didn't like how the other man was eyeing him. In fact, he had a bad feeling that he was about to meet the Baltimore earth alpha.

He inclined his head to Olivia, tall and proud in a long, burnt-orange-and-blue dress that, paired with her copper hair, made her resemble a column of living fire. They exchanged polite greetings and then he raised a brow in the earth shifter's direction.

"Who's the kid?" he asked, just to jerk the other man's chain.

"Lord Adric," she replied, confirming his suspicions.

Damn. Dion's instincts went on high alert, but he inclined his head to the other alpha. "Peace to you and yours."

"Peace to you and yours," Adric returned, the ritual words more of a snarl than a greeting. He stared into Dion's eyes.

Dion stared back. Their gazes locked as they silently tested each other's dominance. Adric looked away first, but Dion didn't fool himself that the other man was conceding supremacy. No, he was merely biding his time.

"Lord Adric has offered his services to help track Queen Cleia," said Olivia.

Dion stilled. He should've expected this. The sun fae couldn't track Cleia—he'd been too careful for that—but another shifter just might be able to.

"So you haven't found her yet?"

"No," Olivia said, lips tight. "As you well know."

Dion returned her suspicious gaze with a bland look of his own. "Now why would you say that?"

The woman simply raised a brow, her eyes dark and very cold against her pale face.

Ice trickled down Dion's spine. He had to stop himself from taking a step back. He hadn't forgotten Cleia's warning, but until now Olivia had been careful to appear harmless. Now she let the façade fall, making it clear she was an old, powerful fae—and that he was the prime suspect in her cousin's disappearance.

"Let's not play games, my lord," she said. "The sun fae need their queen. We must have her back for the midsummer celebration. If not, we'll be forced to find someone else to lead our ritual."

"She's that important?"

"Yes. You don't need to know why, but we *will* find her and bring her back before midsummer."

Dion shot a glance at Adric, listening as avidly as he. Dion knew the sun fae drew energy from the sun, but what did their queen have to do with it?

"I'm sorry, my lady. I'd like to help, but—" He spread his hands.

The lines around the fae lady's mouth tightened. "Name your price, my lord. I promise we can pay it."

"I'm sorry," he repeated, "but I can't help you."

Her aristocratic nostrils flared. "You lie," she hissed. Power crackled in the air and Dion guessed he was moments from being blown to smithereens.

He gathered his own power. There was no nearby thunderstorm for him to draw on, but he could take energy from the flow of the nearby creek, using it to throw up a shield—and then pray to all the gods and goddesses it held.

From the corner of his eye he caught Luis moving but made a slight gesture. *Not yet.*

"Do I?" he asked.

He and Olivia stared at each other, the seconds ticking by in tense increments. Then she drew a breath, visibly bringing herself under control, and inclined her head.

"Very well." Her tone made the phrase a thinly veiled threat. "Thank you for your time. Peace to you and yours."

He bowed his head as well. "Peace to you and yours," he returned, including Adric in the farewell.

The earth fada alpha gave him a cocky grin. "I'm the clan's best tracker, you know. Even our old men"—he emphasized the 'old'—"can't hide from me."

"*Ah, sim*? But even the most skilled tracker should take care lest he step in a pile of shit."

Adric's brows shot up. Then he chuckled. "Thanks for the warning."

He gave a short, deliberate nod in first Luis's direction, then Rodolfo's, making it clear he'd picked up their scent, and then joined Olivia at the edge of the clearing.

The sun fae lady chanted something in an ancient Celtic language. The air brightened and twisted in a way that was uncomfortable to watch. Dion blinked and when he opened his eyes, the two of them were gone.

Luis trotted up and shifted back to a man. "Damn. I thought she was going to blow you into the next county."

Dion expelled a breath. It had been a long time since anyone had made him sweat like that. "She came close. But I was counting on the fact that she's smart. She has to know that if she kills me she'll never see Cleia again."

"You have balls of frigging steel." Luis shook his head in admiration. "I stayed out of her way when I was at Rising Sun. She never raises her voice but she's damn scary. Those cold black eyes make a man want to check himself after she leaves, just to make sure she didn't freeze off the most important parts."

Dion snorted. But he couldn't help glancing down.

"She's not going to wait much longer," Luis pointed out. "She's going to make a move."

Dion nodded and motioned for Rodolfo, still in otter-form, to go ahead of them, and strolled with his second toward the house, where he dragged off the uncomfortable clothes.

"Cleia's more important to them than I realized. More than just their queen. Do you know why?"

"No. I was there during the midsummer festival, but they didn't invite me to the ritual. They threw a helluva party though—it lasted for three days."

"Hm. Maybe they need her to conjure up extra champagne or something."

The two of them left the house and headed back to the creek. Luis shot him an unreadable glance. "The queen's not a bad person, you know. Whatever she did to me and the others, I'd lay odds it wasn't deliberate."

"*Não?*" Dion refrained from pointing out that Luis, having been caught in Cleia's snare, was hardly unbiased. "She still has to be stopped."

"But do you have to keep her underground with her eyes bound? That has to be torture for a sun fae."

"I have no choice, not unless I want her to escape—and blast me to bits on her way out. I don't like it any more than you do, but I can't allow it to continue. You, Rui, Rodolfo...and the children, the vineyards. I had no choice. You of all people should know that."

"You're right, of course. And I supported—*support*—your decision to bring her here. But we can't keep her underground forever. She's a sun fae. If you keep her from the sun too long, she's going to die. Do you want that on your conscience?"

"She'll give in soon," he said, although he was no longer as certain of that as he'd once been. "My decision stands."

He wasn't sure who he was trying to convince—Luis or himself. Because if it came down to it, he was afraid he wouldn't be able to stand by and watch her die.

Luis shook his head but let it drop. The two of them paced forward.

"Tell me," Dion said, "what did you think of Adric?"

"He's hungry—and damn sure of himself for a man that young."

Luis's thoughts mirrored his own. "He's powerful for his age. But then he'd have to be, to bring the Baltimore shifters to heel. I'll tell you one thing, I don't like this alliance he's made with the sun fae."

"You think he's more than the hired muscle?"

"Not right now. But he's got to be hoping it'll lead to more."

"His clan's small," Luis pointed out, "and he's nowhere near your strength. Only a fool would pick a fight he hasn't a prayer of winning."

"He may be young, but he's no fool. Helping the sun fae proves it. He gets a big payment and the sun fae's gratitude besides. Down the road, that might be worth even more than the payment. If he attacks us, for instance, the sun fae would be inclined to favor his clan. Lord knows, they have no love for Rock Run at the moment."

"*Sim.* It bears watching."

Dion nodded. It did indeed. He'd kidnapped Cleia as a last resort. Now he was one misstep from having the whole thing blow up in his face.

He and Luis reached the creek where Rodolfo waited. Dion thanked them and said he'd meet them back at the base. "I'm going for a swim."

"Be careful," Luis said. "Lady Olivia would turn you into a toad if she thought she could get away with it. And Adric is going to be hunting you. If he's as good as he says he is, you're going to have a hard time shaking him."

Dion smiled coolly. "He can't track me in the water—not from land. I don't care if he has the best damn nose in the world. Just to be sure, the three of us will all head in a different direction. Take your time and don't return to base until you're sure you've lost him."

He dove into the creek and shifted to dolphin, Luis and Rodolfo right behind him. They saluted him with a slap of their tails and then sloped off in separate directions.

In this form he could hold his breath for as long as seven minutes. When he came back up, he'd be a half mile downriver.

Sucking in a breath through his blowhole, he dove deep and for good measure, used his Gift to all but disappear.

IN THE FOREST a hundred yards upwind, Adric crouched on a log as his cougar. Leaping to the ground, he crept forward and watched as Dion vanished under the swiftly flowing water.

He swished his tail in irritation. *Fucking river fada.*

The Rock Run alpha was correct. This job for the sun fae had been a gift from the gods.

When Lady Olivia had come around asking about the missing queen, he'd never guessed her chief suspect was Lord Dion himself. But he'd offered his services as a tracker anyway—his clan could always use the cash—and she'd taken him up on it. That's when he'd discovered the Rock Run shifters were in it up to their thick, ruthless necks.

It was the opportunity he'd been waiting for. The river fada were a thorn in his clan's collective paw, interlopers who had appeared out of nowhere some ninety years ago and claimed prime land in what had always been considered earth shifter territory. To add insult to injury, they also competed with his clan for the same jobs.

But his people had been too busy battling one another to go up against them, so as far back as Adric could remember, they'd had to settle for Rock Run's leavings.

Not any longer.

Adric had wrested control of the clan and set about methodically eliminating his challengers—starting with his own brutal and corrupt uncle—until there was no one left to stand against him. Then he'd heard rumors about the river people fighting off a mysterious malady—one that left them open to a takeover by another clan.

And stones, Adric craved their lands.

Not for their vineyards and fishing rights, but for those vast acres of forest and the sweet springs which crisscrossed them. As shifters who turned into big cats, wolves and bears, his people needed land in which to run, prey to chase down, territory they could mark as their own. But small and poor as they were, they could only eye Rock Run's territory with envy. Any attempt to take it over would be suicide.

Then the rumors had started trickling in. Something was wrong at Rock Run. Something that made them weak...vulnerable. He'd already started to investigate when Lady Olivia had contacted him.

Now he watched, narrow-eyed, as Dion disappeared downriver.

But there was no sense crying over something that couldn't be helped. Muscles bunched in his powerful hind legs. He bounded forward, racing along the river's edge, on the off-chance one of the dolphins would resurface. This far from the Atlantic, true dolphins were rare; any sighting was almost certainly a river fada.

But as Dion had said, it was impossible to track a water animal from land, especially if the animal could stay underwater for extended periods of time.

After ten minutes of hard running, Adric admitted the Rock Run alpha had lost him. He let out a vicious snarl and clawed at the grass, tearing great scrapes in the soil. Marking the other man's territory as his in the most primitive way possible.

Dion would recognize the scent as Adric's and know he'd been tracked deep into his own lands. Adric's lips peeled back in a savage smile. To add to the insult, he lifted one leg and pissed on the grass.

When he was finished, he trotted back to where he'd hidden his clothes and motorcycle. There was more than one way to skin a cat.

A half hour later he was at Rising Sun, assuring Lady Olivia that everything was going as planned.

"Now that I have Dion's scent, I can track him to his lair. If your queen is there, I'll find her."

The fae pinned him with her black-ice eyes. "I hope that's true, my lord, and not a young man's crowing."

He bristled. He might be young, but to get where he was, he'd cut down people eons more terrifying than Olivia.

"I don't crow," he returned in a voice as cold as hers. "I've never met a man—or woman—I can't track, once I have their scent."

"Good," was the curt reply. "Because you'll get nothing more from the sun fae if the queen isn't returned to us for the midsummer festivities. Is that understood?"

"Don't worry, I'll find her. You'll hear from me as soon as I locate the Rock Run base." He bid her goodbye, and after first using his quartz to set up a meeting with his top lieutenants upon his return, headed back down I-95 to his den in east Baltimore.

The Rock Run fada weren't what you'd call sociable, but even they didn't stay in their base all the time. In fact, they often visited the Full Moon Saloon, an old establishment near the Baltimore waterfront.

Although the owner, Claudio, was a river fada as well, he'd chosen to live as a solitary with no clan of his own. Claudio was a smart S.O.B. He'd realized he could make a bigger profit if he opened the saloon to all fada and enforced a neutral-territory rule. It was one of the few places in the mid-Atlantic where shifters from different clans mingled freely.

Adric drank at the Full Moon himself. He'd noticed that the normally disciplined Rock Run shifters kept to themselves—except for the young ones, who felt safe enough to let their hair down, flirt with women and get drunk away from the eyes of their alpha and his *tenentes*.

Adric smiled. It was a weakness, one he intended to exploit.

He looked around at his lieutenants—three men and a woman, his sister Marjani.

"Here's what we're going to do…"

13

Cleia trailed her fingers along the stone wall as she made her way to the dining hall. Eleven days she'd been here. She didn't bother counting steps anymore, having long since memorized the route.

Eleven days.

Panic wrapped chill fingers around her throat. Her time underground was beginning to tell. She was noticeably weaker, losing weight no matter how much she ate.

Up until now she'd remained firm in her belief that Olivia would rescue her. But midsummer was just a week away.

What if Olivia didn't find her in time? What would happen to her people? They wouldn't die immediately, of course. But even if she eventually returned, she wouldn't be able to replenish their energy fully for another year. They'd lose the weakest—the children and old ones.

Her head hurt. She realized she was tearing at the binding and that it had started to constrict. With an effort, she brought her hands back to her sides.

She had to have faith in Olivia. Her cousin would move heaven and earth to rescue her. Meanwhile, Cleia's job was to stay strong. Panicking or giving in to despair would only hasten her decline.

As she entered the cavern, several of the cooks called out greetings. As she returned them, her spirits lifted a little. Since shelling peas, she'd returned each of the following afternoons, taking on whatever the cooks assigned her. After the first couple of days, the other women had accepted her presence, although they were still wary around her.

Gabriela appeared and grasped Cleia's hand with her sturdy fingers. "Come," she said in her brusque way. "We could use you in the kitchen today."

It was the first time she'd been invited into the inner sanctum. Curious, Cleia allowed Gabriela to lead her into the kitchen. A few minutes later she was up to her elbows in water, rinsing greens in a large stone sink, but damn if she didn't feel as if she'd been promoted.

Around her the other four women were talking about the things women everywhere discuss when they get together: men, children, how to carve out some time for themselves, men...

Cleia inserted a comment here and there, but mostly she just listened, enjoying their earthy humor.

Across the kitchen, the two male cooks carried on their own conversation, oblivious to the women having a laugh at the expense of their gender.

Cleia tore a head of lettuce into pieces and placed them in a colander, then reached for the radicchio.

Marina came over and asked if she'd like some help.

"Yes, please," she said, and the two of them fell into a companionable rhythm, with Cleia washing the leaves and then handing them off to Marina, who shook the leaves dry before tearing them into pieces and putting them into large bowls for dinner.

To Cleia's surprise and gratitude, Marina had taken her under her wing, bringing Xavier for visits, joining her at meals along with Rosana and Tiago. Marina was sweet and soft-spoken—Cleia's opposite, in other words—but somehow they always found something to talk about. Cleia wasn't sure how Luis felt about their tentative friendship—he rarely spoke to her himself—but he hadn't tried to interfere.

She was starting to realize that much of what she'd heard about the fada was simply not true.

The women, for instance, were far from meek or downtrodden. The men might be stronger physically, but no one spending any time in a fada clan could think the women were in any way cowed by the larger, more powerful males. In fact, Isa practically ran Rock Run in her motherly way. Even Dion deferred to her.

Several people entered the kitchen: a couple of men and a young girl and her mother.

The girl was bragging in English about a large fish she'd caught herself. "With my claws, Mama."

"That's wonderful, Merry," her mother replied in the same language, although her English had a Portuguese lilt. "Now let me give this to Gabriela."

"She can have my fish, too," the girl said.

"I'll make sure you have a taste of it," the cook promised.

There was the sound of baskets being placed on the counter and then the two men wished them all a cheerful "*Tchau!*" and left.

Cleia wiped her hands on a towel and smiled in the direction of the newcomers. "*Boa tarde,*" she said, expecting to be introduced.

But the woman inhaled sharply.

There was a moment's silence, and then Marina rushed into speech. "Four baskets of fish—and such fine, plump ones. You always bring in the best catch, Valeria."

Cleia stilled. *Valeria again.* Who *was* she?

"*De nada,*" the woman replied.

There was an awkward pause in which Cleia sensed the other women looking at one another.

Then Marina, bless her, tried again. "This is Valeria da Costa, Cleia." To Valeria, she said, "Senhora Cleia has been helping in the kitchen."

"So I see," said Valeria.

"And I'm Merry," a voice level with Cleia's navel said. "Like Christmas: M-E-R-R-Y."

Cleia smiled down at her. "What a pretty name."

"Thank you." A small hand touched hers. "I think you're pretty. Is your hair really made out of metal? Trina says it's not real hair."

"It's real." She ruffled the child's wiry curls. "And thank you. I'll bet you're pretty too."

There was a snarl that sent a chill down Cleia's spine, and then Merry was jerked away.

"Don't. Touch. Her," Valeria gritted out.

"I'm sorry." Cleia held up both hands in propitiation. "But she—"

"I don't care," was the fierce reply. "Just keep your hands off her."

"Valeria," Marina said, "calm down. Cleia—"

"Stay out of this," the other woman snapped. "Just because you let Xavier play with her doesn't mean I want my daughter anywhere near her. Come, Merry. We need to get cleaned up before dinner."

"But, Mama—"

"*Now*," Valeria stated.

The little girl grumbled, but went along.

Cleia found she was tugging at the scarf again. She wanted, no *needed*, to see the woman. She sensed the other cooks looking at her and brought her hands back to her sides.

"If we don't get back to work," Gabriela said, "nobody's going to eat tonight. Food doesn't cook itself, you know."

The other cooks chuckled—more to relieve the tension than because it was funny—and returned to their stations.

"Sorry about that," Marina murmured as Cleia turned back to the sink. "Valeria—that's not what she's like. She's normally a nice person, but she's bitter about her mate."

Cleia moved a shoulder but she was shaking inside. She'd known, of course, that she wasn't exactly popular with Rock Run's women, but she hadn't realized how deep the hatred ran with some of them. And to act as if her touch was somehow harmful? What kind of monster would harm a child?

She reached for the radicchio and started to tear off the leaves. "Who was he? Her mate?"

"Rui do Mar."

"I see." She bit her lip, recalling the big, hard-eyed male.

Dion had said something about Rui's mate that first day, but she'd been too upset to pay attention. Of all her Rock Run lovers, he'd been the only one who'd left before she was through with him. He'd wanted her, yes, but it had been only lust. She'd had the feeling he was using her as much as she was using him, and for the same reason—to distract himself from a bone-deep loneliness.

She hadn't been surprised when he woke up one morning and told her he was going home.

But something didn't make sense. "If they were mates, why was Rui out looking for another woman?"

Because he had been, that night in the bar. Her glamour would've brushed right off him if he'd truly not been interested.

"It wasn't official," Marina explained. "They hadn't gone through the mating ceremony. But as for what he was doing that night—who knows? All I know is that he broke Valeria's heart."

Cleia nodded. The mate bond could form even without the ceremony, but the couple often waited to make the final, irrevocable commitment so that it could be witnessed by their family and clan.

"He never said a word. The first I knew of it was when Dion told me last week. But Rui left me over a year ago. If he's really her mate, they could've—"

"I know. I think that's what hurts her more than anything. She waited for him to come back—wouldn't even look at another male. But when he returned, he made it clear they were through. Instead he's sexed any woman he could—fae, fada, human. For a while I thought Valeria would just say the hell with it and leave, but it would be hard for her to find another clan that accepts Merry. She's a mixed-blood."

"I see." Such children—part-fae, part-fada and even part-human—often had a hard time of it, shunned by purebloods of every stripe. "So she's not Rui's?"

"No—and she's not Valeria's either. She's adopted. But she's Valeria's in every way that counts."

"Of course. Still, it's good of your clan to take her in."

"The alpha believes all children are precious. But even if he didn't, we have too few young ones to take them for granted. And besides, Merry's a sweetheart—everyone loves her."

"Mama!" called an excited voice. "Guess what?"

"Uh-oh." Marina chuckled as small feet pounded across the stone floor. "Here comes my ball of trouble."

She let out an "oof" as Xavier ran into her, his head thumping into her stomach. Still chuckling, she swept him up and gave him a smacking kiss.

He started to chatter but she said, "Remember your manners, *menino*. Say hello to Senhora Cleia."

"Hello, Senhora Cleia." His arms wrapped around Cleia's legs.

While Marina thanked the teen who'd escorted Xavier from the creche, Cleia picked the little boy up, gave him a kiss and listened to his news, which was all about a snapping turtle that the creche had seen while swimming in Rock Run Creek that afternoon.

Marina set a chair next to the sink for Xavier and he told the story again, the snapping turtle growing larger and more dangerous to fingers and toes with each telling. Together, Cleia and Marina finished the rest of the greens, with occasional "help" from Xavier.

With the salad done, Marina and Xavier went back to their apartment. There was still another hour until dinner, so Cleia returned to Dion's apartment. In the bedroom, she pulled one of the bentwood chairs under a sunbeam, and then took out the knife she'd slid into her pocket while Marina was distracted by her son.

She weighed it in her hand, knowing it probably wouldn't work and yet driven to try. It was stainless steel, which meant it contained a little iron, which just might break the spell. She was careful to touch only the rubber handle so that she wouldn't blister her own skin in the process.

Raising her hands, she slid the knife under her scarf and dug the point into the material. When that didn't work, she tried sawing at the material.

The spell held firm.

The scarf started to constrict. She jerked the knife from beneath it and with a curse, threw it from her. It clattered on the stone floor somewhere on the other side of the room.

She supposed she should retrieve it. But why bother? So Dion knew she'd tried to escape—what difference would it make?

Her hands were trembling. She pressed them together.

Goddess. What was she going to do? She was so damn helpless.

She thought of the animosity emanating from Valeria, and the panic that had threatened earlier rushed back. She gulped for air but her chest was too tight.

She moaned and shook her head from side to side.

The sunbeam touched her face: warm, calming.

Breathe, she ordered herself, and emptying her mind, raised her face to it.

She was still there fifteen minutes later when Dion returned to the apartment. Her skin tingled in recognition even before he entered the room.

She rubbed her hands over her forearms. He was the only man who'd ever had this effect on her. She didn't want to consider what that meant.

"Good afternoon, my lord."

"Good afternoon." He moved the other chair next to hers and sat down. "I brought you something." He set a paper bag in her lap.

"Oh?" she said dully.

She could tell by the feel that it was fruit. She opened the bag and took one out. It was round and fuzzy in her hand, still warm from the sun.

Peaches. He'd brought her peaches. How had he known they were her favorite fruit?

Tears welled in her eyes. She bit her lip and willed them not to fall.

"They're the first of the season—" He halted and traced a finger down her cheek. "*Querida?* What's the matter?"

Sweetheart. Damn him to Hades.

She closed her eyes beneath the scarf. She could handle his cold dislike, but kindness was unfair.

She turned her face away. "Nothing."

He rose and crossed the room in the direction she'd thrown the knife. She tensed, wishing she'd made the effort to retrieve it. She just couldn't face his anger today.

But when he sat down again, he didn't seem angry. Instead, he took each of her arms in turn and turned the wrists from side to side, examining them.

"I didn't try to kill myself, if that's what you're thinking." Her voice sounded too loud in her ears.

"*Deus*, Cleia." He rested his forehead against hers. "Promise me that you won't. I...just promise."

She touched his face. His jaw was stubbled. He swallowed audibly.

She wanted to ask why he cared. Wouldn't her death solve his problem? But that seemed childish—and besides, she knew why. There was something between them, something that neither of them could deny, however much they might pretend to themselves—or each other.

"All right," she whispered. "I promise."

She felt his exhale of relief. He pressed a kiss to the corner of her mouth and then sat back.

The bag rustled as he removed a peach. "Here. I'll wash you one." He rinsed it in the pool, and then cut a slice and brought it to her lips. "Eat. It will do you good. You're getting too thin."

She turned her head away. "That's because I need sunlight. Food alone isn't enough."

He sat back. "You're in the sunlight right now."

"This?" She made a disgusted noise. "It's not enough to keep a child alive."

"I'd take you above if I could."

"Then why don't you?"

"I can't," was all he'd say. "But I'll tell you what, I'll ask Branco to take a look at you. He's our oldest healer. Maybe there's something he can do to restore your energy."

"Thank you," she said, even though she knew it was hopeless. She was a sun fae. She needed sunlight.

"Now, no more questions. Eat." He brought the peach to her mouth again.

As disappointed as she was at his refusal, she was also smart enough to realize that if Dion was keeping her inside, it was because he was afraid someone would see her. That must mean that Olivia—or whoever she had helping her—was getting close.

The slice nudged her lips. "Please, Cleia."

This time she obeyed, biting off a piece. It was delicious,

sweet and juicy with a hint of tartness. She chewed slowly, savoring the taste.

"That's it," he murmured, holding the slice to her lips again so that she could finish it. Some of the juices dribbled onto her chin and she swiped at them with her hand. "Here...let me." A cloth dabbed at her chin.

She licked the juices from her lips and he drew a slow breath. She heard the knife cut into the peach again and then another slice was against her lips.

"Have another one."

She opened her mouth. This time he was holding the napkin under her chin, ready to catch the juices. But instead of wiping her mouth, he let her finish the slice and then brought his lips to hers and licked them clean with leisurely sweeps of his tongue.

Ah, Goddess. Not today, when she was so vulnerable.

She heard herself moan.

"Here." He urged her to take another bite, and when she did, licked her mouth clean a second time.

Almost against her will, she caught his head and drew him closer, opening her mouth to kiss him, slow and deep. His chest rumbled in a sound that was half-purr, half-growl. His hands remained by his sides but he willingly returned the kiss: sliding his tongue over hers, nibbling at her lips.

When he lifted his head, her heart was slamming against her rib cage. Without speaking, he fed her the rest of the peach, slice by slice. She ate, knowing he watched her—each bite, each swallow, each lick of her lips.

When she was finished, he wet the cloth in the pool and cleaned her face and hands. "Come." He drew her to her feet. "It's almost time for dinner."

She nodded mutely, wanting more than anything to press her body against his, to beg him to do what both of them ached for.

But pride kept her silent. She was this man's prisoner.

If she gave herself to him, she'd be little better than his whore.

14

———

Gaspar tugged on his bushy gray mustache. "I'm sorry, *meu senhor*. There's black rot all through the vines. I have my people spraying, but—" He spread his gnarled hands.

Dion stared at the viticulturist. Gaspar had contacted him early that morning, asking him to come to the largest vineyard as soon as possible. He'd gulped down some breakfast and then grabbed a boat and raced upriver.

He nodded shortly. "Show me."

Gaspar pointed the way and together they walked along one of the rows.

"It's most advanced in this section," the older man said.

Dion scowled at the dark spots riddling the leaves and stems. It was as bad as he'd feared. The spots were still small, but if the fungus couldn't be controlled, it would spread to the still tiny grapes as they matured, eventually causing them to turn black and shrivel on the vine.

The same disease had decimated the crop last year. He himself had supervised the removal of the shriveled grapes and the dead tendrils and canes so that the disease wouldn't overwinter.

But here it was again.

"I've seen enough," he said when they reached the end of the row. "*Obrigado.*"

"*De acordo, meu senhor.*"

As they returned to the vineyard's entrance, he thanked Gaspar. "I know you're doing your best."

The human nodded but his brown eyes were despondent. "I treat those vines like they're my own children. Training, pruning, fertilizing, getting the amount of water just right. But"—he moved a shoulder—"I can't work miracles. It's as if the earth herself is against us."

"Just keep doing what you've been doing." Dion clapped him on the back. "You can beat this this thing, *irmão.* I have faith in you."

"*Obrigado, meu senhor.* I'll do my best."

"Good man."

But as he walked away, Dion's shoulders sagged. The vineyards and the winery were the most important source of income for both the clan and the humans they employed. They were barely hanging on after the loss of most of last year's crop. They'd bought grapes from other vineyards to make into their best-selling vinho verde, but having to pay for the grapes had cut heavily into their profits.

Rock Run couldn't weather many more blows like this before they fell apart and started fighting over scraps like a pack of animals. It had happened with the Baltimore earth fada.

And that brought to mind yet another problem. That arrogant young pup of an alpha had actually dared enter Rock Run's territory. It was Davi who'd discovered the scent mark. Dion had gone with him and Rodolfo to see the mark himself. It was across the creek from the base, near the place where Rock Run flowed into the Susquehanna, and not more than a half mile from the vine-yard: the heart of Rock Run territory, in other words.

Dion's jaw had tightened as he scented the mark, saw how the earth shifter had clawed the grass.

"It's him all right," he confirmed. "Lord Adric."

It was a deliberate challenge, but right now Dion couldn't afford to answer it.

He'd glanced at Rodolfo. "How the fuck did he get this far onto our land?"

Rodolfo squeezed the back of his neck with a beefy hand. "I don't know," he admitted. "But I'm going to find out."

"You do that. Meanwhile, have the sentries vary their patterns, cover all our territory a little more often. But don't put anyone extra on this. Adric's young and full of himself. He's poking at us, seeing what we'll do. If we let him spook us, we're playing into his hands."

"And if we do catch one of the bastards on our territory?" Davi asked.

"Then he—or she—is fair game, of course. But just teach them a lesson. No deaths. I don't want to set off a blood feud. We can't afford that right now."

The two *tenentes* nodded.

"Good morning, my lord." The voice of Gaspar's youngest son interrupted Dion's thoughts, and he realized he'd arrived at the vineyard's dock.

Noah was a sturdy young man with a head of black curls. He held out his hand and Dion clasped it firmly.

"How's it going, son?"

"Good, my lord." Noah unwound the mooring lines and tossed them onto the deck. "Do you need anything?"

"Thank you, but no."

Dion leapt into the boat and took the wheel, and with a nod at Noah, edged out into the river. As soon as he was far enough from shore, he opened the throttle. The hull shuddered in protest, but he knew exactly how hard to push it.

The Susquehanna stretched before him like a broad silver path. The powerful engine vibrated in the boards beneath his feet, creating an answering hum in his veins. He braced his legs, brought the speed up another notch and grinned into the wind, temporarily setting aside his problems as the boat sliced through the water.

All too soon, he was back at the marina. He throttled down the engine and turned toward the dock.

We can beat this.

If black rot took the grapes, he and his men could always hire themselves out to the pureblood fae. At least the purebloods paid well—even if his proud warriors were little better than hired killers.

But money wouldn't cure Luis, or bring back the people who'd already died.

After leaving the boat at the marina, he dove into the river and through the underwater tunnel that led to an entrance on the base's west side. He dried off in the small anteroom and pulled on a pair of shorts before heading for his quarters.

This couldn't go on. There had to be something Cleia could do.

Branco had reported that she was growing weaker—not steadily, but in fits and starts. He'd done what he could to boost her energy, but he'd confirmed what Dion already knew. The woman needed sunlight; it was a simple fact of sun fae physiology. If she didn't receive a full dose soon, she would fall ill.

Eventually, she'd literally fade away.

He found her by the pool with Tiago and Fausto. He halted in the doorway. Cleia reclined on her forearms, Tiago on his side with his head propped on one hand, gazing at her, while the otter gamboled in the water.

Looking at them, Dion had a flash of déjà vu: himself as a

young man—slim, strong, with the same untamed mane of black hair and wildly in love with his first woman.

He just hoped he hadn't made such an ass of himself.

His brother said something and Cleia chuckled, lighting her whole face.

Something tugged in Dion's chest.

Deus, he loved to hear her laugh. He'd been wrong about her being haughty or prejudiced against fada. She never forgot she was a queen, but she was warm and kind to everyone from the toddlers to the frailest elders.

And they responded in kind, with only a few still refusing to have anything to do with her. Even his most battle-hardened warriors went out of their way to please her, making sure her plate was full at meals, bringing her small gifts, telling her jokes just to see her smile.

And he was the worst of the lot. He who lived in shadows and caves and the green calm of the river bed found her as irresistible as a hot, bright flame to a moth.

If only things were different. If the two of them had met as equals, man to woman, without the burden of their respective clans...

He inhaled harshly, aware his face probably mirrored Tiago's.

And that knowledge, along with the shitty morning he'd had, sent him stalking into the bedroom.

"Damn it, Tiago, don't you have somewhere to be?"

His brother jolted and jumped to his feet, stammering an apology. "I—I came back to base on an errand and I—"

"Out," he snarled. "I'm tired of finding you in here every time I turn my back. If you're not scheduled for training, you can help the fishers with the day's catch."

Tiago's hands balled into fists.

Fausto scrambled out of the pool and wound himself around Tiago's legs. Dion glanced down to see the otter's upper lip curled back to reveal sharp incisors. Lord, that was all he needed—a challenge from a frigging otter. He raised his own lip, and Fausto retreated behind Tiago.

"We were just talking," his brother said truculently.

"I know what you were doing. Now get lost before I toss you out by the scruff of your mangy neck."

Tiago reddened. He glanced at Cleia, who was sitting upright, face averted, pretending not to listen.

"Promise you won't hurt her," he demanded in a low, hard voice.

Dion gave a disbelieving shake of his head. "Senhora Cleia is under my protection as long as she's here at Rock Run," he said, unable to hide his hurt. "When have you ever known me to harm anyone—man or woman—who's under my protection?"

His brother's throat worked, but he didn't back down.

"*Prometa*," he insisted. "Whatever you think, she didn't invite me in here. If you're angry at anyone, it should be me."

Dion eyed him with grudging respect. The boy was turning into a man. Although clearly uncomfortable at going up against his alpha, he was willing to risk it for Cleia's sake.

"Believe me," he growled, "I know who's at fault here. But if it makes you feel better, I have no intention of harming the lady. Now go." He put all his dominance behind the command and this time his brother scooped up Fausto and left, albeit reluctantly.

Dion turned to Cleia. She sat a little straighter, sensing his scrutiny. As usual, she'd found a sunbeam to sit in. It illuminated her skin and hair with a hazy golden glow.

She reminded him of a butterfly, all long limbs and wispy yellow dress, sunning herself at his pool. He had the curious fear that if he disturbed her, tried to grab hold of her in any way, she'd flit away and he'd find himself grasping empty air.

She dipped a foot in the pool, tracing a figure-eight on the surface. "Don't be angry with him. He thinks he's in love with me, but it's just puppy love. It will pass."

He sat down a few feet away from her. "Too bad. From now on, he's not to be alone with you."

"Tell him, not me. I haven't encouraged him, if that's what you think. Frankly, I envy him—don't you?" Her lips formed a bittersweet curve. "It seems so long ago, my first love. The whole world seemed brighter, more colorful—and I was happy all the time. It's intoxicating."

"Nothing you can't get from a good bottle of wine."

"You don't have a romantic bone in your body, do you?" she asked, a smile in her voice.

"If it turns me into an ass, then no." But a wry grin tugged at his lips. "I just hope I was never so young and idiotic—but I'm afraid I was."

"You?" she murmured, the laughter still in her voice. "Not Lord Dion."

"I thought I'd die if I didn't have her. My father tried to warn me, but when I refused to listen he let me have my head."

"What happened?"

He snorted. "We fucked each other brainless for a month, but when we came up for air, both of us knew it wasn't the real thing. Not even the possibility of a mate bond. She left with a couple of friends to see what else was out there. I hear she mated with a man from another clan a few years later. She lives in Brazil now."

"Then you understand?"

"It's why I let him out of here with his hide intact."

He watched, fascinated, as she continued to trace slow loops on the pool's surface, the yellow dress bunched up around her thighs. It reminded him of the night he'd had her on the chair as the storm blew in. Her skin had been so soft, those shapely thighs quivering with need...

Blood thrummed in his veins, slow and heavy.

He was tired of resisting what was between them. He hadn't had a good night's sleep since he'd brought her to Rock Run. If he wasn't in the river, dreaming of her, he was tossing and turning on that damned couch, aching to go to her.

He wanted her with every fiber of his being. He craved her sexy body, itched to thread his fingers in her hair and taste her full red lips. Wanted those sunny smiles to be all for him.

And it didn't make it easier knowing she felt the same. He could smell her arousal, see the faint flush on her cheeks.

She cocked her head. "Dion?" she asked in husky tones.

He moved the few feet to her and crouched on his haunches, gripped by a sudden, fierce desire to see her unusual tawny eyes. "Cleia." His voice sounded thick in his ears. "I—we can't go on like this."

Her tongue touched her lower lip, and his whole body tautened. "No," she agreed.

He slid a finger down the smooth silk of her temple. She was visibly thinner, her lovely cheeks beginning to hollow out.

And he was the reason why.

He swallowed sickly. "Help me, *querida*. I'm begging you. Help me and I can let you go. You need the sun, and my people... they're fighting for their lives. I wish you could see how thin everyone is. Even the children."

She held up a hand. "Please...don't. I—"

But he couldn't stop. If he could only make her see...

"I just came from our biggest vineyard. It's being attacked by black rot. We need those grapes, Cleia. We need something to sell besides our bodies as the fae's cannon fodder. A people can't work only as instruments of war. It takes something from you, chews your soul—"

"Stop it." She twisted her fingers in her lap. "Why won't you listen to me? I've told you before, I can't help you. I can't."

"Can't? Or won't?"

"*Can't.*" Her voice was anguished. "I suppose I may have somehow drained energy from your men when they were my lovers, but I'm not doing it now. I swear it. But I can't give the energy back—it doesn't work like that. Why won't you believe me?"

"Why?" He grimaced and rose to his feet. "Because if I do, that means there's no hope."

The cavern was silent save for the sound of the waterfall. His words reverberated in his head like a death knell.

Cleia stretched out a hand. "Dion—"

"Don't," he said hoarsely. "Just...don't." He turned on his heel and strode from the room.

15

———

Tiago shoved his hands in his pockets and stalked into the night. He'd borrowed one of the clan's motorcycles for the trip to Baltimore. On reaching the city, he parked it outside a rowhouse the clan kept in Fells Point and headed for the Full Moon Saloon. A light rain was falling, but it would take more than a few raindrops to bother a water fada.

Damn Dion anyway. Maybe Tiago hadn't seen a hundred turns of the sun, but he was an adult and it was time his brother realized it.

He flushed anew at the humiliation of being scolded in front of Cleia. All he wanted was for her to see him as a man. But thanks to Dion, she'd started treating him like a kid brother.

His hands fisted in his pockets. If only Dion wasn't his alpha. He ached to tell him to stay the hell away from Cleia. But he couldn't. Not unless he was willing to challenge for dominance, and the idea of that made him go cold. Dion wasn't just his oldest brother; he was the closest thing Tiago had to a father.

And besides, Tiago knew damn well he'd lose.

Fells Point hummed with activity: office workers grabbing supper, tourists strolling the cobblestone streets along the waterfront, college students out partying. The humans made way for him, the men eyeing him warily, the women with unmistakable interest. He looked back—he was a fada male, after all—but even the prettiest didn't come close to Cleia.

Glancing up, he saw the howling wolf logo that meant he'd reached his destination. Tiago nodded to the earth fada with the shaved head guarding the door—at the Full Moon, shifters didn't have to show I.D.—and walked inside.

The bar was a dark, cave-like place with low ceilings and the pungent odor of alcohol and lust. It was already full of fada, both water and earth, and those humans who got a thrill out of rubbing shoulders with dangerous men.

Tiago swiped the rain from his face. There was no one from Rock Run except a couple of older unmated women in sexy little dresses, and they'd already staked out two males from another water fada clan. They nodded in Tiago's direction before turning back to the men they were with.

That was fine with him. All he wanted was to be left alone.

He crossed the floor to the long wooden bar and ordered a high-octane beer from the owner, Claudio, an Amazonas fada from Brazil. When it came, he drained it and signaled for a second.

Someone turned up the music and hard-driving rock blared. Like all fae, fada were susceptible to music. Tiago closed his eyes and swayed in time to the beat.

He and Cleia had danced one night, both of them naked save for the colorful scarf he'd tied around her hips. She'd spun around and around, the scarf allowing tantalizing glimpses of her thighs and mound until he caught one end and spun her into his arms. She tossed back her head and laughed unselfconsciously, and he wrapped his arms tightly around her, his erection pulsing against her belly, wanting her so much he thought he'd go mad with it.

And then she danced out of his arms, only to take his hand and draw him toward her big oak bed...

"Thanks, Claudio," someone next to Tiago said.

He opened his eyes to find an earth fada had joined him at the bar. A young man with a hard, sculpted face under dark hair with the tips bleached almost white. Despite the fact it was summer, he had on a leather jacket and combat boots. Everything about him screamed hard-ass.

Tiago stifled a groan. He could think of only a few reasons why a Baltimore shifter would choose to sit next to him and none of them were good. The last thing he wanted was to fend off an earth fada looking for a fight.

But the man gave him an easy smile and raised his bottle at the soccer re-run playing on a small TV behind the bar. "That Neymar's damn good."

"He's not bad."

"No? Did you catch that game against Scotland? He was fucking awesome. Man's a genius with the ball."

"Yeah, but what about—" Tiago relaxed and settled in to talk soccer with the other man.

An hour passed. Two other earth fada joined them, more young men in their twenties. They deferred to the first man, whose name was Ric. Apparently he was a man of high status in the Baltimore clan. A lieutenant, perhaps.

Ric ordered a round of shots. "Him, too," he said, gesturing at Tiago.

"Thanks." Tiago picked up the glass.

He'd never drunk whisky before but he imitated the other men and tossed it down. It was like swallowing a fireball, burning his throat and stinging his eyes and nose. He blinked and struggled to hide his discomfort from the earth fada, who were already calling for another round.

The heat hit his stomach. He blinked again as it spread to his limbs. Okay, that wasn't so bad. Kind of nice, actually.

"Have another." Ric motioned for the bartender to refill his glass. "The second one goes down a helluva lot smoother."

Why not? Tiago picked up the glass. He took a cautious sip, but the burning had changed to a pleasant warmth. He downed the rest in a single gulp.

One of Ric's friends was talking about a woman—a sun fae. Not Queen Cleia, but apparently just as talented in bed.

"Sun fae burn hot," Ric said. "The women can't get enough, if you know what I mean."

All the men laughed knowingly, including Tiago. Then he grimaced, ashamed. He set his glass on the bar a little too hard.

"They're not like that," he declared. "They're...nice. I'm gon— going to mate with a sun fae."

Ric raised a disbelieving brow. "Like hell. Fae don't mate with fada. They're too good for us. They might like our cocks, but when it's time to take a mate, they look to their own kind."

The laughter this time had a bitter edge to it.

"Not Cl—my woman," Tiago insisted. He blinked as Ric's face wavered, then came back into focus, but he was determined to make his point. "She *likes* fada."

There were a couple of snickers and Tiago scowled.

"Shut the fuck up," Ric said mildly. The snickers instantly ceased. To Tiago he said, "We meant no disrespect to your woman."

"Not—mine," he admitted. "But she will be. She tole—told me to come back in a few years. When—when I'm older."

"Tough luck. But she promised to wait?"

"N—not exactly." He thought of how she'd treated him the past couple of weeks and rubbed his nape.

And then there was his brother. He was beginning to think Dion wanted her for himself; he watched her like a hungry wolf.

"Over my dead body," he muttered.

"Something the matter?" Ric asked.

"What—oh, nothing." Tiago pressed his lips together. He

wasn't drunk enough to spill clan secrets, especially to a Baltimore fada.

"You know a sun fae can't stay underground too long. They need the sun—it boosts their life-energy." It was the man who'd had a sun fae lover. "You'll have to live aboveground for part of the time."

Tiago furrowed his brow. It was true. Sunlight was necessary to a sun fae. And Dion knew that but didn't seem to care. Meanwhile, the rest of the clan just stood by and let it happen.

He slid a look at Ric, who met his gaze straight on. For the first time, Tiago noticed how odd the other man's eyes were: a strange, reflective bronze. In the dark bar, they glowed like a cat's...flat, predatory.

Suddenly wary, Tiago set down the shot glass. "I'd better get going."

"Sure," Ric said. "But I get the feeling you need a friend—someone not in your clan."

Tiago moved a shoulder and started to turn away, but the other fada pressed something into his palm.

"Here."

It was a chunk of quartz. Tiago looked at the gray crystal suspiciously. It was about half the size of his palm, with a smooth flat surface on one side. "What is it?"

"A smartphone," Ric said with obvious pride. "You tap this"— he touched a depression on the smooth side—"and you can call me. Say, if your woman is in trouble..."

A smartphone screen appeared as if by magic.

Tiago eyed it, impressed. Rock Run owned some computers and a handful of phones, but for the most part electronics didn't mix with a people who spent much of their time in water—they tended to short them out—so they weren't as plugged in as most of the world.

Ric tapped the screen a second time and it disappeared. "The best part," he told Tiago, "is you can drop it, throw it, take it under water. It's damn near indestructible."

"Thank you." Tiago closed his fingers on the quartz, too drunk to question the gift. He pushed away from the bar only to halt as the room spun around him. He gulped and tried to find his footing. He'd definitely had too much to drink.

"You okay?" asked Ric.

He squeezed his eyes shut, then opened them again. "Yeah. No problem. *Adeus*."

"*Adeus*," the three men chorused. He thought he heard another snicker but he was already on his way out of the bar.

ADRIC WATCHED as the river man wove an unsteady path to the exit. He'd known who he was, of course: Tiago do Rio, Lord Dion's youngest brother. He kept a file on all Rock Run's key members.

He could hardly believe his luck. When he'd set his trap, he hadn't hoped to snare such a juicy morsel.

A smile played on his lips as Tiago lurched past a table which held several of his men along with two flirtatious human females who had no idea they were providing cover.

The river shifter was loyal, he'd give him that. He'd been careful not to admit Rock Run was holding Cleia.

But what a fucking break. Apparently the man was in love with her, and even better, unhappy at how she was being treated.

From behind the bar, Claudio frowned at him. The man made it a point to steer clear of clan politics. If he found out that Adric had deliberately gotten Tiago drunk and then pumped him for information, Adric would be out on his ass, banned from the saloon for life.

But hell, there were other bars, although only a few that catered to fada.

He nodded easily to Claudio, but under the bar, his hand sliced in an order: *Follow him.* The man he'd stationed near the door waited thirty seconds, then rose and sauntered out the door after Tiago.

Horace was one of his best trackers. The young fada would never know he was being followed, not as wasted as he was.

He turned to his two lieutenants. "Get your bikes," he murmured in a sub-vocal voice. Neutral or not, he didn't trust Claudio not to warn Lord Dion that something was up. "We'll give him a head start and then we'll follow him."

A water animal couldn't be tracked from land—unless he had a tracking device planted on him.

16

"*Com licença*." Marina's low, musical voice was edged with tightness. "Excuse me, Senhora Cleia."

Cleia struggled groggily upright from where she was reclined on a couch in the *sala*. She was tired all the time now.

"Marina? Is something wrong?"

"Oh, Senhora Cleia." Tears clogged the other woman's voice. "*Por favor*. My Xavier, he's so sick. Please say you will help him."

"Xavier? What's the matter?"

She hadn't seen him or Marina since that afternoon in the kitchen. When she'd asked Isa about them, all she'd said was that he was sick and that Marina was keeping him in bed. Cleia had figured it was some childhood thing.

"He—he—it started with his head two nights ago. A terrible ache that wouldn't go away. In the morning he said his stomach hurt. He hasn't eaten anything but a little broth for two days. He's so weak now he can barely lift his head. And then this morning—he...didn't wake up."

"No," Cleia whispered. Not Xavier. The three-year-old had burrowed his way into her heart with his clear-eyed observations and bottomless pit of a stomach. She reached out blindly for

Marina's hand and pressed it between her own. "Oh, my dear. I'm so sorry."

"Thank you. I—you say you're a healer. Luis says he saw you heal a man who was close to death. This is true?"

"It depends on what's wrong, but yes, I have the ability to heal —it has something to do with my being the sun fae's Conduit. But you know I can't draw on my magic. Not unless Lord Dion allows it."

"Oh." Marina swallowed audibly. "So there's nothing you can do?"

"I'm not sure," Cleia admitted. "My healing talent is something apart from my magic. It's just inside me. I've always had it, even before I learned how to call on my magic—like my Gift for tongues. But I use the magic to boost it."

"Then you'll try? *Por favor, minha senhora.* My Xavier, he's so sick."

"I'll do my best, but please don't get your hopes up. I've never tried to heal someone without my magic."

"*Sim, sim.*" Marina tugged on Cleia's hand. "Come with me, please. He's in our quarters. Here, take my arm—it'll be quicker."

They set out, Marina walking so fast Cleia had to trot to keep up. She clung to the other woman's arm and trusted she wouldn't lead her into a wall. Their route led them past the dining hall and into a section unfamiliar to Cleia.

"Here we are," Marina said a few minutes and several turns later. She opened a door and ushered Cleia across what must be the *sala* and through another doorway. "She came, Luis. She thinks she can help. Please let her."

Footsteps crossed the room. Marina's arm was jerked from Cleia's grasp.

"Have you lost your mind, woman?" Luis demanded. "You'd bring her here, to him?"

Cleia pressed her lips together, hurt. Luis had been her lover for close to two years. Surely he knew she wouldn't harm a child.

"She's his only chance," Marina argued. "You said yourself she's a healer."

"Her own people," Luis grated. "Not one of us."

"So? We're not so different from the fae."

"But it drains her own energy. She's already weak. Why would she hurt herself to save a fada?"

Cleia decided it was time to speak up. "I wouldn't have come if I wasn't willing to help."

"Is that so?" Luis shot back. "How do I know you're not here to finish him off?"

Cleia flinched. "By the Goddess, Luis. You know I adore Xavier. Truth." She touched her heart. "I'd cut off my own hand before I'd hurt him."

Marina grabbed Cleia's hand and put it on her mate's bare chest. "Feel him. Feel Luis."

"What do you mean?"

"Feel his ribs," she replied. "That. Feel how thin he is. And it's gotten worse since you've been here."

Cleia moved her hand over Luis's torso. The skin felt dry and unhealthy, and beneath, his ribs stuck out like bony ridges.

"But...what's wrong? You're sick?"

"I told her it wasn't you," he said. "That I'd probably picked up a virus. Hell, that's what I thought at first. But the healers can't find the cause. I'm perfectly healthy, just losing weight and getting a little weaker each day—just like some of the other men you had. And now Xavier has the same thing."

"No." Cleia snatched back her hand. "I don't believe it."

"It's true," Marina asserted. "Our own healers have tried everything and Xavier—he only gets worse. Then this morning, Branco went into a trance. His Gift allows him to see deep into the body. He saw Xavier's life-energy being drawn from him, drop by drop. He couldn't see how or why, but we all know why Lord Dion is keeping you here, that you're somehow draining energy from our people."

Cleia felt for a chair and sank onto it. "No. Not Xavier. Not a child. I wouldn't. *I couldn't.*"

But she wasn't completely, one-hundred-percent certain. Yes, her energy was slowly draining away, and had been since the day she'd arrived, but she'd noticed occasional, unexplained surges of energy. "By the sun and all the stars, no."

"Please, my lady." Marina dropped to her knees and clasped Cleia's legs. "Isn't it enough you're taking energy from Luis? Do you have to take it from Xavier, too?" Her voice broke. "He—he's our baby. Our only child. If you need energy, take mine, not his. You can have it freely, as much as you need. Only please let him live."

"But I'm not—" Cleia scrubbed her hands over her face. If only she could take off this blasted scarf, use her magic, she might be able to do something. Without her magic, her healing ability was weak...too weak. She could heal a cut, perhaps—but a dying little boy?

She dragged in a breath. "May I touch him? I'd like to see if I can sense what your healer did."

There was a short silence in which she sensed them looking at one another. Then Luis spoke. "*De acordo.* But if you try anything funny—if you even *breathe* wrong on him—I'll kill you where you stand. I don't give a frigging damn that Dion wants you alive."

She stiffened. *This is his only child*, she told herself, but she still felt lacerated by his distrust.

"It's your decision. I won't touch him without your permission. But I swear I'm only here to help."

Marina rose to her feet. "You have our permission," she said. "Here, sit on this chair."

She guided Cleia to sit on a chair next to Xavier's bed, then sat down beside her. Meanwhile, Luis took a seat on the bed's other side.

Cleia held her hands out, palms down. Even without

touching Xavier, she could sense his own unique energy: a cheerful imp of a boy. It seemed impossible for that lively flame to be extinguished.

She pressed her palms together and brought them over her heart, drawing deeply on her own depleted reserves, before reaching out again. Xavier was curled up in a ball, facing her. She stroked his soft curls back from his face.

"It's me, Senhora Cleia," she murmured, knowing that in the very ill, the hearing was often the last to go. "I'm going to try and make you feel better."

Luis shifted. "Talking won't help. He can't hear you."

"Perhaps. But if he can, he can help heal himself. You have to stay positive. Tell him he's going to get better as often as you can. *Sim*, little one?"

She smoothed the back of her fingers over Xavier's cheek. The skin was petal-soft and very cool; at least he didn't have a fever. But he was too cool, even for a fada. Her fingers drifted over his closed eyes.

She frowned, realizing the quiet sough she heard was the air moving in and out of his lungs.

Her heart turned over. Goddess, his breath was light, barely enough to keep him alive.

She continued down his neck to his shoulders. He was covered by a sheet. Drawing it down, she rolled him onto his back and placed a palm on his bare chest. He was so small and narrow, his heartbeat a slow, weak flutter beneath her hand.

She rubbed that narrow, fragile chest. "Now what's the problem, *meu amigo*? I've missed you, especially at dinnertime. I don't have anyone to share my strawberries with."

Xavier muttered something.

Marina gasped. "He opened his eyes, my lady. Just for a moment. But he knows it's you, I'm sure of it."

"Good." Cleia felt a spark of hope. "That's very good."

She focused on Xavier, rubbing her hand over his bird-like

chest, noting his heartbeat again before going deeper to the blood moving sluggishly through his veins. Drawing in a breath, she went deeper still, seeking his very essence, the layer that was more spiritual than physical even though it was intricately intertwined with his body.

Her brows drew together. His energy was off somehow. A weak, pale yellow when it should have been a warm, vibrant gold.

Instinctively she pulsed some of her own energy into him.

"His eyes just opened," Marina exclaimed. "Xavier? Can you hear me, *querido*?"

Cleia heard a tiny movement against the pillow.

"He nodded his head," Marina reported.

"Good," Cleia murmured, her focus on her small patient.

There was something about his energy, right at the center...a twisting ribbon of light similar to the one that connected her with her own people. But that connection ran both ways, while this one seemed only to pulse outward.

In her direction.

She mentally plucked at it. The twang reverberated in her own being. Beneath the scarf, her eyes widened. By the sun and all the stars, she *was* taking energy from him.

Quickly, she shot energy down the connection, trying to block or even break it. She immediately felt weaker, but Xavier sighed and his energy brightened ever so slightly. She sent more energy pulsing down the ribbon connecting them, but although she was no longer taking as much energy from him, she couldn't stop the flow completely.

She removed her hand from his chest and sat back, shaken to the core.

"Mama?" said a small, fretful voice. "I'm hungry. And I need a drink."

"Oh, Xavier," Marina replied. "Of course, you can—" Her voice broke and Luis took over.

"You've been sick, *meu filho*. But Papa will get you something to eat. Right away."

Cleia heard the two of them gather him into a hug.

"It's a miracle," Marina said in a voice thick with tears. "*Obrigada*, my lady. *Muito, muito obrigada*."

"Start him with some broth." Cleia automatically offered a healer's advice, even though inside, she was reeling at what she'd discovered. "Then in a couple of hours try simple solid foods—rice, mashed fruit, a little fish. A few bites at a time. He needs food—as much as you can get into him."

"*Sim, certo*." Luis strode from the room, leaving Marina to murmur over her son.

"Here, *querido*. Have some water. There, that's better, *não*? Oh, my lady, he's drinking."

Cleia smiled and nodded, but she was numb with shock.

Dion had been right all long. She was draining energy from certain members of his clan.

And even worse, it seemed to be ones she *liked*. Xavier had only gotten sick after the two of them became friends.

Great Goddess above. What was she going to do? If she told Dion the truth, he'd never let her leave. Either he'd keep her underground until she literally faded away, or—she bunched her fingers in her skirt uneasily—he might simply slit her throat and be done with it.

He wouldn't *want* to—it might even hurt him to—but he'd do it if it meant saving his clan.

No, she couldn't tell Dion. She *had* to be back by the summer solstice. Her people depended on her. They'd eventually sicken and die without the extra boost of energy she channeled from the sun each year.

Just as Dion's clan had been sickening and dying. She briefly closed her eyes.

At Marina's urging, Xavier said her name in a weak voice.

She turned her head in his direction. "Yes, sweetheart?"

"*Obrigado*," he told her politely. "For fixin' me."

"*Ah, querido*." She reached out a hand to touch him, then thought better of it and brought the hand back to her lap. "I just want you to get well. Can you do that for me?"

"Sure. I'm a river fada. We're tough."

Cleia couldn't help chuckling. "I know, little one. I know."

She remained until Luis returned with Xavier's broth, then had to sit through another round of thanks from both him and Marina.

"He's still weak," she cautioned, but they were too relieved to really hear her.

Unfortunately, she knew her "fix" would only help Xavier for a few days. Sooner or later, he'd get worse again unless she could somehow break the connection she was using to siphon his energy. She could continue giving him small boosts of energy to keep him alive, but to do so she had to be touching him. How would she explain that to Luis and Marina—or to Dion, for that matter?

And if she escaped, it was as good as a death sentence for the little boy.

At last they let her leave, Luis taking her as far as the dining hall and then hurrying back to his son.

Cleia groped her way back down the hall back to Dion's apartment, her stomach a sick knot.

She couldn't let Xavier die. She couldn't.

Yet to stay—or admit the truth—was to condemn her own people to a slow, painful death. No one else was strong enough to serve as the Conduit. Olivia would try, but she'd almost certainly fail and lose her own life as a result. Without Cleia to channel the sun's energy, the sun fae would wither and die, and her cousin's sacrifice would have been in vain.

It was an impossible choice.

She felt as if she was being pulled in opposite directions, threatening to rend her in two.

Her breath scraped over the back of her throat. She pressed a hand to her mouth and with the other continued to feel her way down the hall until she touched Dion's door. She pushed it open and made her way across the floor, instinctively seeking out the nearest sunbeam.

Light and heat touched her face, but it was weak. Too weak for her needs.

She snarled in frustration, then sank onto the floor beneath it, driven to soak up even that meager amount of energy. Wrapping her arms around her legs, she dropped her head on her knees and wondered dully what to do.

And all the time she was thinking: What kind of monster would harm a child?

17

———

$\mathcal{T}$iago's head felt as if a drummer was having an exuberant practice session on the inside of his skull.

He raised heavy lids and peered at the familiar stone ceiling. At least he was in his own room in the quarters he shared with several other unmated males.

He cautiously lifted his head. He was naked save for a pair of jeans, a sheet tangled in his legs. And for some reason his pillow was beneath one of his thighs instead of his head.

He lifted his head higher and then groaned as the walls swooped queasily around him. Carefully, he set his aching skull back on the bed.

He lay there for a couple more minutes and then took a deep breath and pushed himself back to sitting. This time he remained upright, hands braced on the mattress, until the room stopped spinning.

Something in his back pocket jabbed him. He took it out and stared at it, vaguely recalling that it was a smartphone, given to him by the earth fada—Ric.

He blinked. After leaving the bar, he'd walked around for an hour to sober up, then ridden his bike the thirty-some miles back up I-95. Apparently he'd hung onto the earth fada's gift.

He turned it in his hand, noting the smooth side. Curious, he touched the depression and the screen lit up. Hurriedly, he touched it a second time and it winked off.

Setting the phone on his nightstand, he massaged his aching temples, his mind swarming with the questions he should have asked last night. Chief among them was why a Baltimore shifter would give a valuable communication tool to a Rock Run fada.

He recalled discussing Cleia and how it was unhealthy for her to spend so much time underground. He frowned, then winced as pain gripped his head like a vise.

He hadn't told them her name. He was sure of that.

So why did he feel so uneasy?

He drew in a breath and decided to worry about it later. Right now he had to get his ass in gear. He was due at training any minute and calling off sick wasn't an option. Any fada could scent the reek of a hangover. If word got around, he'd be the laughing stock of his cohort.

He placed the smartphone in a drawer in his nightstand and came to his feet. The room wavered and bile rose in his throat.

He staggered to his bathroom, where he leaned against the wall, swallowing dryly and wondering if it might be better to simply heave it all up. But his stomach settled down enough for him to drink a glass of water. He relieved himself, then filled the sink with cold water and doused his head in it before downing another glass.

That done, he was still unsteady, but his inner clock told him he was past due at training.

But first, he headed out for a cold dip in the creek. It was the only way he was going to get through the day.

~

LATE THAT AFTERNOON, Tiago hobbled painfully back to his room. He was exhausted, his muscles limp noodles.

The instructors had known immediately he was hung over—that damn fada sense of smell—and had been in his face the entire frigging day, riding him until he'd been close to collapse. The clan didn't tolerate lack of control in any form, especially alcohol and drugs, the excesses of the bacchanalia still fresh in people's minds.

But he'd gritted his teeth and hung in there, earning a slap on the back from the ensign in charge. "You'll do, man."

At least he'd sweated out the hangover. Now, after another quick dip in the creek, he pulled on a pair of shorts and went looking for Cleia.

Worry for her gnawed at him. He hadn't forgotten that it was his fault she was here in the first place. If he hadn't overheard a conversation between her and Olivia that led him to believe her magic depended on her ability to see, Dion would never have been able to bind her powers.

He rapped on the door to Dion's quarters. "Cleia? Can I come in?"

There was a pause and then she said, "Yes," in a barely audible voice.

He pushed open the door. The *sala* was empty, so he continued to the bedroom.

To his surprise, she was in bed, the room dark save for a few fae lights. Outside, it was raining, so no sunlight came through the shafts. He peered at where she was curled up in a ball, the covers up to her ears.

"Cleia? You all right?"

She sat up and scrubbed at her cheeks with the heels of her hands. "Oh, it's you," she said flatly.

He swallowed his hurt. "You were expecting someone else?"

She shook her head. But he knew the answer. Lately, every

time he visited, his brother was there, hovering over her like a dragon guarding his treasure.

Then everything flew from his mind as she took a ragged breath and he realized she'd been crying.

"*Querida*?" He sat on the mattress and touched her shoulder. "What's the matter?"

She shook his hand off. "I'm not your sweetheart," she muttered.

He stiffened and pulled back. "I beg your pardon."

She jerked her head in acknowledgment. The cover had fallen to her waist. Her dress was wrinkled, her hair mussed, but she still managed to look like a queen, her spine an elegant line, her fine features regal.

He clenched his hands. If only he had the right to hold her, to comfort her. To kiss her tears away and promise that whatever was troubling her, he'd take care of it.

And then, when she was smiling again, he'd ease her onto the mattress, cover her body with his and love her until she forgot everything and everyone but him...

He tightened his jaw, painfully aware that was the last thing she wanted. But that didn't mean he couldn't help.

"Tell me why you're crying," he coaxed. "Maybe there's something I can do—not as a sweetheart, but as a friend."

"Oh, Tiago." She pleated the cover between her fingers. "I'm not cry—" she started, then spoiled it by giving a forlorn sniff.

He regarded her helplessly. "Cleia..." He looked around for a handkerchief, found a soft cloth that looked like it would do, and pressed it into her hands.

"Thank you." She blew her nose and then sat there, shoulders drooping. He waited patiently and after a few moments she said, "It's just—I'm so tired. I miss my friends. I miss the sun. I miss being able to goddamn see." She gave a savage tug to the scarf binding her eyes. "And now little Xavier is sick—did you know? I tried to help him, but he...it's bad, Tiago."

He swore under his breath. "I heard something yesterday, but—"

"He's wasting away. He must have lost five pounds. And on a little one like him, that's huge."

He gulped. "The healers can't help?"

"They've done all they can—that's why Marina came to me. I was able to help a little. When I got there this morning, he was comatose and hadn't eaten for a couple of days. He's better now, but what I did won't last. It's only a matter of time before he gets worse again."

He touched her arm. "I'm sure you did your best."

"And if he dies, it's not my fault, right?" The savage twist to her voice made him frown.

"But it's not your fault—is it?"

She lifted a shoulder. He waited for her to say something more but she drew up her legs and rested her head on her knees. She appeared worn out, her skin wan. He tentatively patted her back. The muscles were locked tight. When she didn't rebuff him, he rubbed in slow, easy circles.

"Tell me something," he said. "Our own healers—did they do any better?" She shook her head mutely and he squeezed her shoulder. "There, see. A good friend of mine is training to be a healer, and she said that's the hardest thing, accepting that there are some people you can't help."

A strangled sob escaped her lips. He regarded her in dismay. *Deus*, he was making things worse.

"Cleia? What can I do? Tell me, *meu amor*. I can't stand seeing you so sad. I—I love you."

"Oh, Tiago." A tear slid from beneath the scarf. She knuckled it away. "You don't love me. You just think you do. Someday you'll meet your mate and forget all about me."

His cheeks heated with anger. He was sick of being treated as if he were a pup who didn't know his head from his ass. He removed his hand from her back.

"Don't tell me what I feel," he gritted. "I do love you. And I've met my mate—she just thinks I'm too young to know my own mind."

There was a taut silence. "I'm sorry," she told him. "You're right, I don't know what you feel. But I don't love you—and I never will."

"Fine. If that's how you feel, so be it. But at least let me help. Allow me do that much for you."

"Oh, Tiago. Thank you for that." She touched his hand. "But what can you do? Your brother has me trapped. If I could get away, get this damn blindfold off, maybe there'd be something I could do. At least I'd have a chance of figuring out how to help Xavier and the others who are sick. I could consult my own healers, for example. But like this I'm no good to anyone."

Tiago jumped to his feet and paced across the room. "*Deus*, Cleia. I want to help. You know I do. But ask me anything except that."

"I wasn't asking."

But they both knew that wasn't entirely true.

"I'd be banished from the clan, if Dion didn't just kill me outright. Don't get me wrong—he loves me—but he can't allow anyone to get away with such a challenge to his authority. Not even his own brother."

"I understand. Really. Please forget I said anything."

Tiago closed his eyes. He thought of little Xavier, of how much he meant to everyone. He thought of Cleia, imprisoned here by his goddamn stubborn brother, even though the whole clan was starting to mutter that it was time to let her go, that she either wouldn't or couldn't help them.

And then he thought of that gray quartz in his nightstand drawer.

"But if someone else helped you," he said, "someone not in the clan—"

The words seem to come from another man's mouth. They hung in the air, dark, insinuating. He swallowed sickly.

However Cleia escaped, if he supplied the means, he was betraying his brother.

But this was his future mate, damn it. He didn't care what she said about not loving him—sometimes it happened that way, especially if one of the pair was very young. In a few years' time he'd reach full maturity, and then the bond would flower and she'd see he'd been right all along.

And everyone knew the mate bond was supreme, trumping even family and clan loyalties.

"But how?" she asked. "No one knows where I am. I thought they'd find me by now, but it's only a few days to the solstice, and if they haven't by this time..." She spread her hands in defeat.

Tiago crouched in front of the bed and grasped her shoulders. "Swear it, Cleia. Swear that if I help you escape, you won't turn around and take revenge on Rock Run."

"I do." She grabbed his forearms. "I swear that if you help me get home, I'll consider us even. Truth." She brought a hand to her heart.

"You promise that you won't try to harm the clan—or Dion?"

"Yes. I swear it by everything I hold holy."

Tiago drew in a breath. "Then I think I can help."

18

———————

"Please, my lord," implored Lady Olivia. "The midsummer celebration is just three days away. You must help us."

Dion crossed his arms and studied the sun fae noblewoman. He hadn't wanted to meet with her again, but her communications had become increasingly aggressive. Now her obsidian gaze was suspicious, but she was clearly desperate. At least she'd come without Adric this time.

"Must I?"

She shuttered her fierce eyes and dropped to her knees. "Lord Dion, I'm begging you. The sun fae will do anything to get our queen back. Anything. Riches, spells...or take me instead, if you require a captive—just allow Cleia to return before the midsummer festival. Whatever she did, do all the sun fae have to suffer for her mistake?"

"Get back on your feet," he growled. He wasn't some jumped-up fae lord, to require a woman to plead her cause on her knees.

He waited as Lady Olivia rose gracefully back up. Her fine features, so like Cleia's, were somber; her copper hair braided into a shiny rope that fell to the middle of her back; and she was wearing a silky green tunic and pants. She seemed to be trying to appear less powerful, more approachable. It worked, up to a point. Nothing could completely mask the woman's innate authority.

Not for the first time, he wondered why Cleia was queen and not her older cousin.

"Tell me," he asked, "what makes you think your queen is at Rock Run? When last I saw her she was well." Which was the truth, of course. "But who knows? She could be anywhere—even dead." Also the truth.

Olivia's eyes narrowed. "Let us speak freely, my lord. We sun fae may not have your animal-enhanced senses, but we have our own ways of tracking people. As soon as we discovered Cleia was missing, the queen's bodyguards followed her trail. The storm had washed most of it away, but we had enough information to narrow her capture down to you or the Virginia night fae. We've now eliminated the night fae. But just to be sure, in the past two weeks we've visited or contacted every fae and fada clan in the Americas—and many of those overseas as well. They all swear they haven't seen her. Can you swear the same? If so, tell me now and I'll turn my search elsewhere."

Dion kept his face blank, but inside his mind raced, considering his options. Olivia was finally certain enough to force the issue, leaving him with two choices: tell the truth or lie outright, which would exact an enormous personal cost, leaving him sick and drained of energy at the worst possible time.

Yet if he admitted having taken the queen, it meant war. The very war he'd sought to prevent by kidnapping Cleia in the first place.

He forced himself to meet Lady Olivia's suspicious gaze. "I can't," he admitted.

She stiffened. "As I thought."

He inclined his head.

She was silent for a moment. Then she said, "There's no one

else, you know. No one who can take Cleia's place in the midsummer ritual. What I tell you now is known to very few people outside the sun fae. Can I trust you to keep it a secret?"

"Yes, of course." He was desperate for any information that might break this impasse.

"This is for your ears only."

He nodded and flicked his hand. He'd brought only Rodolfo this time, leaving Luis to watch over his sick son. Now he waited until the *tenente* had moved out of earshot before turning back to Olivia. "Go ahead."

"Queen Cleia isn't just our ruler, she's our Conduit. Do you know what that means?"

When he replied in the negative, she went on, "The Conduit is the only one who can link directly to the sun and then only on midsummer's day. As Conduit, Cleia has the ability to tap the sun's energy and then in turn share the energy with every other sun fae. The talent may pass to either a man or a woman, but almost never to someone outside of Cleia's direct line. I can try to take her place, but she's the chosen one. We pray that one of her children...but she's never mated. And like you fada, the fae rarely have children outside the mate bond."

"I'm sorry." He stifled a pang of guilt. This wasn't his fault. He was only doing what was necessary to ensure his own clan's survival.

"Truth." Olivia touched her chest. "If Cleia doesn't return by the summer solstice, the sun fae will die. We'll do anything to get her back."

And this time, Dion understood, she wasn't talking about riches or magic, but war.

"I see."

He scrutinized the sun fae lady's severe face. It went against the grain to let an outsider, especially a fae, know how bad things were at Rock Run, but she'd entrusted him with one of her own secrets. And she needed to understand that he wasn't imprisoning her cousin on some cruel whim.

"The last thing I want, my lady, is to harm the sun fae, but if I allow your queen to go on as she was, my clan will die."

Olivia's brows snapped down. "What do you mean?"

"Each time Cleia took one of my men as her lover, she drained energy from both him and the clan. But worse, even after they came home, she was still drawing energy from at least some of them. Meanwhile, you grow stronger and more powerful, while we're barely surviving. Our crops are failing. Our people are dying. Even"—his throat worked as he recalled Xavier that morning, pale and unconscious, his small body bone-thin—"our littlest ones."

A wasting disease, the healers said, one they couldn't explain or fix—something he'd seen too damn often.

He'd stared down at the small boy, his thoughts a simple prayer: *Not him. Please Deus, not him.* Every child lost was a blow, but losing Xavier—beloved imp that he was—would rip out the clan's collective heart.

And Luis looked almost as bad as Xavier. He and Marina had gazed down at the little boy, their despair palpable.

"I'm sorry," Olivia murmured, "but—"

"Right now there's a boy"—he swallowed thickly—"barely more than a toddler. He's dying and no one can help him. Just like we've seen before. And it all goes back to Cleia. Our oldest and most experienced healer confirmed it."

"Then your healer's wrong. Cleia wouldn't—she loves children. And besides, she has no need for your energy. She can get all she needs from the sun. It doesn't make sense."

"She may not know she's doing it," he allowed. "But that doesn't mean she isn't. She's sucking us dry, my lady. She has to be stopped."

"But—"

He slashed his hand through the air. "My mind is made up. I

admit nothing, you understand, but know that if you choose war, we'll fight you with everything we have. It's either that or stand by and let her drain us without a fight. At least this way we'll die with honor." He inclined his head. "This meeting is over. Peace to you and yours."

She inhaled sharply and then nodded as well. "So be it. Peace to you and yours." But instead of leaving, she searched his face. "At least tell me how she's doing. She's not just my queen, but my cousin and closest friend. She's all right?"

"Everyone loves her," he admitted. "She has the whole damn clan tripping over themselves to please her."

Olivia made a small, amused sound. "That sounds like Cleia."

She turned in a swirl of green silk and walked into the trees. As before, the air shimmered and seemed to twist in a way that was uncomfortable to watch. Dion glanced away and when he looked back, she was gone.

He scraped a hand over his hair and for a long moment just stood there. Then he blew out a breath and stowed his clothing in the stone house before heading back to the creek. High overhead, the blazing sun beat down on his bare skin, a reminder of how close midsummer's day was—if he required one.

Three more days.

Rodolfo had already changed to his river dolphin and was waiting in the water.

"Go back to base," Dion told him. "Tell Davi to double the guards on all the entrances. The sun fae shouldn't be able to break the concealing spell, but it's best to be prepared. Lady Olivia isn't going to wait much longer before she tries something."

Rodolfo nodded and headed off.

Three more days. And he'd be lucky if Lady Olivia gave him another twenty-four hours.

Hell. He dove into the creek, shifting in mid-air to dolphin. With a flip of his tail flukes he dove deep, taking an evasive route that took him past the base into the Susquehanna before he doubled back to Rock Run Creek and home.

ADRIC HAD PLANNED FOR THAT.

He was waiting high in a tree overlooking the creek above the location where Horace had tracked Tiago before he'd seemed to disappear into thin air, along with the signal coming from the smartphone. Horace was too good to be shaken off by an inebriated river fada cub. Rock Run must be using a spell to conceal the base. Together, Adric and Horace had nailed down this as the most likely location of its main entrance.

Now when Dion dove for the last time without returning to the surface, Adric bared his teeth.

Gotcha.

He used his quartz to text his surveyors, waiting nearby. Next he called Olivia so she could temporarily disable the concealing spells. She had it done within minutes.

Quickly, his surveyors swarmed over the area before the river fada discovered their defenses were down, using their crystals to locate and map the large system of caverns that made up the base. When they were done, Olivia removed the disabling spell and the head surveyor sent the map to Adric.

As it came up on the screen, he whistled softly. Holy shit.

The base stretched a good third of a mile along the creek, its average depth forty feet underground. No wonder it was such a well-kept secret. The map was rough; even with Olivia's help, whatever magic the river clan was using left large gaps, but he could see enough to tell it was comparable to an earth fada base.

And that was saying something. His people were master miners, spending even more of their time underground than the river people.

But even though the surveyors had marked several likely

entrances, they couldn't tell him where Cleia was. He scowled. In his cougar form, he could use his heightened sense of smell to sniff her out. But how the hell could he retrieve her in a base swarming with river shifters who could scent him just as easily?

He changed to cougar and loped the eight miles back to Rising Sun. Just before he reached the courtyard he ducked behind a tree, where he shifted back to a man and retrieved his clothes. As he entered the courtyard, Olivia and four of the sun fae's best warriors were waiting, including Cleia's bulked-up blond bodyguards, Artan and Grady.

He bowed to Olivia. "We've mapped their base. But it's big—there's no telling where they have her. We'll have to fight our way through it, looking for her."

"Then we'll fight," she replied.

Adric nodded coolly. He hadn't expected anything different. The sun fae were desperate. This was a suicide mission and they all knew it.

Of course, he had a plan for getting out with his hide intact, but nothing was certain. He'd made sure Lady Olivia had deposited half of the huge fee she was paying him into an offshore bank that only he and his sister could access.

Artan moved restively. "What are we waiting for? The longer that bastard has her, the sicker she—"

Olivia silenced him with a slice of her hand.

"I'm ready whenever you—" Adric halted as the quartz around his neck buzzed. His skin tingled.

He *knew* who was on the other end.

"Hang on," he said and tapped the screen, activating the speaker so the sun fae could hear as well. "Ric here."

DION STRODE INTO HIS QUARTERS, face set. This was going to end. Today.

It was time to get rough with Cleia...make her believe he was going to act on the dark, lascivious thoughts that tormented him night and day. Lord knew it wouldn't be much of a stretch. The queen might hate him by the time he was through, but at least little Xavier would get well. Then Cleia could go home and he wouldn't have her health and that of her people on his conscience.

He just prayed the sun fae would accept that he'd merely sought to right a wrong. As he'd told Olivia, the last thing he wanted was war with the sun fae. Even in their current weakened state, he'd back his warriors against anyone, but Rising Sun had twice their people—and they were fae besides, with powerful magic to call on.

On top of that, with their queen at risk, the six other sun fae clans would join the fight. It was why he'd waited this long before acting.

Isa met him at the door, brown eyes thoughtful.

He jerked his head toward the bedroom. "She in there?"

"She is." The older woman laid a hand on his arm. "But calm down. She's—"

He growled. "Damn it, Isa, I'm a grown man. Stop telling me to calm down as if I'm a five-year-old throwing a tantrum."

She inclined her graying head. "*Desculpe-me, meu senhor.*"

He blew out a breath. "No, I'm the one who's sorry. Go ahead —what did you want to tell me?"

Isa studied him, her round face crinkled with compassion... and a tinge of humor. She opened her mouth, then shook her head. "I think I'll just let you find out for yourself."

"Then can I pass?" he asked between gritted teeth.

"Of course," she said and stepped aside.

He found Cleia by the pool again, face upturned toward a shaft of sunlight, wearing a gauzy pink-and-green dress that made her look good enough to eat.

But as he came closer, he saw her shoulders drooped. He

scowled. She appeared even thinner than last night, and her golden skin had an unhealthy gray tint.

He squeezed his nape, recalling Luis's comment: *"She's a sun fae. If you keep her from the sun too long, she's going to die."*

"Hello, Dion," she said without turning her face. "You met with Olivia again, didn't you?"

He didn't ask how she knew; she seemed to have sixth sense about these things. "*Sim*. She knows you're here."

"Of course. I'm sure she's known for days."

He came closer, disturbed by the dullness of her voice.

"I can't let you go. Even if it means war."

She just lifted a shoulder. His brow furrowed. Something was definitely wrong. All thought of getting rough with her evaporated. Instead, he wanted to enfold her in his arms and promise that he'd make everything better.

He crouched down on his haunches. "What's the matter, *querida*?"

"It's little Xavier. He's sick."

He frowned. He'd instructed Isa to keep Cleia away from Xavier. "I know."

"Yes, of course. I suppose everyone knew but me. But this morning, Marina came to me and asked for my help. I'm a healer in my clan, you know."

He hadn't known. He was surprised Marina had let Cleia near her sick child, but she was desperate—and Cleia had never been anything but kind to the clan's children.

"Were you able to help?"

"Not really." She sighed. "I was able to halt the…disease for a time. When I left, Xavier was awake and eating a little food."

"But that's good news. Why are you so upset?"

"Because I'm pretty sure it's only temporary, that he'll get worse again. I didn't tell Marina and Luis, but—" She shook her head. "Maybe," she said with a sardonic laugh, "you should just slit my throat and be done with it."

His brows snapped together. He might have considered it in the beginning, but only as a last resort—and even then he wasn't sure he could've brought himself to do it.

But things had changed between them. Surely she knew he'd never hurt her physically. Hell, he couldn't even bring himself to threaten her verbally.

"Damn it, Cleia, it doesn't have to be like this. Make it right and you can go. Your people are desperate. The solstice is only three days away."

"Don't you think I know that?"

"Then why not? You're responsible for the energy drain—we both know that. Why don't you stop it?"

"Because. I. Can't," she said in slow, emphatic tones. "Do you think I would've stayed here all this time otherwise? My own people are hurting. And now I have to see your clan, people I've come to like, hurting as well. Do you think I wouldn't help little Xavier if I could? I'd give anything to make him better. *Anything.* But I can't. What I did was like putting a band-aid on a gaping wound."

He sank down beside her. "Then what are we going to do?"

"I don't know. But whatever I did—whatever I'm doing—it's not intentional. I may be draining power from your people, but I swear on everything I hold holy that it's not deliberate. You have to believe me."

He took her chin in his hand and examined her face. Now that he was looking for them, he could see tear tracks on the smooth skin.

He muttered a curse. "Cleia—" He ran his thumb over her drooping lower lip.

"Yes?"

He heaved a breath. "Hell, I do." The words burst from him like a dam breaking. "I do believe you."

"You do?" She caught his wrist and tilted her head, instinctively trying to see him.

"Yes." She'd shown him by both word and deed that she wasn't the shallow bitch he'd believed her to be. And today, she'd tried to heal Xavier, even though it had clearly taken a lot of energy, energy she didn't have to spare.

But if she was telling the truth, there was only one choice left to him. He swallowed over the constriction in his throat. *Deus*, it was difficult to say the words that would let her walk out of here... and out of his life.

"You're free, Cleia. I'm letting you go."

Amazement bloomed on her face. "I'm free? Just like that?"

"If you can't help us, there's no point in holding you any longer. All I ask is that you explain to your people why I captured you. I—I don't want war with you, *querida*."

He started to rise but she kept hold of his wrist, halting him. "Wait."

He came back down on his knees. He raised his free hand to touch her, then curled his fingers and brought his hand back to his thigh. She wasn't his to touch.

Not now and not ever.

"Yes?" he asked gruffly.

She cupped his jaw. "You want me."

"You know I do."

"Then why not? Once more, before I leave."

His throat tightened. Her words hung in the air for a single hard beat of his heart. He couldn't seem to make himself speak, to tell her yes or no.

Her face fell. "I understand," she said, bringing her hand back to her lap. "You have to think of your people."

He closed his eyes for a moment. *Deus*, he wanted her. Surely just once more wouldn't make a difference one way or the other.

A golden lock of hair had fallen over her shoulder. He gave in to his need and fingered the silky strands.

"When we joined before, it didn't seem to harm the clan."

In fact, he'd returned with Cleia to find his people newly

energized. Yes, they'd been upset and worried, but there'd been excitement there, too, and a new sense of purpose. And the fishers had brought back several large catches in a row.

"Actually," he added, "it seemed to boost our energy. At least for a few days."

"Then what's stop—" Cleia gasped as he dragged her onto his lap.

"Not a damn thing," he said and brought his mouth down on hers.

19

Cleia froze, heart slamming in her chest. Then she twined her arms around Dion's neck and kissed him back. Her weariness evaporated before the familiar spark the two of them always triggered. It danced over her skin like the best magic, sparkly, revitalizing.

He drew away. "Are you sure? I—"

She dragged him back again. "I asked you, remember?"

"By the gods, I want you. You're like a fever in my blood..." He inhaled raggedly and laid his cheek against her hair.

"I know, I know." She pressed a kiss to the side of his neck.

Having her eyes covered had heightened her other senses. She drew in a slow breath, taking in his scent: musky and potent. She spread her fingers over his chest. The skin was moist; he must have come to her straight from the water. She pictured him striding half-naked through the caverns, powerful and very male, and her inner thighs constricted.

Sliding a hand under his wet hair, she brought her mouth to the strong cords of his throat, licking and tasting him. His flavor was fresh and clean as his creek, his very coolness exciting to her fiery sun fae senses. He groaned with pleasure and she sucked his skin into her mouth, hard enough to mark him.

His cock lengthened, prodding her hip through the two thin layers of material dividing them.

He swore softly. "Damn, woman. You're going to drive me mad." He speared his fingers through her hair but kept his head tilted, allowing her to kiss and nip his throat.

Desire twisted in her belly, hot and needy. Stars, she craved him. She hadn't burned for a man like this since her first lover, an ice fae lord from the far north who'd only wanted her for the lands the sun fae controlled. Blond and coldly beautiful, the ice lord had been a hundred times her age and a thousand times more jaded than she'd ever be, and he'd demanded she power her glamour to the fullest before bedding her.

Dion wanted her even without the glamour, found her beautiful when she was her naked, unadorned self. It was the most powerful love potion she could imagine.

She twined her arms around his neck and nibbled his earlobe. "Please, my lord," she murmured, knowing how he liked her to beg. For this one afternoon, she'd be anything he wanted, do anything he asked. "Take me."

He rumbled approval low in his throat. His fingers gripped the base of her skull, holding her in place for his seeking mouth. He licked the seam of her lips until she opened to him, then his tongue surged in. She sucked it deep into her mouth and he responded with another growl of approval.

They exchanged leisurely kisses that stoked the heat in her belly even higher. He lifted his head, moving his mouth to her neck to give her love-bites to match those she'd given him.

Her breath sighed out. "Dion, I need—"

"Yes?" he replied in a voice rough with arousal. "What do you need, sweetheart? To be touched here?" He tweaked one eager nipple through the cotton, then the other. "Or here?" He slid a hand beneath her skirt.

She was bare beneath the dress—she disliked undergarments and he hadn't brought any back for her anyway. His fingers nudged her thighs apart, going to where she was slick with arousal.

"Yes. There." She rubbed against his stiff cock.

He took his hand from between her thighs to smack the side of her buttock. "Patience, *querida*. We will make this last, *sim*? I want everything from you. I want to take you slowly, until you're burning for me and begging me to quench the fire. But I'm not that nice. I'll make you wait, keep it slow and easy until you're crying with need."

His finger teased her clit, and she stifled a whimper.

"And then," he continued, "I'll take you hard and fast and so deep you don't know where you end and I begin. I want you to remember this loving for the rest of your life. No matter where you go, who you take as a lover. Because I don't care who he is, he's never going to want you even a tenth as much as I do, never going to give you what I can."

"No...," she breathed. "I mean yes. Please. Anything."

Her chest squeezed with the knowledge that what they did today would have to last for a long, long time. Once she returned home, she'd never make love with this big, arrogant *fada* again. Even if he wished to, he'd never risk harming his people.

She twined her fingers in his hair and brought her mouth to his. Dion returned her kiss slow and easy as he'd promised, his tongue exploring her mouth as if they had a lifetime to learn each other and not just a few short hours.

She moaned low in her throat. He lifted his head and she felt him eyeing her. Her aching heart must have shown on her face because he asked, "Why so sad, *querida*? Give me a smile."

She obediently stretched her lips into the semblance of a grin.

"Not good enough," he chided. He lifted her enough to remove her dress and then caught her waist. "Hold your breath," he warned and, pushing off the ledge with his feet, fell with her backward into the pool.

She shrieked just before the water closed over their heads, but he kicked them back to the surface. She sensed him reaching into himself for his power. There was a pleasant sizzle and the pool heated to a comfortable temperature.

"Ah..." She sighed in contentment.

He smoothed her wet hair back from her face and she felt rather than saw his boyish grin. "Like it?"

She shook her head, thinking of all those cold baths she'd taken. "You've been holding out on me."

He nibbled her throat. "You were my prisoner, sweetheart. I couldn't make things too comfortable for you."

"Has anyone ever told you you're a bastard, my lord?" she returned pleasantly.

"Dion." He gave her a hard kiss. "Call me Dion." When she obligingly repeated his name, he replied, "And yes, I've been called that and more." He kissed her again, this time soft and sweet. When she was limp in his arms, he lifted his head and said, "Now, what should I do with you, my beautiful *rainha*?"

"Anything you want. But I have a request, too—don't call me queen." As ruler of the larger, more powerful sun fae clans, she technically outranked him, but not here—not in this enchanted pool of his. "With you, I'm Cleia—only Cleia."

"Mm." Removing his shorts, he tossed them onto the ledge, where they landed with a soggy plop, and then took her hands, swimming backward with her so that they moved in a slow circle.

When he spoke, his voice was husky; it slid over her skin like rough honey.

"But I can call you *querida*, yes? Or *minha bonita*? Because you *are* sweet...and very, very beautiful."

The warm water felt wonderful flowing over her naked body. She let her head fall back as it caressed her thighs, her breasts.

"Yes, yes. Whatever you like."

He drew her closer for a kiss. She wrapped her legs around his waist, her sex rubbing against his belly, and opened her mouth, sucking on his tongue deep inside until they were both breathless.

She was the one who pulled back, but his mouth only moved to her neck, trailing kisses down her jaw and throat as he slid a hand between their bodies to her breasts.

"So beautiful. I want—*eh, bem*..." She felt him shake his head. He brushed his thumb over her nipples, teasing them with light touches.

When they were taut and aching, he began to move again. This time he drew her through the small waterfall that flowed down the back wall. The water was chilly after the warmth of the pool. She yelped in surprise and he reeled her back in so that their mouths were almost touching, his chuckle a warm touch against her lips.

She laughed, exhilarated. "Stars, I want you. Take me. I'm yours, Dion. You know that."

"Careful what you ask for," he replied, his voice hoarse and yet tender.

She tilted her head. Had she really heard tenderness, or was that just wishful thinking?

If only she could see his face.

Then his mouth crashed down on hers and she forgot everything but his tongue dancing with hers, hot and sexy. His erection touched her soft folds, not entering her, just sliding over the delicate, aroused tissues. She moaned and rocked against its hard length.

He raised her from the water so that her breasts were level with his face and sucked one of her nipples into his mouth. She gasped and gripped his shoulders as he drew on her strongly. With each pull, sensation arrowed downward, tugging on her clit and making her womb clench. She squirmed against him, making little sounds of pleasure.

Just when she believed she couldn't take any more, he shifted his attention to her other breast. Somehow her legs were twined high around his chest, her sex rasping over the wiry hair. She ground herself against him, reaching for the climax that was close, so close...

He chuckled darkly and slid her back down his body until they were face to face again. "Not yet."

She hung limply in his arms. "Screw you," she said without heat.

"Oh you will," he promised. "But only when I'm ready. We're going to do this my way. It's what you want. Admit it."

Desire shivered over her skin but she tossed her head. "I admit nothing," she said as she wrapped her legs around him again. "You're already too full of yourself."

"And you're going to be full of me, *querida*." He nuzzled her neck. "Very full."

Then his cock nudged her opening and his fingers gripped her bottom as he pressed inside, inch by slow inch.

"Oh," she breathed, wriggling a little as she adjusted to him. He was hard and thick, stretching her deliciously.

He flexed his hips and slid the last fraction inside. They both sighed with satisfaction.

And he was right, she was very, very full.

She tightened her inner muscles around him and he rumbled in pleasure. "By the gods, you feel good. Tight and so hot. My scorching little sun fae."

He wrapped an arm around her back, the other arm hooked under one of her thighs, and began to move, holding her in place for his easy, measured thrusts.

"Remind me to tease you some more," he said against her neck. "Next time."

"This is perfect," she gasped. "Sometimes...basic...is best."

He made a sound that was half-laugh, half-groan, and backed her up so she was pressed against the rock wall beneath the waterfall. The cool water washed over her shoulders and breasts, tightening her nipples as he thrust into her, hard and fast now. The contrast of cold water and searing friction made her nerve endings go haywire.

Pleasure whipped through her. She whimpered and dug her heels into his muscled ass, brokenly urging him on.

He hitched her up higher so with each thrust he rubbed over her swollen clit, telling her in guttural tones how sweet she was, how much she pleased him. That if she were his, he'd have her a thousand different ways and she'd love every one of them...

"Yes," she breathed. "Yes, love. *Please*."

She cried out as the sensations built to a fever pitch. He thrust deep and held still as she clenched around him. Then he thrust again, and then a third time.

"Cleia," he groaned, and together, they tumbled into a bright, boundless bliss.

When she came back to herself, she was still wrapped around him, the two of them half-reclined in the water with her on top. She shifted, trying to raise herself up, and he flexed his pelvis against hers, his cock still deep inside her.

He began to harden again. "*Deus,*" he muttered. "I just had you and I want you again."

"Yeah?" She relaxed back against his chest and smiled. "No complaints here."

They shared a kiss, then he gave a leisurely kick, sending them backward in the water until he was against the pool's edge. She touched his face, fingering the strong bones, the stubble on his chin.

Blindfolded sex was incredible, but she longed to see him. Just one more time.

She tugged at the scarf binding her eyes. "Take this off, Dion. Please?"

He tensed and an ache blossomed in her chest. Even now he didn't trust her.

"No tricks, I promise. Truth." She touched her breastbone in the sacred oath of the sun fae. "I swear I won't do anything to hurt you or your people. I just want to see you."

His chest heaved. And then his fingers touched either side of the scarf and he muttered a few words in ancient Greek, the ritual language of all fada. The material unwrapped itself from her head and slid into the water.

She opened her eyes and then quickly shut them again. Even the dim light of the cavern hurt. She blinked several times before trying a second time, this time only opening the lids partway.

At first, everything was hazy, but gradually her eyes adjusted and Dion's face swam into focus.

Her breath hitched.

She'd been right. Without his glamour he was as beautiful as a god. And like a god, his was a beauty edged with danger: smooth olive skin covering thick slabs of muscle, a hard face balanced by a sensual lower lip, a mane of midnight hair and black brows guarding his startling ice-blue eyes.

She touched his collar bone, fingered a flat brown nipple. His eyes slit in pleasure, his lashes dark fans on his cheeks. She spread her fingers over his chest. The muscles were warm and resilient under her palms. She stroked her hands over his torso and then back to his shoulders.

Memorizing him for the long, lonely time after she returned home.

When she glanced at his face again, he was gazing back at her. His eyes were hot, predatory, the iris a thin, clear line around pupils dark with desire. His hand slid up her back and he cupped her nape, saying nothing, just reminding her how much stronger he was than her.

Excitement slid over her skin. He was a powerful man, one who ruled his world.

This was what she'd been searching for in her lovers. He was right—she *had* been looking for a strong man, one not easily controlled.

A man who wanted her for herself, not thanks to magic-enhanced lust.

A man who saw past the queen to the woman.

She'd come close to finding it with some of her other Rock Run lovers. But although she'd enjoyed them all, they'd never been quite enough. They hadn't been Dion.

She rubbed her lips over his. "Thank you."

She knew how hard it was for a fada to trust anyone outside the clan. And for Dion to extend that faith to her, the woman who'd stolen his men and weakened his people, was truly a gift.

His expression softened. "I trust you," he said, seemingly reading her mind, and she nodded, her heart too full to speak.

They kissed again, an unhurried mingling of their lips and tongues, and yet somehow it meant more than any of the kisses they'd shared so far.

Dion set her on the ledge that ran around the inside of the pool so that her head and breasts were above the water. "Can I get you anything? Some wine? Water?"

"A glass of wine would be nice."

He levered himself out of the pool and padded into the *sala*. She watched him until he'd passed through the doorway, unashamedly enjoying the view.

While she waited for him to return, she glanced around, curious to see the rooms where she'd spent so much of the past two weeks. The apartment had been carved out of an existing cave; she could see marks where hammers and chisels had been employed. The stone walls were mainly granite, with streaks and nodules of quartz.

Near the ceiling, a handful of fae lights emitted a diffuse green light that made everything appear as if it were underwater. Natural light entered through several slits in the high rock ceiling. She was, of course, well-acquainted with the location of each of those five rays, but now she saw how cleverly they'd been placed to illuminate the bedroom without making it overly bright.

As she'd observed the first day, it was a sparse, utilitarian space with the only furniture being a bed and two chairs. Shelves chiseled into the wall held a few personal items—a hairbrush, shaving utensils, a toothbrush and a small glass. The room was clearly used by Dion alone, which pleased a possessive side she hadn't known existed. Whatever lovers he'd had previously hadn't made a mark on his most private space.

Dion returned with a glass of vinho verde. He lowered himself into the water and put an arm around her, while with the other hand he offered her the wine, never taking his gaze from hers.

At that intent look, her breath sped up. She sipped the wine, and then he took a sip himself before setting down the glass.

"What now?" He drew her closer. His tongue caressed the sensitive point of her ear and she let out an involuntary moan. "I think I know."

Before she could ask what he meant, he ducked beneath the pool's surface and nudged his way between her legs, placing her feet on his shoulders and wrapping his arms around her hips.

"Dion?" She chuckled and then gasped as his mouth closed over her clit. He did something to make the water heat a little more and started to suckle her, slow and easy. "Oh. My. Lord." She grasped the pool's edge, arching into him.

He eased a couple of fingers into her passage, stroking her, while his mouth continued its slow, sensual seduction. She rocked her hips, urging him on. He wrapped a hand around her thigh, holding her in place as he continued to pleasure her, remaining underwater way longer than a man ought to be able to, so that she wondered if he could grow gills at will.

And then she wasn't thinking of anything but the hot suck of his mouth as he circled his tongue around her aching bud.

His fingers stroked in and out of her, rubbing over sensitive inner walls. She tightened on him, her thighs gripping his shoulders. Heat built in her lower belly, spiraled higher. She gripped the rocky edge, making broken sounds as pleasure twisted through her.

It increased until she broke and came hard, calling his name, her inner muscles convulsing around his fingers.

He waited until she went limp before blowing a few hot bubbles against her clit. She couldn't help giggling, and he must have heard because he squeezed her bottom in retaliation. He surfaced one slow inch at a time, kissing his way up her abdomen until he appeared in front of her.

He took her face in his big hands. "Do you know," he husked, "how beautiful you are when you're aroused?"

She shook her head, mesmerized by the tenderness in his gaze.

"*Não*? Then I'll tell you. Your eyes are big and dark with little gold streaks like stars on a hot summer night, and your cheeks are flushed like a child's. Your nipples are hard points, and your cunt"—he glided his cock over her swollen folds—"is wet and ready for me. If you were mine, I'd love you day and night, keep you like this all the time so that everyone knew who you belonged to."

Her throat constricted. "I want that too. So much."

He rested his forehead against hers. "Ah, *querida*. What are we going to do?"

She brushed his wet black hair back from his face. "Take me, Dion. Take me hard."

He twisted her hair around his wrist and gently tugged her head back. Her skin prickled at the look in his eyes. His lips curved in a feral smile that reminded her that he was a fada and would never be entirely tame.

"As you wish, *minha rainha*."

20

At Cleia's words, a dark lust rose up in Dion. For a few slow, powerful heartbeats, he was more animal than not, his blood pumping hot and wild. His fingers tightened on her hair and his lips peeled back in a savage grin.

He inhaled raggedly, struggling to rein in his animal, as Cleia watched him, her golden-brown eyes wide. Then she swiped her tongue over her lower lip, and he nearly came out of his skin.

He drew a shuddering breath. He had to get himself under control before he did something he regretted, took her in a way that only a fada female would understand. He briefly closed his eyes, waiting until the pounding in his veins subsided before brushing a light kiss over her lips.

In response, she nipped him.

His brows winged up. "What the—" He fingered his stinging lower lip. Damn if she hadn't drawn blood. He rinsed it off in the pool.

"Don't," she demanded. "Don't hold back."

His heart resumed its slow, hard beat. "You want this?" He eyed her strong, beautiful face. "Be very sure, my lady."

Her gaze challenged his. "I'm sure, Lord Dion."

"Bom." He climbed out of the pool with her in his arms and set her on her feet. He tugged her head back again, not hurting her, just reminding her who was in charge, and said, "Open your mouth."

She gave him a slow smile and then opened to him as he took her mouth in a fierce kiss.

"You're mine," he growled when he lifted his head. "Mine for this night. Mine forever. Tell me."

"Yes. You know I am. I wish—" Her voice caught.

He shook his head. "No thinking—just let yourself feel." He took her hand and led her across the room to the sheepskin rug at the foot of the bed. "Now, *minha bonita.*" He turned her around and pressed the middle of her back, urging her down. "On your knees."

She smiled and obeyed. He clenched his fists, her ready submission feeding that dark side of him. Kneeling behind her, he pressed her shoulders so that she was on all fours, her varicolored hair streaming like liquid metal over her back. He cupped her hips and let his gaze roam hungrily over her, moving down her body to where her waist tapered in and then flared into that round, perfect ass.

"So beautiful," he said thickly, caressing one firm globe. "So fucking beautiful."

Her head dropped as she pressed back against his hand. *"Dion."*

He smiled and moved his hands to her breasts, pinching the nipples into furled points. "Such pretty nipples. I'd like to taste them—but not yet. Later, I think."

She moaned and arched her back. "Oh, that feels good. So good."

He came upright again. He squeezed her ass, hard enough to imprint his fingers on the smooth golden skin. She moaned again and he said, "I'll make it even better, I promise."

"Please," she begged. "Don't tease, Dion."

He put a knee between her legs, spreading her further, then drew a finger between her thighs. She was wet and impossibly hot, and his balls tightened.

"But I promised I would," he said against her ear. "And I always keep my promises. Besides, it makes things so much more...satisfying."

She quivered beneath his hand. "But I—"

He slapped her ass. "Patience, *querida*. Trust me."

She drew a sharp breath. "I do."

"That's better," he praised and went back to his leisurely exploration of her sex, brushing his fingertips across the wet, swollen lips, swirling over her sweet little pearl.

She made a sound low in her throat. "Please—"

He smiled, taking a visceral satisfaction in how thoroughly she was his. "Soon, love. Soon."

She drew a sobbing breath and he pressed a kiss to her shoulder, then rubbed his cheek over the soft skin, marking her with his scent. The animal wanted everyone to know whom she belonged to.

"*Minha*," he said against her neck. "You're mine. *Me entendes*?"

She dropped onto her forearms, her head on her hands, her bottom turned up in an erotic invitation. "Yes...yes."

His chest clenched. She was his mate, damn it. He'd felt the tug in his heart that signaled a bond was possible.

He'd finally found her after decades of searching—and he couldn't claim her as his. It made him all the more determined to love her hard and long, to bind her to him so that she never forgot him. She might have a hundred lovers in the years to come —and *Deus* if the thought of that didn't make him half-crazed— but it would be his face she'd see as they took her, his name she'd call out as she came.

He played with her for long minutes, enjoying the high, needy sounds she made, the salty-sweet scent of her sex, the way she instinctively widened her thighs to coax him to enter her.

"Not yet," he murmured and came down over top of her, bracing himself with his hands on either side of her body so he could rub his chest and abdomen over her back and buttocks, his cock sliding through her slick folds without entering.

The pleasure was excruciating. His balls tightened and he gritted his teeth, wanting to draw it out as long as possible. But she was so primed that at the merest touch she shuddered and called out his name, coming in a small orgasm that he knew would be a tease in itself.

Sure enough, she turned her head to look at him through dazed eyes, her shining hair half-covering her face. "Dion, please," she rasped. "I need you."

He smoothed her hair back so he could see her expression: open, wanting, vulnerable—his. A wave of tenderness washed over him. Abruptly he was tired of teasing. He just wanted her.

"Then you'll have me, *querida*." He pressed a kiss to the sweet-smelling skin between her shoulder blades and positioned himself to take her.

Suddenly, the air around him shifted, shimmered...and then they were surrounded by four sun fae, including Lady Olivia, a dart in her hand. Behind them was Adric, a smirk on his lips.

Dion rocked back on his haunches and roared with anger. "*Não.*"

They were already pulling Cleia to her feet. Her eyes met his, wide and distressed. "Dion, I—"

He just had time to spit out the word, "Bitch," before Olivia plunged the dart into his shoulder and everything went black.

CLEIA SUCKED in a breath as Dion slumped to the ground.

"Don't hurt him!" She threw herself between him and her men. She crouched down next to him and ran her hands over his body. His breath was slow and uneven. She shot an accusing look at Olivia. "What did you do?"

"Nothing that will cause permanent damage. He's going to sleep for a while, but he'll be fine." Olivia arched a single copper brow. "An ill-timed rescue, I see. My apologies, cousin. I believed you were a prisoner here."

Cleia grimaced. "I was, but—he was going to let me go." She touched Dion's cheek. He was unharmed. That was the important thing.

She looked up at the group surrounding them: Olivia, Artan and Grady, two sun fae warriors and a fifth man whom she didn't know. Their frowns—save for the fifth man, who was watching the proceedings with a sardonic smile—reminded her she was a queen.

One whose people desperately needed her to return.

She glanced back at Dion, curled up on his side, naked and defenseless. Hot tears stung her eyes.

Stars, what a mess. She pressed a kiss to the top of his head and came to her feet.

Artan held out the pink dress. She put it on, her gaze going back to Dion as soon as she was done.

"Ready?" Olivia asked impatiently. "I cast a misdirection spell to make them think we're attacking from the other side of the base, but we only have a few minutes before they realize it's a hoax."

Cleia nodded, her gaze still on Dion. "He'll never forgive me for this," she said, more to herself than anyone else. Her stomach cramped with regret. She pressed a hand to it and took a steadying breath.

Dion was going to hate her for this—and he'd be downright murderous when he awoke and discovered what she was about to do.

But something he'd said had given her an idea. It just might work. And if it did, she could undo some of the damage she'd unwittingly caused his clan.

She turned to Olivia. "We have to take him with us."

"What?"

"We have to take him with us—back to Rising Sun."

Cleia snatched up one of the nets she'd mended. Chanting softly, she threw it over Dion, using her magic to bind it around him. Even as her heart wept at the brutal interruption of their interlude, it felt good to use her magic again, to feel the tingle as the spell flowed from her heart-center to her fingertips to manifest itself in the physical world, although after two weeks underground, her strength was much reduced.

"What in Hades are you doing?" Olivia stared at Cleia as if she'd lost her mind. "Do you want war with the river fada? Right now we've got right on our side, but if you kidnap their alpha, they'll be out for blood. They're *animals*, Cleia. They'd as soon as tear out your throat as negotiate."

The fifth man, the one Cleia didn't know, shifted position. His odd bronze eyes flashed, but were swiftly shuttered.

Olivia's mouth compressed. "I beg your pardon, Lord Adric."

"Dion's not like that—" Cleia started to say but was interrupted by a hard banging on the door.

"Lord Dion?" a man shouted. "Are you all right? Open the door."

"There's no time," Cleia said. "Everyone, touch a part of the net. *Now.*"

Olivia and the four sun fae warriors hurried to obey, although it was clearly against their better judgment, but the earth alpha hung back.

"You too, Lord Adric," Cleia rapped out. She'd already guessed he was an earth fada—not only did he have that lithe, catlike physique, those odd eyes were a dead giveaway—and as soon as Olivia had said his name, she'd realized he was the Baltimore clan's new alpha. Everybody knew that his clan and Dion's were long-time enemies. She was damned if she'd leave him behind in Rock Run to cause mischief.

The earth fada's nostrils flared angrily, but he stepped forward to grasp the net.

Of the six sun fae, only Cleia and her cousin had the power to teleport. "My apartment," she told Olivia. "The center." Weakened as she was, Cleia could never do it alone.

Olivia jerked her head in assent and added her energy to Cleia's.

The door to the hall burst open and several large, angry Rock Run warriors rushed across the *sala*, Tiago at the rear. She and Olivia hurriedly extended their power to the rest of their group, Cleia focusing all her remaining resources on herself and Dion, relying on Olivia to bring herself and the others through.

Power surged. The air around them opened like a curtain through which they stepped as their molecules shifted to pure energy.

The last thing Cleia saw was Tiago looking at her with stormy eyes that were a replica of his brother's.

21

---

*D*ion's tongue felt swollen to twice its normal size. He tried to swallow, but his mouth was so dry there was no saliva to spare.

He was stiff and aching, with a cramp in his left calf. He moved restlessly, trying to reach his leg so he could massage it, but his arms seemed glued to his sides.

And he was hot, so hot, the skin on his face burning. In fact, his entire body felt as if he'd been hung out to bake in the desert sun.

He forced his sleep-encrusted eyes open and turned his head to avoid the bright sunlight. He couldn't see clearly, but he had the impression of pale yellow walls, immense windows, billowing white curtains. It seemed familiar, but why?

His face was wrapped in something. He tried to lift a hand to it and couldn't. He glanced down at the black mesh entrapping him, and in a rush, everything came back to him. Having sex with Cleia...giving in to her pleas to remove the bespelled scarf around her eyes...and then Olivia and the other sun fae appearing out of nowhere and plunging a drugged dart into his shoulder.

A savage snarl rose in his throat.

Cleia. The *puta* had trussed him up in one of his own fishing nets and brought him home.

He was laid out on a couch in her apartment with the noon sun hammering on his face.

His vision hazed over. He'd trusted her, damn it—and she'd ground that trust beneath her pretty little heel.

The animal in him rose, instinctively trying to fight free of the net. He thrashed about, scratching and biting at the knotted webbing until he fell back to the cushions exhausted, chest working like a bellows. With a tremendous effort, he reined in his animal and forced himself to think rationally.

It was his only hope.

Okay. The animal's right.

He did need to escape the net—but panicking only made things worse.

He took a deep breath and braced his arms and legs against the netting, straining with everything he had to break it—even just a small opening that he could rip wider. But it held fast.

He kept pushing, refusing to give up until his muscles gave and again he dropped back onto the couch, heart pounding and the room swooping crazily around him.

He steeled himself for a third round. This time he tried to shift to otter so that he could claw his way out of the net, but whatever magic Cleia had woven into the strands slammed him back into his human form before he was even halfway changed.

He swore viciously. His fingers clenched and unclenched. If he ever got free of the net, the sun fae witch had better be far, far away.

The door opened and light footsteps entered the apartment. He pushed himself partially upright, his back against one of the couch's arms. The room did another dizzy gyration.

He swallowed a wave of nausea and watched narrow-eyed as his captor approached. She'd changed into a simple white shift and dressed her hair in a single braid that hung over one shoulder. Her lovely sun-touched eyes were large and wary. She appeared as innocent as a child.

His lip curled. If Queen Cleia was innocent, then he was a just-hatched minnow.

She drew in a breath, causing her firm breasts to press against her shift, and he cursed the way his stomach clenched, how he wanted her even now, knowing what she was. A lying, betraying bitch.

Anguish gripped his chest until his heart felt like a cold, heavy lump instead of a living organ.

He was a fool for this woman—and his people were going to suffer for it. Thanks to his weakness, his stupidity in trusting her, she'd been able to capture him, leaving his people leaderless at a time when both the sun fae and the Baltimore earth fada knew where the base was and that the river clan was vulnerable. Even now the earth fada could be attacking—and he was trussed up like a pig on a spit, helpless to prevent them.

"You're awake," Cleia said, then clucked her tongue. "The sun —I'm sorry, I didn't think."

She crossed to the windows on the sunny side of the room and pulled the curtains across them. He heaved a sigh of relief as the searing light was muted.

She walked back to him, stopping a few feet from the couch. "How are you feeling?"

He stared at her without replying. Surely she wasn't going to behave as if he were a frigging guest? But apparently she was.

"You must be thirsty," she said. "You've been out since yesterday evening." She went to a small kitchen, returning with a glass of water.

He glared at her through slit lids. "Just...enjoying your hospitality, Queen Cleia," he said, speaking with difficulty around his swollen tongue. "It's most...restful."

She regarded him somberly, and then waved her hand,

removing the net from his face. "Drink," she urged, holding the glass to his lips.

He growled lowly and considered refusing, but he craved that drink with every cell in his body. Water fada were easily dehydrated. His skin was so dry and tight it was painful, his mind sluggish from lack of fluids. Just the act of sitting partway up had left him shaky, so he swallowed his pride and took a tentative sip. The water was ice-cold with a hint of lime. It slid down his parched throat, cool and blessedly moist.

"More," he croaked. She brought the glass back to his lips. This time she murmured something and he felt the unmistakable whisper of magic slide over his skin. He reared back. "What the fu—?"

"I infused the water with a strengthening spell. You're weak from being out so long."

He pressed his lips together. "I don't need your goddamn magic."

She sighed. "Please drink it. I swear there's nothing in it to harm you."

He hesitated, but he couldn't scent the metallic taint of dark magic. And however low his opinion of the sun fae queen, he'd bet his life she didn't dabble in the dark arts. He gave in and emptied the glass.

"That's better, isn't it?" She gave him an encouraging smile as if he were a child. "Would you like more?"

He nodded, already feeling better. As she helped him drink a second glass, strength flooded into him.

When she turned to set the glass on a nearby table, he sat up straighter, surreptitiously flexing his muscles. If he could just break out of this blasted net... But the binding spell was too powerful.

"You must be hungry, too." She gave him an assessing look. "I'll order some food. My chef doesn't have your cooks' way with fish, but he's quite good."

He dropped his head back on the couch and regarded her through lowered lids. "Cut the crap, Cleia. You drugged me and dragged me back here trussed in a net. Your cousin gave the location of our clan base to a sneaky, murderous S.O.B. who'd like nothing better than to move in on Rock Run's territory. And to top it all off, you lied. *No tricks,*" he mimicked. "*I promise. I just want to see you, Dion.*" He shook his head. "I'm the world's biggest ass. So stop acting like I'm a goddamn dinner guest and tell me what the hell you want."

"Fine." She dragged a hand over her braid. "I'll admit you've got a right to be angry. I did bring you here against your will. But I did *not* lie to you. I couldn't—I made a sacred oath that would've left me ill for days if I'd broken it. Olivia and Lord Adric found the base on their own—he was tracking you after each meeting. And then one of your own people told them where you were keeping me."

"*No.*" He swung his bound legs to the floor and struggled to sit the rest of the way upright, wriggling on the couch until he faced her. "I don't believe you."

"I'm sorry, Dion, but it's true. You know what it costs a fae to lie."

He eyed her. She should be trying harder to convince him. The fact that she wasn't made his fingers clench on the net.

"Who?" he demanded in hoarse tones. "Tell me his name."

"I didn't say it was a man. But what does it matter? You were going to release me yourself."

"It matters."

She shook her head. "Let it go, Dion. What's done is done."

"I can't," he said flatly. "I'm alpha. My word has to be law. I can't allow a traitor to live. I'd be seen as weak for allowing it, and every warrior unhappy with his place in the hierarchy would start challenging for dominance."

To the fada, a weak leader needed to be culled. The clan would split into factions, each supporting a different man, and pretty soon they'd be at one another's throats. It had happened with the Baltimore shifters.

"Then I'll have to make sure you never find out who it was."

"You're welcome to try."

They stared at each other challengingly. She looked away first. "Look, I didn't bring you here to argue with you."

"Then why? You say you didn't lie to me, but it was you who bound me in this net, you who brought me back here, *sim*?"

"Yes, but—"

"If you're not trying to harm Rock Run, then why take me—the alpha—when we're at our most vulnerable? Adric could be attacking even now. What's the matter, *querida*, couldn't the queen live without her pet shifter?"

She winced. "I can explain—"

"*Por favor*." He settled back on the couch and lifted a mocking brow. "I've always enjoyed a good story."

She blew out a breath but said, "First, let me order your food."

She crossed the room and opened the door. After speaking with a servant there, she returned and sat down on a chair across from him. A weary look crossed her face and she gave a small, almost imperceptible sigh.

He frowned. If anything, she looked more tired and wan than she had yesterday, and even a little thinner. If keeping her underground had been the problem, shouldn't she be starting to get better now that she was home and getting plenty of sunshine and fresh air?

He opened his mouth to ask if she was sick, and then closed it again. Why should he care about the *puta*'s health? But it bothered him all the same. Hades take the woman anyway. It was going to be difficult to remove the claws she'd sunk into his heart.

She cocked her head to one side, considering him in turn.

He narrowed his eyes at her. "Talk."

"I have an idea, Dion." She leaned forward, hands on her

thighs. "I think I know a way for your people to regain their energy."

"Yes?" he replied in an unencouraging tone. As her captive, he had no choice but to listen, but the rivers would flow backward before he'd trust the deceitful queen again.

She opened her mouth, then closed it again. "Not like this, with you trapped in that net. Give me your word that you'll stay within the compound until the midsummer ritual and not try to communicate with your clan, and I'll free you from the net."

"And after the ritual? What then?"

"You'll be free to go."

"That's it?" He eyed her, his mind probing for loopholes, tricks. "I remain here for two days and then I can leave?"

"Yes. That's it. I swear on the Mother Goddess herself that you'll be free to leave after the ritual."

"My people will be worried. They'll try to rescue me whether or not I contact them."

"You can let them know about our bargain but nothing else. You can send them a message using fae magic. They'll see and hear you talking as if you were in the room with them. All right?"

He scrutinized her for another few seconds and then jerked his head in assent. "All right."

After all, his alternative was to remain ensnared in a net—and he'd go crazy if he remained bound much longer. Already the animal was rising again, urging him to kick and scratch and bite his way out of it, chew his own limbs off if he had to. Anything to break free.

"Say the words. Swear it."

He inclined his head. "I swear on my honor as the Rock Run alpha that I will stay within Rising Sun territory until the summer solstice, and I will not communicate with anyone of my clan, save to tell them of our bargain."

She hesitated, examining his words for any hidden meaning

before giving a satisfied nod. "Thank you. This is going to work—you'll see."

She waved a hand and the net disappeared.

Yes... He pushed himself to standing, his muscles protesting their confinement, and raised his arms for a long, bone-cracking stretch.

He was still naked, and angry as he was with Cleia, he couldn't help enjoying how her eyes darkened. He drew out the stretch until her breath quickened and he began to harden.

He brought his hands to his hips. "Did you want something, *querida*?"

She licked her lips and he smiled to himself.

"Yes," she said absently. "I mean no, I—" She dragged her gaze from his rapidly growing erection. "I—you remember where the bathing room is."

"*Sim.*"

"You probably want to—to—" She waved a hand in the room's direction. "I—I set out some clothes for you, too."

He'd never seen her so flustered. The animal in him preened, while the man grinned wickedly. He sauntered across the apartment to the bathing room, aware of her gaze on his ass the entire way.

Inside the shower, he cranked the water to hot and let it cascade over him, soothing his stiff muscles and washing away the stale odor of a man who'd been unconscious for almost a day. Damn the woman anyway.

Although now that he had calmed down a bit, he couldn't help feeling a grudging respect at the way she'd turned the tables on him. He shook his head. *Capturing him in his own fucking net.*

There were several cakes of soap to choose from. He lifted each of them to his nose in turn. One had the tangy aroma of fresh oranges: Cleia's scent. He inhaled deeply before setting it back down and choosing one without fragrance.

But her scent lingered in his nostrils, and his mindless cock bobbed in response. He cupped the hard flesh with a soapy hand, wishing...wanting...

Deus, he *was* a fool.

He finished washing and turned off the shower.

It was as he reached for a towel that he realized Cleia hadn't made him promise not to touch her. In fact, he could do anything he pleased to her—as long as he stayed within the sun fae compound.

His mouth curved.

22

____

Dion returned to the main room dressed in the T-shirt and shorts that Cleia had left out for him. By the time they had sent the message to his people, the food had arrived—plump oysters on the half-shell, oversized lobsters, grilled scallops, and mussels cooked in a wine-and-garlic sauce and served over pasta. Rounding out the meal was a loaf of crusty bread, a large bowl of salad and another of summer berries, and a carafe of vinho verde.

The sight and scent of all that food made him lightheaded. His hollow stomach rumbled.

Cleia waved a hand at the table. "Eat, please. You must be starved. You were out for almost eighteen hours."

"*Obrigado*." He took a seat and heaped his plate as she reached for the vinho verde.

"It's one of yours," she said as she handed him a glass. "Our wine steward has a standing order with Rock Run."

He sipped the crisp, slightly sparkling liquid. "What little there is of it these days."

He reached for an oyster and tipped the shell to his lips. The meat slid down his throat, briny and delicious. He chased it with the wine and reached for another.

"Isa told me about your vineyards," Cleia said. "That it's not just the one that has black rot. The problem is deeper than that. Your vineyards and farms have dropped in fertility and you're constantly fighting fungi and diseases. She blames the move from the Mediterranean, says the old ways are being lost. But that's not the real reason, is it? You were here for years before you had any problems. Isa said it all started around two decades ago, around the time I took the first one of your men as a lover. She didn't make the connection, but you did."

"That's right." He speared a grilled scallop. "It was bad enough that you stole some of my best men, but as you said, they were adults and capable of making their own choices. But one of our healers sensed an energy drain. He told me and eventually we traced it to the times you had one of our men under your thrall."

The skin around her eyes tightened, but she ignored the veiled insult. "I see."

"It lessens after they come home, but it never stops completely. And with each man you take, it gets worse."

"There's a cumulative effect, then."

"*Sim.*"

She met his eyes. "I'm sorry, Dion. If I'd known, I swear I wouldn't have kept taking your men as lovers."

He inclined his head. She may not have known she was doing it, but the end result was the same.

They ate in silence for a few minutes. Cleia was the first to speak.

"I'm curious—why haven't we met before now? We've been neighbors for close to a century. The fada were often invited to our festivals. Some of your people came, but never you—or anyone in your family, for that matter."

"I'm too busy to go to parties."

"No one works all the time."

"No? We fada don't have your magic to help us build. We had to hollow out the caverns ourselves, build or trade for our own furniture, help the humans who emigrated with us to plant our vineyards and plow our fields."

His people had magic of a sort, but it tended to manifest itself in the ability to hunt, to track and kill prey. The fada were the world's best hunters and fishers, but when it came to farming, they had to labor as hard as any human to prosper. And of course, once Dion had made warrior, he'd been required to train several hours a day when not on a mission.

"We aren't so different," Cleia said. "Our magic is useful, of course. I can teleport and work energy. Others can create gold from straw—or conjure a building from thin air—but it's a huge energy drain. We try not to call on it unless it's absolutely necessary. But from what I could tell, your base is finished except when you need to carve out new apartments for mated couples. So why not accept one of our invitations?"

He set down his fork. Fine. If she wanted the truth, he'd give it to her.

"In the beginning, I was too busy. And don't forget, we fada have our own parties."

She nodded. "The bacchanalia."

"The bacchas, yes, and also other celebrations that are for ourselves alone. But mainly my family stayed away because my *pai* didn't trust you worth a damn. You fae may not lie, but you twist the truth to suit yourselves. And you think the fada are a lower form of life. You're happy to use us to fight your wars or for a good fuck, but you don't see us as equals."

"That's not true. Perhaps some fae are like that, but my parents always treated you fairly. I've continued that, and encouraged my people to do the same."

His mouth twisted. "So it was fair to lure our men with your glamour, and then keep them for years at a time? Once I saw what was happening, I wouldn't have touched you with a ten-foot pole. I warned the others to stay away from you—but you can't blame an unmated male for seeking out a willing woman."

"I—" She had the grace to look ashamed. "They came of their own free will. They were free to come and go as they pleased."

"But your glamour made sure they stayed stuck to you like a pup at its mama's teat."

Her chin jutted. "So I used a touch of magic to draw men to me. It's not like you fada are so damn innocent. I've seen what happens at a baccha. Years ago, when I was barely more than a girl, I snuck into one. It was like a nightmare. Drugs. People screaming for mercy. I—I saw a man whipping a woman until she—"

She swallowed and glanced away. "I was so scared they'd come for me next. I tried to teleport out but there was some kind of barrier that prevented me. All I could do was cast a glamour to make myself as old and ugly as I could and hide until Artan and Grady found me."

"For God's sake, woman, what were you thinking?" He scowled. "You could've been carried off and never seen again. The combination of wine and magic cause a frenzy—for anyone, but especially for fada. Our dark side takes over. It *is* a nightmare, the worst you ever had…but also the most carnal, addictive pleasure. Even being an old woman wouldn't have saved you once the *Delírio* was on them."

"Then why hold the bacchas?"

"We don't. Not for twenty-some years. My father banned them —with the full support of the clan—and I've continued that ban."

Her tawny brows arched. "I didn't know that."

"Most of the fada clans have, save for a few renegades."

"But everyone still thinks that you hold them. I don't under-stand—why keep it a secret?"

He moved a shoulder. "We prefer not to share our business with outsiders."

"And it's another reason for people to steer clear of you," she added shrewdly.

He inclined his head.

He'd almost finished his dinner, but she'd barely touched her own food. He frowned, remembering her appetite when she'd first come to Rock Run.

He selected a fat lobster claw, cracked it open and put the meat on her plate. "Eat. Your people depend on you."

She shot him a look, surprised and hopeful. He glanced away and the hopeful expression faded.

He swallowed tightly, the food he'd eaten an uncomfortable ball in his stomach. But he refused to let her read anything more into his actions than his instinct to protect and care for a woman —any woman.

And if he was lying to himself as much as her, so be it.

She sighed and took a bite of lobster.

"I am weaker," she confessed. "My time underground sapped my strength. Sun fae need natural light, as much of it as possible. Especially me. The rest of the sun fae draw from me, you see. I'm the Conduit."

"Olivia told me something about that. But I thought it was just at the midsummer ritual that they draw from you?"

"That's not quite true. All of the sun fae draw energy from the sun—but not enough. They depend on the Conduit to draw the extra energy they need to be truly healthy. As Conduit, the sun's energy is constantly flowing through me to the rest of my people. But yes, the midsummer ritual is where I renew my bond with the sun, and through me, the rest of the sun fae. Without that bond, the flow of energy would gradually cease."

"By Hades, I never intended to—"

"Harm me?" She gave him a straightforward look. "Forget it, Dion. You did what you had to. I understand."

He dragged a hand over his hair. He *had* done what he thought necessary, but that didn't mean he felt good about it.

"But you're home now, getting all the sunlight you need. Why aren't you getting stronger?"

She shook her head and looked down at her plate.

"You *will* get better, won't you?" he pressed.

"Of course. I'm just a little weak today because of Xavier."

"Xavier? But—"

"I went back to see him—to give him as much energy as I could spare. That's where I was this morning."

He scowled. "Luis just let you 'port in and out of there?"

"I waited until he left. Only Marina knew. Please don't be angry with her—she'd do anything to keep Xavier alive."

"You think I don't know that? But damn it, you can't just flit in and out of our base at will." He paused and then reluctantly thanked her. "That was good of you, especially when you're low in energy yourself."

And it *was* kind, damn her anyway.

"Don't thank me. I'm happy to do whatever I can for him." Tears shimmered in her eyes. "He's such a bright spirit."

"It's in *Deus*'s hands now. But thank you for trying."

She lifted a shoulder and didn't answer.

"And my clan?" he asked. "The base—everything was quiet?"

"Yes. Why wouldn't it—?" Understanding dawned on her face. "The earth fada. You think they're going to attack."

"I know they will. You don't know how a fada thinks. Thanks to you and Olivia, Adric knows we're weak—and that I'm not there to lead a defense. That makes us fair game."

"Not if he can't find his way back to your base."

He snorted. "Trust me, it's embedded in his brain."

She hesitated, then said, "I can help with that. Or rather, Olivia can. Her primary Gift is spells—casting them, neutralizing them. She has a spell that will wipe Adric's memory, just a crucial few minutes. He'll know he was at your base, but he'll have no memory of its layout, or exactly where it was. And any records that he kept will be wiped out as well."

"That's a hell of a Gift. But why would your cousin help us?"

"Because I'll ask her to. And besides, our policy is to remain neutral in the politics of other clans."

"*Sim*?" He raised an ironic brow.

"Yes." She shot him an exasperated look. "I'm not your enemy, Dion, which you'd know if you'd look past the end of your goddamned nose."

She crossed the room and sat before a fae-powered computer. She tapped the screen, calling her cousin, and explained what was needed.

He couldn't see Olivia, but he could hear her reluctance. "You're sure? Better to keep the fada at each other's throats so they're too busy to bother with us."

He snarled lowly and Cleia shot him a look. "I'm sure," she replied. "It's only fair. It's because of us that Lord Adric knows where the Rock Run base is and that Lord Dion is our...guest."

"Very well," said her cousin.

As Cleia returned to her seat, Dion whistled softly. "The two of you are some pair, aren't you?"

"We wouldn't have survived this long if we weren't strong. Your father made it clear he'd like to expand into our lands."

"Did he? I didn't know."

It must have been years ago, before he became his father's second.

"We convinced him it wasn't worth his while."

Dion's mouth quirked. "I'd have loved to have heard that conversation."

She grinned. "It wasn't precisely a conversation. More like a demonstration."

He chuckled outright. "He always said that fada and fae don't mix."

"And do you agree?"

His face hardened. "I do now."

"I see." She went very still. Her expression remained impassive, but it was as if she'd curled into a protective ball.

Shame slapped at him. He'd have preferred her to push back, tell him to go to the devil. He was still feeling the humiliation at being captured—in a net, yet. He wanted to hurt her, punish her, and yet each time he did, he hurt himself as well.

He pushed his plate away.

Cleia concentrated on cutting another tiny morsel of lobster. She hadn't eaten enough to keep a bird alive—a small, underweight bird.

He regarded her morosely. "For God's sake, woman, if you're not going to eat, go sit on the balcony. Get some sun. I'll be damned if you get sick because of me and my clan."

She set her fork down without eating the lobster. "It won't help."

"Why the hell not? You need sunlight for energy and it's hot enough to fry eggs out there. Why won't it help?"

"Because...I need you, too."

"What do you mean?"

She lifted her gaze to his. "Don't you feel it?"

"What?"

But it was there in the space between them—not yet tangible, but the possibility tantalizing them both. The mate bond, the magical bond linking mind to mind, soul to soul, heart to heart.

"No. Oh, no." He tore his gaze from hers and pushed away from the table to pace agitatedly around the room. "Don't even *think* it. You—me—our very joining would be a death sentence for my people. I would never agree to it. *Never*."

And the bond couldn't form without both parties' consent.

"But it's different between you and me." She rose to her feet as well. "You said it yourself—when *we* join, your people get a boost in energy. And from what I can tell, it seems to be spread evenly between your people and mine. My guess is that those other men weren't strong enough, so the energy just flowed one way. With us, it's different. Just the two of us together yesterday made a difference. Marina told me this morning that the black rot has almost disappeared. Gaspar's telling everyone it's a miracle, she said. And last night the fishers brought in a huge catch, the biggest in years."

He swung around to eye her. "This is true? Swear it."

"It's true." She touched her breastbone.

He raked his fingers through his hair. "It could be a coincidence."

"Stars, Dion, what will it take to open your mind?"

"All right. Suppose it's true. If this energy exchange is mutual, why are you so weak? And it's not just because of Xavier—it started before you tried to heal him."

"I'm not sure. Part of it was being underground for two weeks —and remember, you didn't touch me until the last day. But my guess is that we need to consciously direct it, the way I do at the midsummer ritual. That's why I need you at the ritual."

"Stop right there." He threw up a hand, palm out. "I never promised to take part in your ritual."

"Please, Dion. Hear me out. This is the answer, I know it is. The two of us can proclaim our mate bond there. I'll draw the sun's energy and together, we'll use it to replenish both our peoples."

Or, he thought cynically, she could drain his entire clan's energy in one fell stroke. What she asked required trust—and he might want to fuck her, but he was damned if he'd entrust her with not only his life-energy, but his entire clan's.

He shook his head. "It's too unpredictable. Even if it's true that the two of us having sex somehow benefits my people, who knows if that will continue? Because mostly it's been a one-way street—a slow, unending suck from us to you until we're weak... sick...dying. I can't take the chance."

Her chest heaved. "Damn it, Dion. This will work. I know it will."

He gazed back at her without speaking.

"All right." She rubbed her palms over her arms. "I—there's something you need to know. Xavier wouldn't be sick if it weren't for me. He's going to die if we don't do something."

He grabbed her shoulders. "What do you mean?"

"I mean you're right, Dion. I'm taking energy from Xavier. I've been taking energy from your men, and probably even from some of the women through their men. I realized it yesterday when I went to heal Xavier. I saw the flow—in my direction." Her big eyes pleaded with his. "I swear I tried to stop it, but I couldn't. All I could do was slow it down."

He stared at her. At last she'd admitted it—flat out, with no equivocations. He should have felt a grim satisfaction, but instead he felt depressed, drained, as if the last drop of hope had been squeezed from him.

And not just his hope that she could help Xavier.

No, this was the last, stupidly optimistic cry of his heart, which against all evidence had still been praying that somehow, someway, the two of them could work this out.

He released her and paced away. "So he's going to die," he said flatly.

"No. Not if we join. We have to accept the mate bond and then together, we can feed energy into your clan."

"Like hell. There has to be another way."

"So you refuse to even try?"

"That's right."

She muttered something that sounded like "pigheaded fada" and turned to leave. "I'll see you at dinner, then."

"Not so fast." His mind was roiling, but he was damned if she was going to walk out on him. They might never be mates but that didn't mean she wasn't his for the next two days. He grasped her arm and spun her to face him. "We have some unfinished business, you and me."

They stared at each other for a charged moment. Then she

glanced at his hand and raised a brow, the haughty queen once more.

Everything masculine in him rose in response. His blood pounded in his veins. His breath seared in and out of his lungs.

If she only knew how that haughty look roused the dominant male animal in him, goading him to show her who her master was. He itched to jerk her up against his body, fist his hand in her braid and take her mouth in deep, drugging kisses until she was whimpering with need. And then he'd bend her over a chair and take her fast and hard until she understood just how hazardous it was to provoke a fada male.

Whatever she saw in his face made her swallow audibly. "Remember your promise, Dion."

"But of course." He repeated it back to her, and her eyes widened. He nodded. "I see you understand."

She took a step back, then another and another, him following until her back was against the wall. He was so close he could feel her body heat all down his front—his chest, thighs, and most of all his groin. So close he could see how large and black her pupils were, the irises thin amber bands around the outside. So close he could smell the tang of her arousal.

And even now, with him crowding her against the wall, she didn't betray a hint of fear. No, she lifted her chin and looked down her straight patrician nose at him.

"Aren't you afraid I'll suck out all your energy?"

His mouth quirked in spite of himself. Damn, he loved her spirit.

"Not if it's just for a couple of days. It's the mate bond I'm worried about. That kind of connection can never be broken. Even if it were hurting my people I wouldn't be able to sever it. But for two days, I'm willing to take a chance."

He placed his hands on either side of her head, caging her in...and smiled.

She finally seemed aware of the danger she was in. Her eyes

went even larger, if that were possible. She moistened her lower lip and his whole body went rock-hard.

He had plans for that luscious red mouth. He hadn't forgotten how she'd boasted of her skills that first night.

"Dion," she said, "I—"

"Oh, no, *querida*," he crooned. "You can't talk your way out of this one."

He pressed closer so that his erection nudged her abdomen.

"You could call your guards, of course. They'd love to beat the crap out of me. Or you can take what you have coming. Which will it be, *minha rainha*?"

23

*D*ion's body crowded Cleia's against the wall, two hundred-plus pounds of hard, angry male. His mouth descended, his eyes a feral silver that signaled his animal was in control.

She could call for help, but he was right. Artan and Grady were already furious that he'd stolen her right from under their noses. They'd love a chance to pound on Dion. She had no doubt he'd give as good as he got—maybe even win—but two against one was never fair, and her bodyguards fought dirty.

And besides, she knew he wouldn't really hurt her. He was alpha, a warrior, but also a protector, especially of women and children. He'd never harm her, at least not for anything she'd done to him personally. Of course, if he decided it was the only way to save his clan...

Then his mouth covered hers and her mind emptied of everything but his body against hers: the firm, muscled chest pressed against her aching nipples; the hips rocking slowly against hers; the lips teasing hers, sensuous, knowing.

She'd expected a rough, punishing kiss. She'd seen his face when she'd entered the apartment. Subjecting a proud man like him to the indignity of a net had been a mistake, but there'd been no time to weigh the pros and cons. And when she'd released him, she'd been so sure he'd see the benefit of her plan that she hadn't extracted a promise from him not to seek revenge—another miscalculation.

But he surprised her by keeping the kiss light, delicate, his mouth brushing over hers in butterfly touches that made her whole body soften.

"Dion," she said against his lips, "I'm sorry. So sorry. I didn't mean—"

"*Silêncio.*" He grasped her wrists and pressed them to the wall on either side of her head. "I don't want to hear your excuses. I just want to hear you begging for mercy."

Her heart thumped against her rib cage. "What do you mean?"

His smile was wolfish. "I should punish you, my queen. That you dared capture me in one of my own nets. You deserve to feel my hand on your ass for that. But there's more than one way to teach you a lesson."

He kissed her again, harder this time. She closed her eyes as his tongue swept into her mouth, demanding her response. His body pressed hers against the wall, his erection thick and urgent against her belly. He bent his knees so he could grind himself against her mound.

She moaned his name and kissed him back with everything she had.

When he lifted his head, her breath sawed in and out of her lungs. His eyes glinted; both man and animal pleased with her surrender. *Bastard.*

Her head dropped back against the wall as she strove to calm the wild beating of her heart. If this was punishment, she'd never survive his idea of pleasure.

"Keep your arms raised," he told her.

She nodded weakly. The time to resist was past. And she

wanted this, even knowing it was all he intended to give her. Damn her foolish, needy heart anyway.

He grasped the hem of her dress and yanked it over her head. She wasn't wearing anything beneath. He dropped it on the floor and looked at her. He drew a slow breath.

"*Bonita,*" he muttered thickly. "*Muito bonita.*"

His big hands moved over her body, brushing her ribs, tweaking her nipples. She made a small sound of pleasure and his lips curved. One rough palm slid down her abdomen to the junction of her thighs to cup her firmly, claiming her —owning her.

She shuddered with arousal and he murmured, "Do you want it, *querida*?"

She jerked her head in assent, and he smiled—not a nice smile. "How bad? Tell me."

"Bad," she admitted in ragged tones. "I'm afraid...you're the only man...I'll ever want."

His dark brows snapped together and he stared at her, unmoving. She dropped every defense and met his gaze, bravely exposing her innermost self to him, instinctively knowing it was the only way to overcome his distrust.

His eyes flickered and she felt a surge of hope. Then he shook his head dismissively. "You'll find someone else."

She shut her eyes. "Perhaps." She refused to let him see how he hurt her.

He gave a low growl of displeasure but didn't say anything.

His palm was still on her mound. She rocked against him, urging him to continue what he'd started. If she couldn't have his heart, at least she'd have his body...for today and tomorrow. Because if he didn't agree to her plan, in two days she was going to have to allow him to leave, and she knew she'd never see him again.

His middle finger delved lower. He grunted with satisfaction.

"You're so hot and wet. So ready for me. Spread a little more, *querida*."

He nudged her inner thighs with his hand. Lowering her arms, she braced her palms against the wall and obediently widened her legs.

"That's it." He stroked a long finger into her, then out again. The work-roughened tip dragged over her clit. Her womb clenched as sensation streaked through her.

She rocked her hips, wordlessly begging for more, and he gripped her hip with his other hand to hold her still.

She drew a jagged breath. "Dion..."

"Always so impatient," he chided. "Didn't anyone ever teach you to wait for your pleasure?"

"Yes, but—" They hadn't been Dion. Until him, sex had been a diversion for her, her partners to be enjoyed until she tired of them. But with Dion, it was different.

Until Dion, she hadn't known what it was to want so badly it was a firestorm of need raging in her veins, wild and hot and sweet.

Until Dion, she hadn't loved.

He didn't wait for her explanation. Instead, he chuckled. "If you were mine," he informed her, "I'd cure you of that."

She shivered at the dark promise in his voice. But she refused to go down easily. She tilted her chin. "If I were yours, I might let you try."

He brought his mouth to her neck, scraping his teeth over the sensitive skin. "You wouldn't have a choice."

But finally, blessedly, his finger began to move, sliding in and out of her feverish, needy sex. She writhed beneath his touch.

"Yes...that's it. Just like that. Please." Her whole body tightened and she was about to climax when he removed his finger to rest his hand on her mound again.

"Dion," she pleaded. She lifted her gaze to find his eyes glittering at her.

"Not yet," he told her.

Her breath sobbed out. "Damn you." She tried to touch herself but he grabbed her wrists and pressed them against the wall again.

"A lesson, *minha rainha*...in who is master here. Tell me."

"Go to Hades," she said in sweet tones.

"Fine." He held onto her wrists with one hand while with the other he rested his hand on her mound, strumming her lightly with his fingers. Her tension ratcheted up. She tried to press against him but he kept the touch tortuously light.

Her breath jerked in and out of her chest.

"Tell me," he commanded softly.

She blew out a breath and gave in. "You are, Dion." Anything to reach the orgasm that was just a touch away.

"Good girl." He tapped her sex once, twice, and then withdrew his hand. "Now, down on your knees. Show me just how good you can be." He took a step back and eyed her, one hand fisted around himself as he slowly stroked up and down.

She blinked at him dazedly. Then she narrowed her eyes; two could play this game. "All right."

She placed a hand on his abdomen, guiding him to lean against the wall, before sinking to her knees on the wood floor. His cock was long and thick, a deep, purplish red. She put one hand on his leg and wrapped the other around the base. His thigh tensed beneath her hand. A thick drop of fluid gleamed on the broad head.

She smiled and leaned forward to swipe her tongue over it. "Mm," she purred against his skin. He tasted of the sea, warm and salty.

She slid her tongue down the hard, engorged length, skimming over the veins, inhaling his rich, wild scent.

His knees locked and his hand came to her head, holding her in place. "That's it, sweetheart," he husked. "Show me how sorry you are. Show me how much you want to please me."

She hummed her assent and sucked him in for a few seconds, then released him again, teasing him with her tongue, reveling in having him under her power. She might be the one kneeling at his feet, but he was the one who was going to be begging before she was finished.

He murmured something inarticulate. His breath rasped in and his hands fisted against the wall. She glanced up to find him gazing down at her, his eyes a smoky silver-blue.

"Say please," she said cheekily, and swirled her tongue over the cap.

His nostrils flared. "I don't think so." He reached down and gripped her braid, gently but firmly pulling her head back. "Now enough playing. Or I'll tie you to the bed and show you what it's like to be teased until you're screaming for release."

An erotic thrill shot down her spine at his words and the firm way he handled her. Heat bloomed between her thighs and she clenched them together.

His erection prodded her lips and she willingly opened to him. He swore under his breath and gripped her head with both hands, guiding her to take him deeper. She settled into give him the best damn blow job he'd ever had, so that he'd never have another woman without thinking of her, Cleia, and what he'd given up by rejecting her.

She sucked deeply, swirling her tongue over him, letting her teeth scrape lightly over the sensitive skin. Meanwhile she worked her hand up and down the base of his cock while with the other she played with his balls, stroking them, rolling them between her fingers.

"That's it," he said in a guttural voice. "Take me, Cleia. Take me deep." He thrust into her mouth. "I'm going to come," he warned.

She sucked harder, all thoughts of teasing and control forgotten, a woman intent on pleasuring the man she loved.

"That's it," he praised. "Take it. Take all of me. Ah, *querida*."

He rocked his hips, fucking her mouth in slow, careful strokes. She squeezed his balls and he groaned and arched his back, giving several hard thrusts before he spurted into her mouth, hot and salty and slightly metallic. She swallowed, once, twice, as his cock jerked and continued to release semen.

When he was done, he eased out of her, one hand still on her head.

She sat back on her heels and slanted him a look from under her lashes. "Told you I was good."

He sank down onto the floor and pulled her between his legs, his back against the wall. "*Madre de Deus.* You made a believer out of me."

She turned so she could wrap an arm around him and rested her head on his shoulder. She inhaled slowly, taking in his familiar, spicy scent.

By the Goddess, she needed this man. She'd still been relatively young when her parents had passed on some forty-odd years ago—first her mother, and then her brokenhearted father soon after. She'd become the Conduit, and the seven clans had selected her as queen as well. Suddenly, instead of the adored, pampered daughter, she was the ruler, the one everyone relied on. Olivia had been wonderful, both best friend and a trusted advisor, but Cleia hadn't realized until now how lonely she'd been.

She stroked his cheek, rough with black stubble. "If we mated, I'd—"

He squeezed her nape to silence her. "No more," he said, his voice cold. "Otherwise I'm out of here. I may have to remain within your territory until the day after tomorrow, but nothing in that promise says I have to stay in this apartment."

Stars, the man was stubborn.

A soul-deep sadness filled her. Was she never to have what most people—fae, fada or human—took for granted? A mate, children?

She swallowed around the jagged lump in her throat. "No more," she managed to say.

He rose to his feet and carried her across the room to an armless chair. Sitting down, he turned her so she straddled his legs. One large hand slid between her thighs.

"Now, *minha querida*, I believe we have some unfinished business..."

24

———————

*D*ion reached for a bar of soap and lathered his hands. He brought them to Cleia, reclined against his chest, and moved them over her breasts, lazily washing her.

It was the afternoon of the following day, and they were in her big bathtub. A hazy aqua light came through the tinted windows and a sultry Brazilian love song emanated from speakers hidden in the tiled walls.

He gave a contented exhale and nuzzled the moist skin of her neck. Her breath sighed out in turn and her muscles softened even more, her head lolling against his chest. He gently pinched her nipples, flushed from the hot water.

"Enough." She flapped a hand weakly. "I'm worn out."

His mouth curved. "Should I say I'm sorry?"

They'd spent most of the past twenty-four hours in her apartment, fucking like otters. He'd had her in her bed, up against the wall, in the bathtub, bent over the couch...

But they'd talked as well, and he'd had a chance to observe her with her people, catching up on what she'd missed while she'd been gone. He was impressed. She was a smart, pragmatic ruler, one who was both liked and respected by her people.

"No," she replied. "It would be a lie."

"True." He lifted first one, then the other of her breasts, cleaning the curved undersides. Leaning forward, he blew a breath over one wet, soapy nipple.

A fine tremor ran over her skin. "You're a bad man."

"Also true. But you like that, no?"

She reached behind her to link her fingers behind his nape, causing her breasts to lift in an interesting way. He tweaked the nipples again just to watch them stand at attention.

Her breath hitched. "You know I do."

He smiled and rinsed her breasts. Then he soaped up his hands again and moved them down her ribs. Her body enthralled him—the golden color, the satiny texture. He could spend a decade simply memorizing the shape of her: the convex curve of her lower abdomen, the shelf of her pelvis, the lush slope of her hips.

He slid his fingers between her thighs, opening her legs, and carefully washed her tender, swollen folds.

She gave a low moan even as she shook her head.

Heat curled through his belly, even though he'd had her not a half hour earlier. He glided his fingertips over her sex. "*Não*?"

"A very bad man," she asserted and turned her head to kiss him, a slow tangling of tongues that had his cock springing up to press against her round bottom. Then she spoiled it by saying, "About tomorrow, I—"

He nipped her neck. "We agreed not to discuss that."

"But—" She unlaced her fingers from his nape and tried to sit up.

"Cleia," he warned. He tightened his arms, keeping her between his legs, and drew the skin of her throat into his mouth, gently suckling. His fingers kept up their slow stroke over her sex.

A quiver ran over her skin but she didn't back down. "Dion? If you won't do this for me, do it for Xavier."

His face hardened even as a certain lower part started to

deflate. Damn her for trying to use Xavier as a lever. She knew how worried he was about the boy.

He lifted his head. "Enough, Cleia."

She gave a growl worthy of a fada and pushed out of his arms. This time he let her go. Sliding to the opposite end of the tub, she turned to glare at him.

"Stars. What would it take to convince you?"

His hands clenched on the water. His arms felt empty without her, and that only increased his annoyance. Reaching for the soap, he washed himself with short, irate strokes.

"How about this? You give me the name of the person who helped you escape and then we'll talk."

He'd racked his brains, trying to decide who'd betrayed him to the sun fae. The short list included Cleia's former lovers—Rodolfo, Luis, Miguel, Emmanuel, even Rui.

But he couldn't believe one of them was responsible. Rodolfo or Luis would confront him straight on—as they already had—and Miguel was off on a mission in South America. Emmanuel hadn't even tried to talk to Cleia; his mate was the jealous type. And Rui was too busy wallowing in wine and women to plot anything but his next conquest.

That left—but his mind skittered past the name, refusing even to think it.

Cleia drew in a breath. "Go. To. Hell," she rapped out and practically leaped out of the tub.

He spread his hands. "Okay, so that wasn't fair."

"No, it wasn't. The one has nothing to do with the other." She snatched up a towel and started rubbing herself dry. "We have to try. Don't you understand? If we don't, Xavier is going to die."

"Do you think I don't know that?" He heaved himself out of the water and grabbed another towel. "If this were just about us, I'd do it in a heartbeat. I'll admit that yesterday I suspected a trick. But you've convinced me that you honestly believe our joining is the only way to help my clan."

"Thank you for that at least," she muttered.

"But it's not just about us. If you're wrong, it's not just me who will be hurt, but my entire clan. What if you *can't* control it? If something goes wrong, it will be my people who'll suffer—not yours."

"But we have to try. Xavier is going to die." She said it slowly, as if he were a difficult child.

He clenched the towel. "You think I don't know that? I couldn't love the boy any more if he were my own son. But I can't take the chance."

"So you'll just let him die."

He met her accusing gaze straight on. She couldn't be any harder on him than he was on himself.

"I pray it won't come to that. But I'll do what's best for the clan."

AFTER THAT, they each went their separate ways, she to work on the final details for tomorrow's ritual and he for a walk.

He started at random down one of the paths crisscrossing the sprawling compound. His thoughts were a jumble, but one thing was clear. He'd do almost anything to keep Xavier alive—except mating with Cleia. He couldn't risk his entire clan for one child.

But *Deus*, he was tempted. She was offering him the one thing he most wanted—a mate bond with her. His very soul clamored for him to accept it and to hell with the rest of the world.

Gradually he began to take in his surroundings. Besides the white mansion, the grounds included a half-dozen condo buildings, state-of-the-art exercise facilities, a cultural center, and that ballroom Rosana was so interested in. It was basically a small, exclusive village. At the moment it was packed to the brim as those sun fae who lived elsewhere arrived for the coming ritual, doubling up with those who lived at Rising Sun year-round as well as bedding down in elaborate tents erected throughout the grounds.

Everything was clean and well-kept, with jewels and precious metals used liberally as embellishments. The sheer bulk of the sun fae's wealth still took his breath away, but he was coming to see that their extravagance was underlain by an innate generosity.

They didn't just scatter gold and jewels everywhere like shells on a beach, they scattered hugs and smiles as well. They were like a tribe of light-hearted children, always talking and laughing with one another.

As he approached the playground, a fantastic assortment of towers, swings, merry-go-rounds and other play equipment, a child's voice sang out, "Lord Dun, wait for me!" It was little Gracie, who'd christened him "Lord Dun" when she couldn't quite get her mouth around the two syllables of his name.

She skipped toward him, beaming. They'd met earlier at the mansion, where she lived with her parents on the second floor. She was adorable, with wheat-blond curls, a Cupid's bow mouth and big golden-brown eyes that were a replica of her cousin Cleia's.

He smiled down at the little girl. "Hello, *menina*." He glanced at Gracie's mother, hustling up the path after her. "Good afternoon, Lady Amelie."

"Good afternoon," she replied with a smile.

They spoke for a few minutes about the weather and the upcoming celebration. He was surprised at how readily the sun fae had accepted him. If they were angry with him for taking their queen captive, they hid it well.

This morning, when Cleia had taken him around the mansion to introduce him to her family, he'd felt a bit like a dark visitor from Hades until he realized they were genuinely pleased to meet him. It made him wonder what, exactly, Cleia had told them.

Gracie tugged on his shirt. "Up, Lord Dun," she commanded and raised her arms.

"Gracie," chided her mother. "Where are your manners?"

"Please?"

He chuckled and tossed her lightly into the air. "How's that?"

"Yes!" she said with a happy chortle. "More!"

He tossed her again and then set her back on the grassy path, but she pouted up at him. "More, Lord Dun."

"Gracie," said Lady Amelie, "Lord Dion doesn't have to—"

The tiny blonde gave him a winning smile. "*Por favor*?"

"Well, since you asked so nicely—" He scooped the girl up for another few tosses. On the last catch he saw Cleia watching them from a few yards away, a corner of her mouth lifted in an unreadable smile.

He set Gracie down and patted her small behind. "Off with you now. Your mama's waiting."

"Thank you." She lifted her face, presenting her cheek. He bent down and gravely planted a kiss on the baby-fine surface. She darted to Cleia for a kiss as well, and then returned to her mother, skipping ahead of her to the playground.

Cleia remained where she was, her expression serious now.

He gave her a stiff nod. "You've finished your business?"

"Yes." She came forward and slipped her hand into the crook of his arm. "Don't be angry at me. Please?" She shot him a look up from under her lashes.

His lips twitched. "Do you know how much you look like Gracie right now?"

Her expression didn't change. "Is it working?"

"*Sim*." He gave her a hard kiss.

When he lifted his head, she twined her arms around his neck. "I don't want to fight with you, Dion."

He kissed her again. "Me neither."

"Good." She caught his hand and tugged him away from the playground to a fork in the path. "I have something to show you."

After a few minutes' walk, they arrived at a small garden encircled by a high boxwood hedge. In the center was a mosaic depicting a tree of life composed of thousands of pieces of pottery, colored glass and the occasional semiprecious stone.

Dion's jaw slackened as his gaze followed the trunk out to sinuous branches hung with leaves of hammered copper and dripping with precious stone "fruit." Fat rubies and citrines. Chunks of emerald and topaz. A silver half-moon framed one side and on the other was a sun of beaten gold.

"My God," he said reverently.

Cleia leaned her head against his shoulder. "My parents made it. On their five-hundredth anniversary. I miss them—so bad— but at least I have this."

He wrapped an arm around her waist. "It's beautiful."

"But? It's a little too flashy for you? Wasteful?"

"Not at all. This is art. And even the rest—maybe you seem wasteful to someone like me, but I've come to see that it's because you take such pleasure in pretty things. You want to share them with everyone."

"Exactly." Her smile was pleased. "We believe art feeds the soul. The whole Rising Sun Clan pitched in to help my mom and dad, donating jewels, weaving straw into gold, trading for what we didn't have. We knew my parents were nearing the end of their lives and we wanted to honor them. And we do try to make sure everyone has what they need before we spend resources on something like this."

"You don't have to defend yourself. You're a good ruler, Cleia. Anyone can see that. And I'm sure your father was as well."

"He was. I just try to live up to the example he set. You're every bit as good, though. Even with the troubles your clan's had, they're still behind you all the way. They trust you to find a solution."

His mouth twisted. "If only I knew what that was."

She was wise enough not to press her case. He wondered if she sensed his wavering.

By mutual accord they continued walking. Dion threaded his fingers through hers and put everything out of his mind—the traitor, his worry about Xavier, his fear that the earth fada might still attack, the desire to claim this woman as his mate. The animal in him wanted to enjoy her while he still could, and the man knew there was nothing he could do until tomorrow anyway.

He scented the stream where he'd hidden that first day and instinctively turned in its direction, craving a taste of its free-flowing water. It wasn't often that he spent more than a day away from his creek.

When they reached the stream, he released Cleia's hand and shucked his shirt and shorts.

"Mm." Her gaze moved down his naked body. "I like the way you think."

He flashed her a cocky grin and waded in up to his waist to scoop up handfuls of the fresh, cool water. After drinking his fill, he did a shallow surface dive and shifted. He was larger than a wild dolphin, the stream barely large enough to hold him, but he was in the mood to play.

He beckoned with his head for Cleia to come in.

Her eyes widened. "Wow...you're beautiful."

Beautiful? He gave a disdainful snort through his blowhole.

She grinned and waded in, holding her skirt up around her thighs. He nudged her with his head. She stroked her hand down his back before moving to his head, instinctively finding his most sensitive places: his snout, around his blowhole, beneath his jaw.

"You're so smooth. It's like petting an olive."

An olive? He snorted again. The woman had a lot to learn about dolphins, powerful predators in their own right.

She chuckled and wrapped her arms around him, placing her

head next to his. "How about you take me for a ride, *meu senhor*?" she murmured in a suggestive voice.

For answer, he pressed his body into hers, inviting her to climb on his back. She gripped his dorsal fin and twined her long legs around his belly. He gave a flip of his tail to get them moving and swam a few hundred yards upstream until the water became too shallow.

Cleia made a sound of pure amusement. "Could you take me into the bay?"

He rolled slowly onto his back so that she stayed upright and shifted back to man. "Not today."

She sat astride him, his wanting obvious against her belly. Her pale yellow dress was soaked, the material practically transparent. He could see the shadow of her nipples, her navel, the coppery hair between her thighs. With a couple of backstrokes, he brought them to the bank and lifted her up to sit with a leg on either side of his.

He spread his hands on her breasts, fingering her beaded nipples through the wet cloth. He squeezed them—just hard enough. She sucked in a breath and he scented the sharp tang of her arousal.

"Take off the dress," he ordered softly.

Her dress was held on by a slender tie at each shoulder. Her eyes held his as she raised her hands to one. He loved how she submitted to him, even as she let him know she was strong, unafraid. That anything she did—even letting him be the dominant when it came to sex—was her choice.

She tugged at the tie and it came undone. The dress fell open, baring a single slick breast. He cupped it. She was cool from the water, but already her inner heat was warming her skin. She brought her hands to the other shoulder and undid that tie as well. The dress fell open to her waist.

His breath hissed between his teeth. He took her breasts in

both hands and flicked her nipples, teasing the sensitive points, and her eyes went dark with pleasure.

His erection was pressed between her thighs. She came up on her knees and rubbed against it, her skirt bunched up around her thighs. She was hot and wet for him.

He let her play while he continued to toy with her nipples, until it was too much and he gripped her hip, opened her with his other hand and slid inside with a leisurely thrust.

She moaned. "Oh. My. Lord."

Her inner passage constricted around him, hot and tight and wet, sending wildness spiraling through him. He curled up and pulled her against him, and kissed her, hard and deep, as he started to move within her.

The stream bank was cool and damp against his buttocks and feet, Cleia hot on top. Behind her the sun had commenced its slow slide down the afternoon sky. A breeze ruffled her hair so that the individual strands caught the sunlight, gleaming filaments of gold, silver and copper, like an angel come down to earth.

"*Deus*, you're beautiful," he said in a thick voice and speared his fingers in those shining strands, holding her still for his kiss. She kissed him back, meeting his passion with her own.

He released her, breathing hard now, and lay back, hands on her hips again. They moved together and apart, finding a mutual rhythm. Cleia brought her hands to her breasts, watching him through slit eyes and fingering herself in a pose that was about the most erotic thing he'd ever seen.

He brought his hand between them and used his thumb to stimulate her.

"Dion," she rasped, and squeezed him more tightly. He thrust harder, a wild, ecstatic excitement burning in him like the *Delírio*. But this was better, untainted by darkness or drugs.

Just pure, incandescent sex with his woman.

He growled low in his throat, and she met his gaze, unafraid, even though he knew his eyes must be showing the animal in him.

"Yes," she said. "Yes."

He groaned and thrust into her hard and they went over the edge together.

When he came back to himself, he was on his back, half in the dirt, half in the water, with Cleia resting on his chest. He rose to his feet with her in his arms and carried her back into the stream. They rinsed each other off, taking their time, splashing and playing with each other. Then she put her dress back on, not caring that it was wet, and they walked back to the path to retrieve his clothes.

They reached the immense willow tree he'd seen the first day. He slung an arm around her shoulders and nuzzled her hair, unable to stop touching her.

"This is where I first saw you—under that tree. You and Olivia."

"Here? But when?"

"A couple of weeks before we met. I wanted to get the lay of the land. I was in the stream when the two of you walked by."

"So that first meeting wasn't an accident..." Her chuckled held no humor. "I made it so easy for you, didn't I?"

He lifted a shoulder, let it drop.

She glanced at the stream. "But it's so shallow. It barely comes up to your waist. Why didn't we see you?"

"I took the form of a fish. And I have a Gift for blending into the rivers and marshes."

"It must make you practically invisible."

"It does."

"What about your other Gift? The one you used on me?"

"It's not two Gifts but one—that of the hunter. The one power allows me to conceal myself, and the other allows me to draw raw energy from the moisture in clouds to stun the victim before finishing it—or him—off."

Her brows crawled into her hairline. "I see. So if you'd wanted to, you could've killed me that day. Artan and Grady wouldn't have been able to stop you."

"Probably."

Her gaze assessed him. "Why tell me now?"

"Because I want you to be more careful. Your wards against intruders are powerful, yet I was able to get through them simply by shifting to a fish. The wards didn't work against my animal form. I think you could've sensed me if you'd tried—you're strong enough—but you thought you were safe and that made you careless." He hesitated, then added, "And because I want you to know what my Gift is."

It was something he'd never before shared with a fae. Even within his clan, few people knew how strong his Gift really was. Together, the two powers made him the perfect hunter—and assassin.

"Thank you." She pressed a kiss to his neck, accepting his disclosure as the offering it was. "Your secret's safe with me. I give you my word."

"I know it is."

She slanted him a look. "The fae underestimate you fada, don't they? We think we're the powerful ones, but you have Gifts we aren't even aware of."

"Perhaps." He took her by the shoulders and turned her to face him. She tensed and he gave her a little shake. "Cleia? Hell, you're not afraid of me, are you? You must know I'd never harm you. Not now and not in a hundred years."

Her mouth twisted. "Even if it was for the good of the clan? For Xavier?"

His stomach clenched. He released her and stepped back. He wasn't angry; she'd only stated his own dilemma. But it hurt to hear her say it, to know she must have been thinking it all along.

She scrubbed her hands over her face. "I'm sorry. You didn't deserve that. You were good to me even that first day at your base, when you had every reason to hate me. I know if you—if you had to...it only would be because you believed there was no other way to save your people."

"*Deus*, Cleia."

Crossing the short space between them, he jerked her to him and crushed his mouth to hers, thrusting his tongue between her lips and tasting her with all the desperation in his heart.

A low moan vibrated in her throat. The sizzle of energy that the pair of them always generated ignited into flame so that he had her back against the willow, his cock grinding into the soft cradle of her abdomen before he realized what he was doing.

He dragged his mouth from hers and buried his face in her neck. Licking her, nipping her, rubbing his skin against hers so that she was covered in his scent.

Marking her as his in the most primitive way possible.

Mine.

"I'd choose you, damn it," he grated against the warmth of her throat. "That's what fucking scares me."

25

———————

*D*ion opened his eyes and squinted at the sunshine streaming in the east windows. It was going to be a beautiful day. Cleia and her clan would be delighted. *Thrice-damned fucking sun.*

Sorrow rolled over him like a rogue wave, threatening to suck him so far under he'd never see daylight again.

He swallowed and rolled onto his side.

Beside him, Cleia stretched like a cat. A ray of sunlight had found her—of course—to slant across her face like an exotic gold tattoo.

He wrapped an arm around her. She was warm and supple and *his*. The animal rose up, urging him to drag her close, bind her so she'd never get free. To claim her in every way a male could a female.

With an effort, he forced it under control and set his lips against the crook of her neck. "Morning."

"Mm," she said without opening her eyes.

He kissed his way up to her mouth, brushing across her full lips. Her lashes were a gold-tipped fringe against her cheeks. He pressed a kiss to each soft, delicate lid, and they opened.

"I was still asleep," she chided, but her mouth curved.

He rubbed his lips over hers, taking the imprint of her smile onto them. She flowed into his arms, opening to him. He tightened his grip on her, tasting her with leisurely sweeps of his tongue, until she was moaning low in her throat and the scent of her arousal filled his nostrils like an exotic perfume.

When he lifted his head, she was flushed and heavy-eyed, her breath coming in sexy little gasps. He gave a slow, no doubt arrogant smile and ran his thumb over her kiss-swollen lower lip. She drew the digit into her mouth. He groaned as sensation shot to his groin. She took a couple of slow sucks before releasing it.

She smiled at him. "Before I forget, I have a surprise for you."

"*Sim*?" He rubbed suggestively against her. He was all for surprises when they occurred in bed.

She chuckled. "You're insatiable."

"For you, yes." He touched his mouth to hers in a kiss as light as a butterfly's. "*Te amo*," he surprised them both by saying.

She stared at him, her eyes bright with tears. "Oh, Dion." She gave him a hard hug. "I love you, too."

He rolled on top of her and cupped her face, wiping the tears away with his thumbs. "It's not supposed to make you cry," he said gruffly.

"They're happy tears."

He grunted, not so sure. But what was the point in making her admit it? He felt a curious ache behind the eyes himself.

"So, what's the surprise?"

She scrutinized him and then shook her head. "I think I'll make you wait."

"All right," he said, his focus on something else right now. He traced her mouth with his tongue, soft and slow.

Her lips clung to his for a moment and then she drew back. "Dion?" She stroked his hair back from his face. "Come to the ritual. Please? I promise nothing else will happen—unless you want it to. Truth." She brought her palm between them to her heart.

He opened his mouth to refuse, and then closed it. They both knew she couldn't compel him to accept a mate bond. For one thing, he was too strong for her, and for another, every fae lord and lady on the planet would be gunning for her should she try to force a sacred bond. The fae took the right to free will seriously, however fond they were of trying to bend the rules.

"Fine. But only to watch—*entendes*?"

"Of course—and thank you."

"Mmph." He moved his mouth to her ear, nipping the lobe, then slid his tongue up the outer edge until he reached the rounded point at the top. Damn, he loved that point. It practically begged a man to play with it. And to his delight, he'd discovered that she was extra sensitive there. He drew it into his mouth and suckled strongly.

The cadence of her breathing changed. Her hips lifted and he pressed them back down with his own, stilling her. Her head moved back and forth on the pillow. He allowed it and then caught the rounded tip between his lips again.

Her throat worked. "Dion—"

"*Sim*?" He moved to her other ear and flicked the point with his tongue.

"Come inside me."

He was fully erect now, his hard flesh cradled in the warm cave of her thighs. He lifted on his forearms, rubbing back and forth across her soft folds without entering her. She was slick and ready.

"Put me there."

She reached between them and brought his tip to her entrance. He took over, pushing inside her with easy nudges until he was fully embedded. He stilled and they both inhaled.

Cleia moved first, lifting her hips and clenching her tight, wet passage around him. Heat balled at the base of his spine, spread through his belly.

His breath hissed out.

He slid one arm under her shoulders and with the other hand, brushed her hair away from her face so that it spilled across the pillow in an iridescent waterfall. He flexed his hips and started to make love to her slowly, tenderly.

"*Amo-te*," he said against her throat. "Always and forever, *meu amor*."

She entwined her arms and legs around him so that he was caught in the sweetest net imaginable. He buried his face in her hair and breathed her in, achingly aware that this was the last time. The last time he'd inhale her tangy scent. The last time he'd have her long golden body under his. The last time he'd hear her cry out his name as she climaxed.

She hummed. "Stars, that feels good. Just like that...please."

"Mm." He loved her with long, deliberate strokes, prolonging the pleasure for both of them. Time stretched, spun into dream-like strands. He had the curious sensation that he'd been making love to her for eons, would be making love to her until the world ended—and that was exactly how it should be.

Her breath quickened and she ground her hips against his, sobbing out his name. "Please, Dion. I need—"

"*Sim, sim*," he soothed. "*Acalme-te*. I know what you need, *querida*."

He slid his hand between their bodies and swirled his fingers over her hot, swollen nub.

"Ah, Goddess." She dug her heels into his thighs, keening out her pleasure, and then she was convulsing around him, each heated contraction sending darts of ecstasy up his spine. His balls drew up and he raised onto his hands to pump into her hard and fast.

Sparks burst behind his eyes and he emptied himself into her with a tortured groan. He slumped over her, his breath scraping in and out of his lungs.

Deus. How was he going to live without her?

When he lifted his head, she gave him a wobbly smile. A single tear slid down her cheek. His heart squeezed. He licked the glistening droplet, tasting the salt and regret.

He rolled to one side and cradled her in his arms. Neither of them spoke.

After a time, Dion slipped into sleep and when he awoke, his heart was a crushing weight in his chest.

Even before he opened his eyes, he knew he was alone in the apartment.

He was stepping from the shower when someone hammered on the apartment door.

"Dion? It's me, Rosana."

He pulled on shorts and strode to the door. "Rosana? What the—"

She was already inside the apartment. She gave him a quick hug and then danced away, turning in a circle as she took in her surroundings.

"*Ohmigod.* This is awesome. But look at the windows—how do they keep cool with all that sun? And the furniture." She dropped onto a couch and ran her palm over the textured silk-and-linen fabric. "The sun fae sure are rich."

He folded his arms. "Rosana," he said warningly. "Why are you here?"

She slanted him a grin. "Queen Cleia invited us, of course."

"We?"

"The clan. Didn't she tell you? Not everyone is here—Rui said we had to leave some of the warriors to guard the babies and old people, but most everyone else came. He stayed home along with a few other men."

"Rui?" he repeated, dumbfounded. "Rui do Mar?"

"Uh-huh. Everyone's saying the old Rui is back. Well, all the old ones, that is."

Which meant anyone over age twenty, he reflected wryly.

"He said that since you weren't going to be back until today," she continued, "and you weren't allowed to communicate with us, then somebody had to guard the base."

"And Luis agreed?"

Dion was still trying to wrap his mind around the fact that his old friend had taken charge.

"Rui didn't give him a choice."

Dion gave a snort of laughter. "That sounds like Rui all right."

"Besides, Luis and Marina wanted to bring Xavier to the ritual. Queen Cleia thinks she can cure him, but she needs all of us to help."

"She does, does she?" He took a deep, calming breath. He should've known the woman wouldn't give up. She was convinced her idea would work. "So you're all here?"

Rosana nodded. "There's going to be a ball after the ritual and the best part is she had them make a dress for me. In jade, just like I wanted. See?" She rose on her toes and spun, dark curls flying, the pleated skirt swirling around her slim legs. "And I'm going to wear emeralds in my hair—won't that be pretty?"

"*Certo*," he said automatically. "You're pretty no matter what you wear. But that's a very nice dress."

"Thank you, my lord." She grasped the hem and inclined her wiry body in a dignified curtsey, making him grin in spite of his rising anger.

As she bounced back upright, he walked to the windows overlooking the meadow where the ritual was to be held. Rosana was right. Most of Rock Run was there, the women in colorful blues or greens or purples, the men in darker hues but looking no less fine. The five *tenentes* had placed themselves around the perimeter to scan the crowd with cold eyes, but the rest were being greeted by the sun fae.

Darting among them like schools of cheerful little fish were the children, making friends, uncaring of whether they were fada or fae. He could see Isa and her family, and Marina and Luis with little Xavier wrapped in a blanket and held securely in his father's arms.

This must be Cleia's surprise.

He squeezed the back of his neck, wondering what she had planned. He could order his people to return home, but Cleia was right. They needed to interact more with their nearest neighbors. Isolation had its own dangers. For example, the Baltimore shifters would think twice before attacking Rock Run if they were allied with the sun fae.

"C'mon." Rosana skipped across the room and tugged his arm. "Everyone's already gathering. The ritual starts at noon."

He glanced up at the sun. He had another half an hour. "You go ahead. I'll be down as soon as I'm dressed."

Cleia had left clothes for him in the bathing room: black pants in a material that looked like leather but was surprisingly light and comfortable, and a royal blue dress shirt in a similar soft, light fabric. No shoes, but he wouldn't have worn them anyway.

He left the shirttail out and started for the door, which Rosana had left open in her rush to leave.

A movement caught his eye. He spun around to see Tiago leaning against the wall, arms crossed, his expression hard.

"Have you mated with her?" he demanded.

Dion suppressed a sigh. "That's none of your business."

"No?" Tiago's light eyes blazed. "She's mine. I had her first."

"But I'm the one she wants," Dion returned, intentionally brutal. It was time his brother faced facts.

"No." Tiago pushed off the wall, hands fisted at his sides.

"That's a lie. She said she'd wait for me. That if I came back in seven years—"

"That was before. We're mates, Tiago."

As he said it, he realized with a shock that the tenuous connection running between him and Cleia had strengthened, another few strands woven into the emotional rope linking them. He'd had no idea how hard it was to deny the mate bond.

He didn't know how Rui had done it for two years. He could barely manage two days.

"Damn you." His brother's voice shook. "If I were older, I'd—"

"What?" he asked in soft, dangerous tones. "What would you do?"

"I'd take her from you, treat her how she should be treated. You don't deserve her. She should be mine."

"Face it, *irmão*." Dion shook his head, suddenly weary. "She's not yours and never will be. But if it makes you feel any better, she's not going to be mine, either."

"Why not?" Tiago raked him with a derisive look. "Are you like the old man? 'Fae and fada don't mix.' She's good enough to fuck, but not to mate with?"

Dion's breath hissed out. He crossed the few steps between them and grabbed the front of Tiago's shirt.

"You know nothing about it." He squeezed the words between clenched teeth. "*Nothing*. But you couldn't be more wrong. I love her, damn you."

His brother stared back, cheeks flushed, mouth set in a stubborn line. He held Dion's gaze for a tense few seconds before breaking. His eyes dropped and he stood with his head bowed, chest heaving.

Dion thrust him away. "Get the hell out of here."

Tiago gave a noisy gulp and rushed from the room, head down.

Dion exhaled harshly. At this rate, Tiago was going to go the way of Nic and Joaquim, and he'd lose his last brother.

Then he tensed. *No.*

But he had the horrible feeling his suspicions were correct. This was why Cleia had refused to tell him who'd helped Adric, why she'd been so adamant that he wouldn't want to know.

The traitor was Tiago.

He let out a string of vicious curses. Damn it to Hades. He couldn't allow the boy to go unpunished. But neither could he execute him. Not a stripling of only twenty-one turns of the sun.

Not his little brother.

He groped for a chair and sat down. He curled his fingers onto the armrests and dropped his head back, eyes squeezed shut. A sound emanated from his chest, half-groan, half-howl.

No. A thousand times no.

Cleia watched from the mansion's first floor as the meadow filled with sun fae and river fada. Later, other fae and fada would come for the three days of festivities that followed the ritual, but for this she'd only invited Rock Run and her own people.

The river people were reserved at first. However, she'd instructed her clan to make them welcome, and the fada soon unbent enough to exchange small talk as they sipped cold drinks and the children of both clans zoomed merrily to and fro.

Of course, being fada, several stern-faced warriors—a woman and four men—had spaced themselves around the meadow's periphery. She assumed there were others seeded throughout the crowd. But she'd expected that. Trust would come with time, when they understood she considered them her people now.

Her own warriors were on alert but also aware that only a fool would attack the sun fae on this day of all days. The sun was at its greatest potency and so was she, energy humming in her like an exhilarating melody. By the time the sun reached its peak, only a few of the most powerful fae could match her strength.

Gracie trotted up to Luis and Marina, standing a few yards

from the window. Cleia suspected her little cousin was going to be a healer. Already she was drawn to the sick and injured, and her mere presence seemed to calm them.

The small blonde touched Xavier's hand. "Are you all right?"

He lifted his head. He was still thin, his dark eyes burning unhealthily, but his life-force was strong—for now. "I'm sick," he announced with a touch of pride.

Cleia pressed her knuckles to her mouth, not sure if she wanted to laugh or cry.

"I'm sorry," Gracie replied. "But Aunt Cleia will make you better."

"I know. She likes me."

"She likes everyone," Gracie agreed.

Cleia bit her lip. Stars, the two of them were adorable. She just prayed their faith in her was borne out.

Turning from the window, she paced restlessly, the bias-cut satin dress swishing about her calves. Traditionally, the Conduit spent the last hour alone, meditating and preparing her- or himself for the concentration the ritual demanded.

She took a few deep breaths and then gave up. She was too keyed up to meditate.

She returned to the window. People were gravitating to the natural amphitheater where the ritual was to be held. A circle was forming with the sun fae on the inside, the Rock Run fada on the perimeter.

She searched the crowd. Where was Dion? Everything depended on him.

And then she saw him striding barefoot across the meadow: her hard, beautiful man, his mane of hair blue-black in the sunlight, his powerful body perfect in the clothes she'd chosen. He looked every inch an alpha, his authority as much a part of him as his ice-blue eyes.

She could feel his emotions vibrating through the bond:

anger, distrust—and hope. She closed her eyes and prayed the hope would win out.

Yesterday afternoon by the stream, he'd opened to her for a few moments, long enough for her to see what he truly desired. She just hoped that what she'd planned for today would do the rest.

Please. Keep his heart open. Give me a chance at least.

Olivia thought Cleia had lost her mind. "Are you mad?" she'd demanded when Cleia had explained what she planned to do. "Wait, maybe he still has some kind of hold on you—"

She'd muttered a defensive counterspell that brushed over Cleia, but when it found nothing, dissipated. Her cousin had folded her arms over her chest.

"You seem to be clean. But the man kidnapped you, kept you underground so long you became ill—not to mention what would have happened to the rest of us—and now you're going to risk your life for his clan?"

"He was only doing what he had to. Be honest, Olivia. If it were us, if you discovered someone—say a night fae—was draining our clan of energy, what would you have done?"

Olivia's mouth tightened. "I'd have gone after them with everything I had," she admitted. "But this could kill you, Cleia."

"I'll be fine."

"And if you're not? What about Rising Sun and the rest of the sun fae? You know we don't have another Conduit."

Cleia moved uneasily. That was the one thing she hadn't let herself think about. But there was really no choice.

"He's my mate."

"A fada?" Olivia closed her eyes. "Please tell me you're not serious. No"—she raised a hand—"I apologize. A mate is a mate."

But she'd stopped trying to convince Cleia to drop her plan. She'd even congratulated her on finding her mate, albeit grudgingly.

Now Cleia brought the heel of her hand to her heart as she

watched Dion cross the lawn. Massaging the ache that seemed to live there now.

This had to work. If she failed, both of them would be condemned to the bleak half-life of an incomplete mating. And she'd have to live with the fact that she'd been responsible for the death of an innocent little boy—and maybe his entire clan.

Even before Dion reached the ring of Rock Run fada, people were turning, pointing, exclaiming with joy. And then he was surrounded, the men pulling him into bear hugs, the women grasping his shoulders and kissing him on both cheeks.

Isa's voice carried across the lawn. "We were worried, but the *rainha* Cleia promised...see you today...knew it would be all right—"

She could no longer sense Dion's emotions, but he visibly relaxed as he saw that everyone was fine and in good spirits. That was good. Knowing his people were all right would go a long way toward easing his suspicions.

Then he glanced at Tiago, standing a little apart from the others, and his shoulders tightened. The mate bond flared with anger and a deep hurt.

He knew.

Cleia swallowed. She'd known he'd figure it out sooner or later. But did it have to be now, when so much depended on his approaching the ritual with an open mind?

Olivia opened the French doors. "It's time, Cleia."

"Coming." She didn't require her cousin's reminder. She knew in her very marrow the exact moment the sun would reach its zenith.

Her palms were sweating. Swiping them against her dress, she set her shoulders and stepped through the doors.

A MURMUR WENT through the crowd.

It's time. She's coming.

Ah, she's beautiful. *Como ela é bonita.*

Dion turned to see Cleia approaching. His lungs seized. She was always beautiful to him, but today she was gut-wrenchingly gorgeous in a dress of gold and copper that flowed over her body like liquid silk, leaving her arms and feet bare. On her head was a simple gold crown and her sun-colored hair had been left unbound to cascade down her back.

He blinked, trying to reconcile this goddess with the woman who'd taken him into her body just hours ago.

He felt an unfamiliar humility; who was he to love this golden creature? Then her gaze sought his across the crowd and she gave him a quick, apologetic smile, and she was just Cleia again, the woman he loved with his entire being—but *must* resist.

She took a spiral path through the assembled crowd, greeting everyone with a smile or a hug as she made for the grass circle at the amphitheater's center. Her friends among his clan greeted her in turn, Rosana opening her arms to give her a fierce hug before passing her on to Isa, Luis and Marina smiling widely as she ruffled Xavier's hair. As she continued to the other fada, there was a great deal of laughter as they helped her match voices to faces.

Gabriela folded her arms over her ample breasts and announced for all to hear that the queen had the makings of a decent cook—with enough training—before dragging Cleia into a bear hug. Cleia laughed and hugged her back before moving on, greeting all the cooks in turn.

Valeria, standing with Merry and the Greek sea fada, watched the queen's progress with an expressionless face. Dion had scented her dislike of Cleia more than once, but she was low in the clan's dominance chain, not likely to cause trouble unless pushed—or unless Merry was threatened. As Cleia neared, Valeria went taut as a bow and gripped her daughter's shoulders.

Dion frowned. They were the sun fae's guests; he would not tolerate any disrespect to Cleia. Valeria shot him a look and averted her face, refusing to meet Cleia's eyes but offering her the respect due a fae queen, and he relaxed.

Cleia stopped by Tiago, standing a few yards from Dion. Tiago grasped her hands and kissed her on each cheek, carefully avoiding Dion's eyes. Dion kept his expression blank; this wasn't the time or place to confront his brother.

And then she reached him. She brought her palms together over her heart and inclined her head in a formal greeting. "Peace, Lord Dionísio. I thank you for coming."

His mouth curled. He'd had time to recall that she'd invited his people behind his back, when she knew damn well he'd have refused to allow them to attend.

"I had a choice?"

Her gaze burned into his, gold flames flickering in the brown so that the tiny hairs on his nape lifted even as his blood hummed in response.

"You always have a choice."

"See that you remember that."

"I never forgot," she returned and continued on to the inner circle of sun fae. They hailed her warmly, thanking her for her care of them as they exchanged greetings.

Exactly at noon she entered the grass circle. As she stepped into the center, the sun flared. Light streamed over her in a brilliant column, illuminating her face and turning her hair into a fiery halo that lifted from her shoulders to blow in an unearthly wind. She closed her eyes and remained still for several moments as the crowd watched in rapt silence.

Dion watched, achingly aware of both her beauty and her power. Against his will, the mate bond curled like a hand around his heart, urging him toward her. He planted his feet and remained determinedly where he was.

Cleia opened her eyes and raised her arms. "Welcome, Rising Sun fae," she called, and continued down the list of the seven sun fae clans. Then she continued, "And an especially warm welcome to the Rock Run fada. How wonderful to have you join us today. Blessed be."

"Welcome," returned the crowd. "Blessed be."

"Today we gather to perform the ancient ritual of the sun, which nourishes the sun fae like a mother her child. But this day is special for another reason. I have an announcement to make to you all as well."

She turned and looked straight at Dion. The crowd parted so that they faced each other across the short distance, she at the circle's center, he the perimeter. Her gaze met his. She lifted a hand, beckoning him.

"I invite Lord Dionísio to come forward."

He narrowed his eyes and remained where he was. She knew damn well his promise had been to attend the ritual and nothing else.

She swallowed visibly. Then she stretched a hand toward him. "Please, my lord?"

The sun fae looked uncertainly from her to him, murmuring in dismay when he glared back without moving. Meanwhile, the river fada edged closer to Dion, prepared to defend their alpha.

Isa sidled up beside him and stuck an elbow in his ribs. "*Idiota.* Go to her."

With a curse, he strode forward, not because of Isa's urging, but because he couldn't deny Cleia any more than he could deny what was in his heart.

He grasped her outstretched hand. "What the hell are you playing at, woman? If this is a trick, I'll—"

"No trick." Before he could stop her, she faced the crowd and raised their linked hands. "Hear me well, sun fae and river fada," she stated in ringing tones. "I declare before the sun and stars and the circling planets and all of you that Lord Dionísio is my mate."

He jerked in denial but she hissed, "Let me finish." To the crowd, she continued, "But he doubts me. Some of you know that

I inadvertently drained life-energy from his clan, harming his people and their vineyards—even their fishing grounds."

There was a shocked murmur from the sun fae, and she nodded. "It's true. So to prove to Lord Dion that my heart is his, I will now return the energy, starting with the fada child that I harmed."

She'd finally admitted it so all could hear, know that his capture of her had been justified. Dion should've felt triumph, but instead he wanted to clap his hand over her mouth, his instinct to protect her from the ripple of anger emanating from his clan.

Cleia released him and beckoned to Luis and Marina. "Bring Xavier to me, please."

He flung out a hand, stopping them. "Touch him and it's war," he growled at Cleia.

Her chin tilted stubbornly. "I can heal him. But only today, when I'm at my strongest."

He turned to Marina and Luis. "And you—you agreed to this? What if he dies?"

Marina dropped her gaze, unable to confront her alpha head on. But her sweet, Madonna-like face was set in obstinate lines. "It's his only chance, *meu senhor*."

"It's true," Luis asserted. He risked holding Dion's eyes for a long moment—indicating how important this was to him— before he too dropped his gaze.

"I discussed this with our top healers yesterday," Cleia said, "and this morning I spoke to Branco. It's risky, but they all agree it's the only way."

He turned back to where Marina and Luis were awaiting his decision. He could scent their desperation but knew that if he commanded, they'd take Xavier home without letting Cleia touch him.

He glanced at the child lying limply in Luis's arms, his big brown eyes gazing trustingly up at Dion. He'd thought the boy was better, but now he saw it was the feverish energy of someone fighting for his life.

Dion's mouth opened, then shut again. He just couldn't say the words ordering Marina and Luis to take their son and leave.

"Branco agreed?" he asked Luis.

"He did, yes. He remained at the base to tend to those too old or sick to come to the ritual, but he told us that it's Xavier's best chance."

Dion stepped aside. "Fine. It's on your heads."

"No," Cleia contradicted. "It's on my head. And it *will* work. It has to," she added in an undertone.

She turned to Luis and Marina. "Set him on the grass. No one but me can touch him."

Luis hesitated, and then at a nudge from Marina, he kissed Xavier and obeyed. Marina gave her son a hard hug and then lifted a face wet with tears and whispered, "Thank you, *minha rainha*. Whatever happens, I know you will do your best."

Cleia gave a tight nod, and then knelt down beside Xavier. Drawing a breath, she placed her hands on the boy's chest and lifted her face to the sun like a flower, drinking in its energy.

Around them the crowd stilled. The sun fae exuded a quiet confidence that their queen could heal the little boy. Dion's own people appeared more skeptical, but he sensed their hope, their *need* to believe this would work. He crossed his arms over his chest but inside he prayed to all the gods and goddesses that Cleia could pull this off.

She murmured something Dion didn't understand and the air around her shimmered, then dimmed. She set her jaw and tried again.

Dion's nerves sparked to life. He glanced around but no one else seemed to feel it. The energy must be coming through the mate bond.

Alarmed, he instinctively shut it down.

Cleia gasped, her whole body jerking as if she'd been shocked. But she didn't stop feeding energy into Xavier.

"Dion." Her gaze sought his. "Please, love. Don't fight it. It'll be all right, I promise."

"You can't know that."

It was exactly what he'd feared. The energy increased, became a low thrum in his blood, and then intensified. As its power grew, he sensed he was about to lose control and clamped down on the bond with everything he had. The low thrumming stopped.

Cleia jerked again. She threw back her head and keened low in her throat, lungs heaving, but still she kept her hands on Xavier.

Dion lunged for her.

"Don't touch her!" Olivia darted forward and grabbed his arm. "If she loses control, you could all three go up in flames."

"What's wrong?" Panicked, Dion glanced from Cleia's anguished face to Olivia. "Help her, damn it."

Olivia ignored him to crouch next to her cousin, careful not to touch her. "Stop this—*now*. It's too much. You can't sustain it."

"No." Cleia forced out the words between pale, strained lips. "Promised Xavier. Make him...better."

Olivia jumped to her feet and turned on Dion, her midnight eyes blazing. "Don't you understand? She needs you to help control it. They're connected somehow. If you keep fighting the bond, she's going to die, and take the boy with her."

"What do you mean? She's your Conduit. Why can't she use whatever energy she gets from the sun to help him?"

"I don't know, damn you. But the boy's a fada. His body wasn't designed to channel energy like a sun fae's. From what Cleia said, the energy flow between your clan and her moves in one direction only—toward her. My guess is she needs another fada to help turn the energy back toward him. And not just any fada—her mate. The connection between you two is the key."

Dion turned back to where Cleia knelt in the grass. Cleia's face was set. Her breath was coming in shallow jerks and she seemed to be losing weight before his very eyes.

He glanced at where Luis and Marina had come to their knees as well. Silent tears dripped down Marina's cheeks. She reached for Xavier, then at a hiss from Luis, curled her fingers into tight balls and brought them back to her thighs.

His hands fisted. *Deus*, what should he do?

As he hesitated, Cleia's eyes rolled back in her head and he *knew*, with a mate's sure instinct, that she was a heartbeat away from going into a fatal convulsion.

In that moment, the decision was made for him. He lunged across the grass and caught her by the shoulders. Energy surged into him, arching his spine and snapping his head back. He gritted his teeth and hung on.

Cleia drew a shuddering breath. "That's it," she gasped out. "Steady me. Focus on...healing Xavier."

"*Pelo amor de Deus*," he rasped, "it's like...grabbing a fucking tiger...by the tail."

It was as if he'd taken hold of a live wire. He had a moment to be thankful that at least they hadn't all burst into flames. Then the pain increased and he was afraid he'd be forced to let go—or even thrown from her against his will.

No. Hang on—or she dies.

He dug deep, his animal throwing itself into the struggle to save the mate. For a few seconds he thought he'd gained control, then the power increased, the pain screaming through his nerves.

His groan seemed to come from somewhere outside of himself. "Can't," he heard himself say. "So sorry, *querida*."

"Work the energy," she gritted. "Don't...fight it."

But his fingers started to open, the pain so great he could no longer control the muscles.

He sensed Cleia's despair. Somehow he forced his fingers to close on her shoulders again.

Work the energy.

Of course. This was energy, and he had a Gift for working it. True, a storm's energy was a wild, elemental vortex, while this was more like an eruption of lava, a fast-moving, searing stream. But at their core, they were the same. Energy. The essence of life.

If he could channel one, surely he could channel the other.

He closed his eyes and called on his Gift with everything he had, visualizing himself gathering the energy to him as he would that of a storm. But the solar stream bucked and twisted, refusing to be controlled. Bracing his legs apart, he clung grimly to Cleia and tried again, this time visualizing himself as the stream bed through which the power flowed.

And suddenly, he was doing it.

The tremendous flow narrowed into a workable stream. It still flowed from the sun through Cleia, but he was able to guide it now.

"*Yes,*" Cleia breathed. "Now—Xavier."

Together, they directed the energy stream toward Xavier. Dion felt the connection running from the little boy to her to him and back again, saw how she'd been taking energy from Xavier, and how she'd given it all back to him and then some.

"Enough," Cleia muttered.

There was a tangible snap as she disengaged whatever was connecting her to Xavier.

The breath left Cleia's lungs in a whoosh. Her hands dropped from Xavier and she swayed under Dion's grip. He held onto her shoulders, steadying her, both their gazes on the boy.

Xavier's chest lifted, then fell. Then he raised his head, and the entire crowd released its collective breath.

He grinned. "I knowed you'd fix me, lady."

"Thank the Goddess." Cleia sat back on her heels.

"*Sim,*" Dion echoed, his heart almost too full to speak. "*Graças a Deus.*"

The crowd murmured excitedly. As Dion helped Cleia to her

feet, Marina burst into tears and gathered her son into her arms, covering his face with kisses while Luis enveloped them both in a tight hug.

"You did it." Dion took both of Cleia's hands in his.

She smiled up at him, bright eyes gleaming. "*We* did it."

His grip tightened. "I thought I was going to lose you." His stomach was still in knots, recalling the moment when her eyes had rolled back in her head.

"I'm not that easy to kill."

There was only one answer to that. He brought his mouth down on hers and kissed her. Hard.

Behind them, Marina and Luis came to their feet, Marina still holding Xavier. Dion put his arm around Cleia and turned toward the little family.

Luis dropped to his knees before them. "*Saúde, minha senhora,*" he said to Cleia. "Bless you with all of my heart." He took her hands in his and kissed them. "We'll never forget this. Never. And you, *meu senhor.*" He looked at Dion. "*Muito, muito obrigado.*"

"You don't have to thank me," Cleia said as Luis rose back up. "Just love him."

And then it was Marina's turn. She handed Xavier to Luis and turned to Cleia, laughing and crying and thanking her somewhat incoherently until Luis nudged her out of the circle and back to where their relatives were waiting to exclaim over the little boy's recovery.

Xavier squirmed to be set down, making everyone grin.

"Thank you." Cleia smiled up at Dion. "For trusting me."

"No." He touched a finger to her lips. "I'm the one who should thank you. You didn't have to help Xavier. Most fae wouldn't, not for a fada, even if it was their fault he was sick. Especially"—his throat worked—"if it meant risking their own life. You almost died, Cleia. Promise me you'll never, ever, put me through that again."

His hands were on her shoulders now, gripping her a little too tightly. "*Eu te amo*," he said in a voice thick with emotion. "I meant it, you know."

Her gaze met his. But instead of telling him she loved him in return—or even better, melting into his arms for a hot, tongue-tangling kiss—she laced her fingers through his and turned to face the crowd, raising their interlinked hands.

When she had everyone's attention, she said, "I have one more announcement to make. Lord Dion is my love and my mate. We each love our people, would die for our people. But the sun fae are strong, while Rock Run is still struggling to come back from twenty years of ill-luck—damage I caused. And so, I will perform this ritual and then return with him to his river caverns as his mate—if he'll have me. I'll still be the Conduit, but you'll have to choose a new ruler."

She brought their hands down and faced Dion.

"It's your choice," she told him with a lopsided smile.

All around them, the sun fae broke into angry exclamations but all Dion could see was Cleia. He grasped her by the shoulders, his chest tight.

"No," he rasped. "You can't. I won't let you."

Her jaw set. "I can and I will. Unless you don't want me—"

He gave her a little shake. "Of course I want you. But your people need you and I won't be responsible for you fading away again. I—it would break me, too."

"Oh, Dion." A smile dawned on her face. She brought her hands to his wrists on her shoulders. "Thank you for that. But I simply need to bathe daily in the sun. I assume you won't be keeping me imprisoned underground this time."

His gaze searched hers. By healing Xavier, she'd proven that together, the two of them could use the links that bound her to various members of his clan to boost their energy rather than taking it from them—and that she could sever the link when necessary.

Now his last misgivings evaporated as he understood what she was willing to give up for him. He'd walk through Hades itself before he'd let her get away.

Uncaring of their audience, he threaded his fingers through her hair and drew her to him. "Of course not," he said against her lips. "Although I might tie you to the bed now and then—"

She exhaled and he realized she hadn't been as sure of him as she'd appeared. "Then it's settled."

"Not quite." He placed an arm around her waist and spoke to the assembled crowd.

"Hear *me* now, people of Rock Run and Rising Sun and the rest of the sun fae clans. I declare before the rivers and oceans and the rain-giving clouds and all of you that Queen Cleia of the sun fae is my mate. But I will not take her from her people any more than she will take me from mine. If the sun fae wish it, she will remain queen, and we will spend half our days here and half our days at Rock Run."

The crowd drew in a collective breath and then everyone roared with approval.

Cleia's irises glinted with tiny gold stars. "You'd do that for me?"

"Of course." He drew her close for a deep kiss. As their lips touched, his heart lurched and the mate bond clicked into place.

Warmth filled his chest. He stared at her in wonder as energy hummed from him to her and back again.

She linked their fingers and, keeping her gaze locked on his, raised their hands above their heads. The sun flared again and the energy increased a thousand fold, streaking along his neural pathways.

His nerves hummed like a tuning fork and his cock began to harden. Elation filled him.

He grinned back at his mate and pressed his body against hers. She undulated against him, blatantly sensual, as the sun fae began to chant an ancient verse welcoming the sun.

The energy increased until the elation became pain that scoured his nerves like gritty sand. He stiffened and clenched his teeth.

Cleia squeezed his fingers. The stars in her eyes expanded and spread until her irises glowed a preternatural gold.

"Trust me," she mouthed.

"Always," he mouthed back.

And with that one word, he let go, entrusting her with both himself and his clan.

As if he'd flicked a switch, the mate bond came into full being. Energy began to flow from the two of them to the surrounding crowd. The sun fae threw up their hands in jubilation and swayed like plants in the wind. Behind them, the river fada linked arms and roared. Dion's head swam but he kept his gaze on his mate and hung on.

She spoke some sacred words. The stream of energy parted, flowing through the crowd to give an extra boost to those who needed it most, especially those among Rock Run's people whom she'd drained.

Dion muttered a prayer of thanks.

But the flow continued, so that even those who'd remained at the base received their share of the life-giving energy. Then it continued to the rest of their territory, infusing the water and surrounding lands with much-needed vitality as well.

The solar flow continued for several minutes and then gradually dissipated. Cleia slanted him a private smile that had him aching to get her alone, and then released him to face the crowd.

"It is done," she called. "May the coming year be filled with blessings. Peace to you and yours—and you're all invited to our mate ball!"

"Peace to you and yours," the crowd returned joyfully.

The next moment, Dion and Cleia were surrounded by well-wishers who hugged and kissed and squeezed indiscriminately.

Rosana was especially gleeful, babbling about how she'd always wanted a sister.

Cleia hugged her. "Me too, sweetheart."

Only Tiago didn't offer his congratulations. Instead, he gave Cleia an anguished look that she met with a rueful smile. He pushed his way through the crowd and hurried away.

Dion set him from his mind. This was his mate-day. There would be time enough to deal with his brother tomorrow.

He endured the congratulations for another few minutes, but the energy was still fizzing and buzzing in him in a decidedly sexual way. As everyone headed toward the meadow where the midsummer festival would take place, he placed a hand on the small of Cleia's back and guided her in the opposite direction to a secluded glade he'd noticed on their walk yesterday.

She slid him a teasing look. "Aren't we going the wrong way? I'd like to dance at my own mate ball."

He drew her into the shade of a large tree. "Oh, you'll dance at your ball," he informed her, cupping her ass through the silky dress. "Later. First there's something you need to take care of, *mate*."

He pulled her closer so that his aching cock was cradled in the soft curve of her belly.

"Oh, yeah?" she returned. "Then tell me, *mate*, can you do that thing with the electricity again? Like you did the first night?"

He nipped her neck. "That was bad of me, hm?" And he grew even harder just recalling it.

"Very bad," she agreed. "Of course, not so strong. I'd like to remain conscious this time, if you don't mind."

She pulled out of his arms long enough to wriggle out of her dress, emerging with her long, golden-skinned body bare so that his breath snagged in his throat. He stared at her, churning with lust...and love.

Mine.

But there was no desperation now, just gratitude mixed with wonder that he'd somehow won this amazing woman's heart.

Cleia was still speaking. "But that was the most incredible—"

He recovered his power of movement and tore off his own clothes.

"As you wish, *minha rainha*," he said and followed her down onto the soft summer grass.

EPILOGUE

A hard, tribal beat rolled across the lawn, overlaid by guitar, bass, and the husky voice of a woman singing a Latin American love song.

Tiago stood under a tree, drinking a beer and watching as fada and fae mingled over the feast set up under a large white tent. Nearby, people were already dancing on a polished wood floor topped by another billowing tent.

The sun fae dazzled in shimmering golds and reds and oranges, their bright hair and beautiful faces set off by glittering jewels; the river fada dark foils in deep greens or blues or blacks with only the occasional jewel or leather bracelet to adorn them. But everyone was smiling, the two clans mixing easily—or at least pretending to, for Dion and Cleia's sake.

Other fae began to arrive for the midsummer festival. The night fae, with their black hair and eyes and milk-pale complexions. Ice fae, equally pale but with blond hair and scary light eyes. A trio of dryads who lived on islands in Rock Run territory, barefoot and dressed in various shades of green, their sun-streaked hair tumbling down their backs.

An ethereal blonde strolled by, her gossamer wings furled

against her back, a member of one of the few winged clans. There were others, too—gremlins, pixies and even a few nightmarish beings like the Celtic *púca*, a shapeshifting black horse that even fada avoided.

Xavier darted by, bare feet pounding on the grass, and nearly collided with a tiny sun fae with a big pink bow in her hair. The two of them careened off to join a group of other kids in an uninhibited dance that ended in everyone on their backs, waving their legs in the air and giggling uncontrollably.

Despite his inner turmoil, Tiago's lips curved. At least something good had come of this mating.

A sun fae man swept Rosana onto the dance floor. She laughed up him, her lithe body striking in an iridescent green dress.

Tiago raised a brow. His baby sister was growing up.

Dion and Cleia were nowhere to be seen, but he'd seen the two of them disappear into a grove of aspens. It didn't take a genius to guess what they were doing.

Tiago's fingers clenched on the beer glass. He felt as if his heart were being strangled by a giant fist, but there was nothing he could do now—the two of them were mated, bonded for life.

Worse, defying his brother to free Cleia had been a worthless act. The queen had informed him earlier that Dion had been about to release her.

And although she'd sworn she hadn't told Dion who'd helped her, he knew. Tiago had seen it on his face.

He figured his brother had two choices—kill him or banish him. Well, he'd save Dion the trouble of having to decide. He'd only remained to keep an eye on Rosana. As soon as the newly mated couple returned, he was out of here.

A shock of bleached hair caught his eye. *Ric.* No, make that Adric—*Lord* Adric. The man had apparently been working for the sun fae all along.

Tiago swallowed sickly. He didn't deserve to live. Not only had he let Dion down, he'd given a rival alpha the coordinates to his brother's quarters.

Adric inclined his head mockingly at Tiago. He jerked his gaze away and pretended he hadn't seen.

"Who'd ever think a fada would mate a fae?" His friend Chico appeared, a plate of raw oysters in one hand and a beer in the other.

Tiago took a gulp of beer. "The two of them"—he couldn't bring himself to say their names—"together will benefit both clans."

Chico tipped an oyster into his mouth. "You okay?" he said after swallowing.

Tiago shrugged. The last thing he wanted was pity. "She was never really mine." *But she would've been*, something dark and dangerous muttered. *If not for Dion*—

"Tough luck. She sure is hot." Chico elbowed Tiago in the ribs. "Pun intended."

He grunted. Chico was a good friend but right now he wished the man to Hades.

Thankfully, Chico was eyeing the sun fae women now. A lush redhead caught his eye and he strolled off to ask her to dance. When Tiago glanced at Adric again, he was staring at Rosana with an arrested expression.

A growl rumbled low in his throat. His sister was still a kid, and even if she wasn't, no earth fada was going to get within ten feet of her. Especially not Adric.

If the man even got close enough to breathe on her, blood would flow.

Tiago pushed off the tree. But before he went more than a few feet, Cleia and Dion appeared. All their clothing was in place, but he could smell the sex on them from ten yards away. And you couldn't miss the fact that his normally poker-faced brother was smiling and that Cleia's cheeks were flushed.

The people around them exchanged knowing grins but

contented themselves with congratulating the couple on their mating.

Glasses were raised. A mating was a rare, special thing. Everyone would be celebrating long into the night and for the two remaining days of the festival, and there would be more than one couple slipping off to express their joy in private.

Adric stepped forward. Tiago caught his breath. The other man could out him in front of the entire clan, in which case it might all be over right now.

But the earth alpha was more interested in testing Dion's dominance. The two of them glared at each another for several tense seconds, and then Adric gave a jerky nod, acknowledging Dion as the stronger. Cleia smiled at Adric. He stepped forward to offer congratulations to them both, and the moment passed.

As Adric and Cleia spoke, Dion glanced over the crowd straight at Tiago. Tiago lifted his beer and withdrew behind the tree. It was time to leave. Dion or one of his *tenentes* would keep an eye on Rosana.

Setting down the glass, Tiago strode toward the creek a half mile away. He followed it a couple of miles and then removed his clothes and tucked them into a pack before focusing inward. Power shivered over his body. His spine elongated and grew more flexible, his limbs shortened and sprouted claws, and his skin grew a sleek brown pelt until he'd taken the form of a large, heavily muscled otter.

He picked up the pack with his teeth and loped toward the Flats. He'd swim upriver to Fausto's den, go to ground with his friend's family.

He needed time to lick his wounds...and to decide what he was going to do, now that he'd lost his last brother—and his clan.

CLAIMING VALERIA (EXCERPT)

BOOK 2

The Rock Run Trilogy continues with the dark, troubled shifter Rui and his mate Valeria...

TWO YEARS EARLIER

The night fae lord materialized in the darkest corner of the alley.

But Rui was expecting that. The night fae were creatures of the moon. You rarely saw one in the daylight, and even at dusk they sought the shadows.

This man could've been the pattern from which his people were cut: tall and lean, with chalk-white skin, midnight hair and sharp features. And dressed in tight black jeans and a long duster even though Baltimore was in the middle of a heat wave.

Rui's lip curled. He didn't like any fae, but he especially didn't like the night fae. Still, a job was a job.

He inclined his head. "Lord Tyrus."

"Do Mar?"

"That's me. Peace to you and yours."

Tyrus hesitated just long enough to be insulting before returning the ritual greeting. "Peace to you and yours."

Rui's jaw tightened. But he hadn't become Rock Run second by indulging his emotions. "You wanted to hire me?"

Tyrus flicked his fingers and an image of a man appeared in Rui's palm. "His name is Silver. He's in Baltimore somewhere—my people have tracked him this far, but we can't get a fix on him."

Rui studied the image. The man—Silver—had dark hair and pale skin, although it was clear he wasn't a pureblood. His face was too broad, his eyes a muddy brown rarely found in a fae.

"He's a half-blood," Tyrus said, confirming Rui's guess. "His mother was human." His voice held a sneer.

"Anything I can use to scent him?"

"I have a few strands of his hair. You can use it to do whatever it is you shifters do." The sneer was more pronounced now. The fae looked down on anyone who wasn't a pureblood, but they had a special disdain for the fada with their mix of human, fae and animal genes.

Rui ignored the scorn. Tyrus might sneer at his animal genes, but that was why he was hiring a fada assassin. Rui wouldn't be the hunter he was without his animal. And although hunting a man mainly involved old-fashioned legwork—questioning known associates, tracking him through credit cards and bank accounts—even a few strands of hair would make things easier, allowing him to track the man through his scent as well.

He wasn't sure why he asked the next question. He'd already talked it over with Dion, his alpha and best friend, and together, they'd decided to take the job. But something made him say, "What did he do?"

The image in his hand dissolved.

"The S.O.B. ripped me off," Tyrus snarled. "He knows what that means. Now, do we have an agreement?"

Rui stared back at him without speaking, his face expressionless, but he felt his eyes going night-glow gold, a sign his animal was aroused.

Tyrus took a step back.

Good. He might be the son of a fae prince, but he needed to remember whom he was dealing with. As clan second, Rui was answerable only to Dion. No one—especially some asshole pureblood from Virginia—spoke to him like that.

The night fae gave an audible swallow. When he spoke again, his tone was more polite. "You don't need to know what he stole. All I want you to do is send a message—no one steals from Lord Tyrus."

So Silver wasn't going to be given a chance to make things right. Rui didn't even blink. If he'd ever been squeamish about acting as a hit man for the fae, he'd long since made his peace with it. Hunger had a way of making a man hard-hearted, especially when his women and children were suffering, too.

"All right."

"Then we're agreed? You'll take the job?"

"Of course." What did he care if the fae picked one another off?

"Good." Tyrus's black eyes flickered with an unholy glee that raised the tiny hairs on Rui's nape. Something was off here. But the night fae was tossing him a small black pouch. "That's the deposit. You'll get the spell when I confirm the kill."

Rui opened the pouch. Inside were three small but perfect diamonds. Purebloods loved expensive, shiny things. Frankly, he and Dion would've preferred a direct deposit into the clan account.

He closed the pouch. "I'll let you know when it's done. We expect the rest of the payment within the week."

"Don't contact me directly—go through Hunter." Hunter was a Baltimore earth fada who worked at the Full Moon Saloon, a bar catering to shifters.

Rui jerked his head in acknowledgment. As long as Tyrus

kept his part of the bargain, he was just as happy not to have to deal with him again, although it went against the grain to let the Baltimore fada have anything to do with Rock Run business.

"And, do Mar?" Tyrus stepped closer.

Rui's nostrils flared. Night fae stank, an acrid mix of metal and decay. Rumor had it they made their homes in crypts, and smelling Tyrus, Rui could believe it.

"What?"

The reply was low and cold. "Don't fuck this up—or you're next."

Rui's fingers tightened on the pouch. For the amount the diamonds would bring, he could slip a blade in Tyrus's aristocratic chest and walk away with the clan twenty-five thousand dollars richer. Not even a pureblood could survive a knife to the heart.

But Rock Run desperately needed the second half of Tyrus's payment—a promise to renew the concealing spell that hid their base from intruders. The clan was gripped by a mysterious malady that was slowly weakening them. And not just the people themselves, although that was bad enough. Even their crops and river had been affected. The grapes that produced the wine that was the clan's main source of income were rotting in the vineyards, and every year the fishers brought in less fish and crabs.

If Rock Run's troubles became generally known, they'd be easy pickings for the Baltimore shifters, who'd long coveted the clan's large tract of land in northern Maryland.

And to top it off, Rui had recently met his mate, a sexy Portuguese shifter named Valeria. Their mating celebration was in a couple of weeks, which made him even more eager to get that concealing spell. It wasn't just other men's families he was protecting now. It was his own woman and their future children.

Right now, the spell was as valuable to Rock Run—and Rui— as a thousand diamonds.

Still, he couldn't resist peeling back his lips to display two sharp canines. Tyrus went whiter, if that were possible. But he was a pureblood fae, taught from birth that all other life forms were inferior. He held his ground.

Rui gave Tyrus his back—a grave insult, implying the other man was too weak to worry about—and stalked out of the alley.

THE HALF-BLOOD WAS DAMN good at hiding. It took Rui almost a week to find him.

But Rui's primary animal was a shark. He was calm, cold, relentless. As a water fada, he tended to short out computers and other electronics, so he paid a human hacker to track Silver through the digital crumbs he'd dropped. That got him close, and then he kept at it until his questions—and his nose—led him to a shabby little rowhouse on a street less than a mile from the alley where he'd met Tyrus.

Now he studied the narrow house, one of a row of twelve that stretched from one corner to the next. So this was where Silver had gone to ground. The house was as sad and neglected as the surrounding area—a sagging roof, a chipped and faded Form-stone exterior and a yard that was more dirt than grass.

Whatever the half-blood had stolen, he sure hadn't cashed in on it.

Silver roomed with a human who worked nights. Rui slipped into the backyard and waited until the man left. One by one, the lights went out. Rui waited another half an hour before skimming across the lawn to the back door. It was locked, but it was a few second's work to dig out the rotted wood around the bolt and ease the door open. A simple warding spell halted him on the threshold. He withdrew a pinch of precious counterspell dust from its packet, sprinkled it on the doorjamb and stepped into the kitchen.

The air inside was hot and close, not much different than the humid summer night outside. Rui took in his surroundings with his animal-enhanced senses: the red plastic table with three mismatched chairs...the greasy remains of a pizza on the counter...the smear of chocolate ice cream in a bowl in the sink. From upstairs came the sound of a man snoring, the ragged buzz a counterpoint to the distant hum of a window air conditioner.

He glanced down and jolted. A small face was staring up at him. Then he realized it was a doll.

Deus. He scrubbed a hand over his face. He wasn't usually so edgy.

He picked up the doll. It was a clown, its baggy satin suit tattered from much handling. He brought it to his face and inhaled, scenting the child who owned it: sweet, happy innocence.

He cursed under his breath. Tyrus hadn't said anything about a child—a girl, from the scent. Children were rare and special gifts. There was no way in hell he'd harm one.

And how had he missed the fact that a child was here? He was working alone, he and Dion having agreed that since Baltimore was technically earth fada territory, the quieter they kept this the better. Still, Rui had spent the past couple of days observing the house, studying the occupants and learning their routine. The half-blood couldn't have brought her in without him knowing—unless he was working some kind of fae magic to hide her.

Rui placed the clown on the kitchen table and headed for the stairs. With any luck, its owner was somewhere else—with her mother, perhaps.

As he reached the top of the stairs, he slipped a switchblade from his pocket and pressed the button. The blade slid out with a soft snick.

Down the hall, the sleeper mumbled something.

Rui stilled, his back against the wall.

Five minutes ticked by, then ten. The only sound was the bedroom air conditioner and the slow drip of a faucet in the bathroom across the hall. Rui waited, unmoving. His Gift was tracking. With it came a predator's patience, whether his prey was animal—or man.

The sleeper resumed snoring. Rui palmed the knife and continued down the hall. He passed two bedrooms, one empty save for a sagging couch. The other must be the human's room; it was sparsely furnished with an ancient dresser and a mattress and box spring covered by a colorful Indian bedspread.

Rui reached the bedroom where the half-blood slept. The door was closed, presumably to keep the cool air in. The snoring had stopped again, but he could hear the slow, steady breath of someone in a deep sleep. Soundlessly, he turned the knob and pushed the door open a few inches. He drew a breath, checking for the half-blood's unique scent: a mix of iron (from his human half) and silver (from the fae half), along with a touch of salt.

But the girl's sweet scent filled the air as well. The iron and silver notes told him she was related to the half-blood, that he was almost certainly her father.

Rui's hand tightened on the knife handle.

Fucking fae. Tyrus had to have known that the half-blood had a daughter. But he apparently didn't give a shit.

He almost said to hell with it and left. But Tyrus would make a powerful enemy—and Dion had asked Rui to do this job for a reason. He was Rock Run's best assassin—and they needed that concealing spell. They'd never be able to pay the huge amount demanded by the night fae to cast it.

No, they'd been forced to barter: a job for a job.

And in the end, an assassin didn't judge the rightness or wrongness of a kill. He just did what he'd been hired to do.

The door jerked open. Rui released the handle and jumped back into the hall. A shadow barreled out of the darkness, knocking him to the floor. He rolled, barely avoiding the other man's clawed fingers.

Something else Tyrus had neglected to tell him. Silver apparently had the fae Gift of wayfaring, which included the ability to move lightning-fast. At least Rui knew how he'd gotten the girl in without him knowing.

Silently consigning Tyrus to whatever hell would take a night fae, Rui rolled again and with an agile twist was back on his feet, bobbing and weaving as he tried to get a fix on the half-blood.

But the other man was impossibly swift, shifting first to one side, then to the other.

The hairs on Rui's nape stood straight up. He spun around to find the half-blood behind him.

The two of them settled into a deadly dance, searching for a weakness. The half-blood's speed made him damn near invisible as he moved from place to place. A human assassin would've been dead by now, but as a fada, Rui had a touch of fae blood as well, so could track the other man's movements—barely—now that he knew what to expect.

He slashed out with the knife, slicing Silver's arm to the bone. The other man inhaled sharply and hugged the arm to his stomach. Blood dripped to the floor. Rui scented a hint of decay beneath the iron-silver. So Silver had some night fae in him.

The other man fought on for another silent, desperate minute but his breath was rasping in and out of his chest, his movements much slower, his injured arm pressed uselessly to his abdomen.

Now, whispered Rui's animal. He feinted left, and when the half-blood shifted to avoid him, plunged the blade beneath his breastbone and up into his heart.

Silver fell to his knees. His good hand latched onto Rui's wrist. "Please." He dragged in a breath. "Not. Mary." His gaze flicked in the direction of the sleeping girl.

Rui hesitated, but there was no harm in telling the man the truth. "She's safe. The contract didn't include her."

Relief softened the half-blood's sharp features. "Thank the gods." His lips moved but nothing came out but a gurgle. He took a last, harsh breath, and then his chest heaved and he released Rui and crumpled the rest of the way to the floor.

Rui stared down at the dead man, wondering why he didn't feel more: remorse at having killed a man, satisfaction at a job well done, guilt about the girl sleeping in the bedroom. But he felt—nothing, as if his heart were encased in chill gray ice.

He retrieved his knife, rinsed it off in the bathroom and returned it to his pocket. He should get the hell out of there—but instead he hesitated, listening to the girl's soft, light breaths.

Drawn by something beyond his control, he stepped into the room and stared down at her.

She was younger than he'd expected—maybe five turns of the sun. She was sprawled on her back in the boneless sleep of a child, a nightgown twisted around her legs, her hair braided into five stubby pigtails that stuck out at angles around her head like an off-kilter crown. Like her father, her face hinted at fae blood— sharp chin, pointed ears and wide, tip-tilted eyes—although her skin was golden-brown where the half-blood was pale.

But like him, she was thin. Too thin.

As he gazed down at that small, skinny body, something in Rui clenched. If a child of his were that underfed, he'd do anything to get her food—lie, cheat, steal, even murder.

Which was apparently what the half-blood had done.

Delicate eyelids fluttered. "Daddy?"

Hell. He couldn't leave her here to find her father dead in the hall.

"Shh," he murmured, "it's all right." He lifted her from the bed. She weighed next to nothing, her arms and legs knobby brown sticks.

Her eyes popped open and rounded in terror. Her lips peeled back in a feral hiss. Light shimmered over her skin and suddenly he was juggling an angry, spitting jaguar cub. She hissed again and struck out with her claws. He cursed and tried to hold onto her, but she twisted out of his arms to the floor where she shook off the nightgown and dashed into the hall. She crouched next to her father and raised her upper lip in warning.

He ruefully rubbed his wrist. The little devil had drawn blood. Not that those tiny claws had done much damage, but still...

He followed her into the hall and crouched down on his haunches. "Easy, little one. I'm not going to hurt you."

Her ears flattened and her mouth opened to bare small canines. She growled, a high, baby growl that would have been cute if it weren't aimed at him.

He put out a hand, palm out. "Everything's going to be all right. I just want to help you."

She snapped at his hand, her little tail whipping back and forth in agitation, but he kept it near her face, allowing her to take in his scent. She took a cautious sniff, then growled again, her eyes flashing the green of her jaguar. Keeping her gaze glued on Rui, she inched backward until her head was next to her father's.

He remained still, knowing she needed a few moments to come to terms with what had happened, even as his animal urged him to grab her and leave—now.

The little jaguar licked the dead man's cheek, trying to heal him in the way of a cat.

That's when he realized she'd shifted to jaguar, which meant she was a fada, a shapeshifter—but not a river fada like him, or even some other form of water shifter. No, she was an earth fada.

He briefly closed his eyes. Could this night get any worse? Water and earth fada didn't get along at the best of times, but Rock Run and the Baltimore earth clan were longtime enemies. At the moment, the Baltimore shifters were in disarray, wracked by a brutal internal war. But it was only a matter of time before they regrouped and tried—yet again—to wrest control of Rock Run.

He had to take the cub and get out of here. *Now.* The last thing Rock Run needed right now was war with another clan.

He seized the little shifter by the scruff of her neck, grabbed the nightgown and loped down the stairs.

She yowled the whole way. In desperation, he snatched up the clown and stuck it in her face. To his relief, she snagged it with her front paws and quieted.

He gripped her neck lightly and stared into her eyes, letting her see his dominance. Water or earth shifter, he was her superior in size and strength, and her animal needed to recognize that. Her gaze dropped and she whimpered, all the fight leached out of her.

He reached the back door and then halted. Someone waited on the other side, someone who smelled of metal and decay.

The cub's tawny head jerked up, sensing the danger. She whimpered again, a small, heart-rending sound.

He swore under his breath and dashed back upstairs. Thank the gods, there was an open window in the human's room that let out onto the roof at the front of the house. He stuffed the nightgown in his back pocket, hefted the cub in one arm and climbed out.

Setting her down, he inched up to the peak and risked a look down. Night fae had eyes like a cat, but the two men below had their gazes trained on the back door.

Just two of them. The S.O.B.s were damn sure they could take him. If he hadn't had to get the little earth shifter to safety, he'd have enjoyed allowing them to test that theory.

He jerked his head at the jaguar, knowing she could easily keep up in her cat form. "This way," he said in a subvocal voice only she could hear. The half-blood's rowhouse was a few from the end. The two of them moved soundlessly down the roofs in the other direction.

The second-to-the-last house had a small dormer jutting out of its roof. Rui dropped to a crouch on the far side, the cub hunkered next to him, her small body shivering despite the warm night.

He passed a hand over her fur. *Deus*, she was young. She felt as thin and breakable in this form as she had as a girl.

"Don't worry," he murmured in the same low voice. "They won't find us here. But you have to be very quiet. Don't move. Can you do that?"

Night fae were like vampires, but rather than sucking blood, they sucked energy. The only way to hide from them was to freeze, slowing your breath and heart rate so they couldn't track you—and pray like hell that it worked.

The cub nodded solemnly and pressed against him. To his relief, her shivers slowed and her breathing calmed. It occurred to him that she'd done this before, and the ice around his heart cracked open enough to send pity stabbing through him.

Although it was nearly midnight, the sidewalks were dotted with people enjoying the cooling night air. He heard the murmur of voices, the sound of footsteps. From somewhere nearby a cat in heat screeched, and a man threw open a window and hollered for it to shut the fuck up.

The noises quieted. Then the crack of a door being kicked open shattered the night. The night fae had gotten impatient.

Now was their chance. "Climb on my back," he told the cub. "We're going down."

She took the clown between her teeth and obeyed. He shimmied down a drainpipe, moved the cub to his arms and dashed the few hundred yards to the alley where he'd stashed his motorcycle.

He set the cub on the pavement. "Shift," he ordered.

She shifted. It took her a long time, her small reserves nearly depleted.

When she was a girl again, he dropped the nightgown over her head. It was pink with a cartoon princess on the front, underlining how very young she was.

He felt another unwelcome stab of pity, and it made his voice gruffer than he intended. "Tell me where your mama lives."

She screwed up her face. Fat tears rolled down her cheeks. "I don't have a mommy."

Rui tensed, knowing he wasn't going to like this. But he softened his tone. "What do you mean, *menina?*"

"She died. The bad men hurt her and she died."

Hades. Rui stared down at the girl, flummoxed.

He could leave her near a Baltimore earth fada's den. They had dens scattered all over the city, unlike his clan, who preferred living together in a single underground base. They would know who her mother was.

But with her mother dead, would the earth clan accept a mixed-blood child, especially one with night fae in her? For all he knew, her mother had been caught up in the savage internal war the Baltimore shifters were fighting, one that had left whole families dead. It would explain why Silver hadn't asked the clan for help hiding his daughter.

Handing the little girl over to the Baltimore shifters could be signing her death warrant.

And apparently the night fae were after her too.

That's when it hit him. The half-blood hadn't stolen a *thing* from Tyrus. He'd stolen this child.

Which meant that Rui had killed a man simply for protecting his own daughter.

His whole body went rigid.

The little girl gave a moist sniff.

He scraped a hand through his cropped black hair. "What's your name?"

"Merry Jones," she said with a tremor in her voice. "M-E-R-R-Y. Like Christmas."

He swung her into his arms. "Well, Merry Christmas Jones, I guess you're coming home with me."

~

Rock Run was about an hour north of Baltimore at the top of the Chesapeake Bay. The clan owned a large, pie-shaped piece of land edged on one side by the bay and on the other by the Susquehanna River, with Rock Run Creek running through the center. The clan base was deep underground in the caverns that ran along Rock Run Creek.

By the time Rui had reached Rock Run, Valeria had already gone to bed. But as he entered his quarters, she emerged from the bedroom, rumpled and adorable in one of his T-shirts, her dark hair tumbling around her shoulders.

"Rui?" She yawned. "What—" She froze, hand still covering her mouth, as she saw the little girl.

"This is Merry. I—" He licked suddenly dry lips. "I found her. In Baltimore."

Valeria's brows lifted but the look she turned on Merry was kind. "*Olá*, sweetheart. Are you lost?"

The little girl shook her head.

"She's part earth shifter."

"*Sim?*" Valeria's brow furrowed. "And a bit fae as well, no? But why—" Merry whimpered and Valeria's face softened. She gathered the child into her arms and sat down in a nearby chair, rocking her gently back and forth. "It's all right, *menina*. It's all right."

Merry had been mute the whole way up from Baltimore, perched before Rui on the motorcycle, one hand clutching his arm around her waist, the other fisted around her clown. She hadn't even complained when he brought her through the narrow tunnel that was the only way for a land dweller to enter the base.

But now she burst into tears. "I...want...my daddy."

"Shh," murmured Valeria. "Of course you do. Don't worry, we'll find him for you."

"Can you?" Merry sniffed. "Please?"

"Of course. *Senhor* Rui will help me. He's the best tracker in the clan."

Rui swallowed something sharp as glass. "I can't," he said, and switched to Portuguese so the girl wouldn't understand him. "*Ele está morto.*"

Valeria sucked in a breath. She glanced at Merry and replied in the same language. "Does she know?"

"She was there. She didn't see it happen but she saw him after."

"Poor baby." Valeria pressed a kiss to the little girl's head. "But why bring her here?"

"She's mixed—human, night fae, earth fada. I asked about her mother, but she told me she's dead. I was afraid to leave her with the Baltimore shifters."

Valeria nodded. She'd only been at Rock Run a couple of months, but she'd heard about the local earth fada and their problems.

Then her full lips pressed together. "Her papa." Her gaze was accusing. "It was you, wasn't it?"

He looked away. "*Sim.*"

"*Madre de Deus.*" A horrified whisper. "How could you?"

The bond between them was still tenuous, not complete until both of them accepted it during the mating ceremony—but he felt her recoil from him.

It sliced at the deepest part of him. Valeria had grown up in a prosperous clan in Portugal—an old, rich clan, where the warriors didn't have to hire themselves out as assassins and mercenaries just to survive. She didn't understand that he'd had no choice.

"*Querida*—" He reached out a hand.

She ignored it to murmur to Merry.

His animal rumbled, puzzled and angry. She was the mate. She should know that if he killed, it was for the good of the clan.

"Valeria," he said, louder this time.

She stiffened but resolutely kept her gaze on Merry. He let the hand drop back to his side.

Merry lifted her head from where she was cuddled close to Valeria's heart to scrutinize him with hazel eyes slashed with shards of green, her jaguar very close to the surface.

"Are you a bad man?" The question hung in the air.

Rui opened his mouth, then shut it again. He shook his head and took a step back. At the door, he said, "I have to report to Dion."

Valeria finally lifted her head to look at him. He blinked. His warm-hearted, sensual, *maternal* woman looked as unforgiving as the harshest judge.

"You do that. And then don't come back. Not tonight, anyway. She needs time."

He stared back, despair an icy sludge in his veins. It was then that he realized how much he'd counted on her warmth to balance the coldness in him. He glanced from Valeria to the tearful little girl and then wrapped the familiar chill around him like a shield and with a curt nod, left the apartment.

He made the walk to the alpha's quarters encased in that same chill gray ice. Despite the late hour, Dion answered on the first knock. He took in Rui's tension with one sharp look. "What happened, *irmão?*" He waved him inside and closed the door.

"It's done. But—" Rui explained about Merry Jones.

"She's our clan now," his friend said immediately. "I'll go to her, mark her with my scent so the others know she's under my protection."

Rui nodded. He'd expected Dion to see it that way, even though the last thing they needed was another mouth to feed— and an earth shifter at that.

They discussed the night fae. They both figured Tyrus had sent the two men after Rui to make sure no one got out of the house alive. Dion was furious, but there wasn't much he could do.

Tyrus was a powerful fae, the son and heir of the night fae prince himself. The clan was too weak to go up against him. All they could do was take the bastard's payment and then never work for him again.

And then Rui left Rock Run and went to a bar in nearby Grace Harbor. He started to toss back shots of whiskey, but no amount of alcohol could drown out Valeria's accusing face and Merry's small, clear voice asking, *Are you a bad man?*

But he couldn't blame the whiskey. He was sober enough when the sun fae queen, Cleia, strolled into the bar on the prowl for another fada lover, dressed in a flirty little red nothing. He couldn't take his eyes off her. He'd seen what she'd done to the men before him—how they returned drained, and fit for little but fishing—but he hadn't cared. All he wanted was to sink himself into that long, golden body and sex his brains out.

So he went home with Cleia, intending to stay for a night. He told himself it was to give Valeria a chance to cool down. But even then he knew he was lying to himself. What he was really trying to do was forget all the men and women he'd killed—and the children he'd left father- or motherless.

Are you a bad man?

Just one night, he told himself. What harm could that do?

But Cleia was a powerful fae, with a glamour that made her damn near irresistible. He'd lost himself in their dark, hedonistic play. The night turned to a week, and the week to a month.

Each evening he told himself: *Tomorrow. Tomorrow I'll go back to my mate.*

But each morning he found himself staying another day, caught in the fae queen's seductive net.

In the end, he stayed a year.

An entire fucking year.

He returned to find he'd lost his mate—and he had no one to blame but himself.

Keep reading *Claiming Valeria*!
(rebeccarivard.com/shapeshifters)

ALSO BY REBECCA RIVARD

THE FADA SHAPESHIFTERS

Stealing Ula: A Fada Shapeshifter Prequel (Nisio & Ula, set in Ireland)

The Rock Run River Fada

Seducing the Sun Fae (Dion & Cleia)

Claiming Valeria (Rui & Valeria)

Tempting the Dryad (Tiago & Alesia)

Sea Dragon's Hunger (Cassidy & Nic)

The Baltimore Earth Fada (The Darktime Trilogy)

Saving Jace (Jace & Evie)

Charming Marjani (Marjani & Fane)

Adric's Heart (Adric & Rosana)

Fada Shapeshifter Short Reads

Lir's Lady (#3.5—Lir & Isleen)

Shifter's Valentine (#3.6—Jenny & Chico)

Find out more and read exclusive excerpts: https://rebeccarivard.com/shapeshifters/

The Vampire Syndicate Romances

Pursued (Gabriel)

Craved (Rafael)

Taken (Zaquiel)

The Vampire Blood Courtesans

Ensnared: Star (Star and Remy)

Compelled: Cerise (Cerise & Bard)

Find out more: https://rebeccarivard.com/vampires/

Join **Rebecca Rivard's newsletter** to stay informed and be eligible for giveaways and sneak peeks of upcoming books. As a thank you, Rebecca will gift you with "Lir's Lady," a steamy short story!

Sign up at rebeccarivard.com or go to this link: Rebecca's newsletter

ABOUT THE AUTHOR

USA Today bestselling author Rebecca Rivard read way too many romances as a teenager, little realizing she was actually preparing for a career. She now spends her days with dark shifters, sexy fae and other magical creatures—which has to be the best job ever. When she's not writing, she walks, bikes and kayaks in the Chesapeake Bay area with her guitar-playing, storytelling husband.

Her debut novel, *Seducing the Sun Fae (#1, Fada Shapeshifters)*, was a 2016 EPIC Awards finalist for Best Fantasy/Paranormal Romance, and her novella *Ensnared: Star* was a *Night Owl Reviews* Top Pick (5 stars).

Five of her novels have been awarded the coveted Crowned Heart Review from *InD'Tale Magazine* and the FADA SHAPESHIFTER SERIES was voted Best Shifter Series in the Paranormal Romance Guild Reviewer's Choice Awards.

Her books have also won the prestigious PRISM Award (*Charming Marjani*) and the PRG Reviewer's Choice Award (*Saving Juce*), and have finaled in both the RONE and the HOLT Medallion.